TAKE MY HAND

TAKE MY HAND

CROSSROADS SUSPENSE: BOOK ONE

BY

KRISTEN HOGREFE PARNELL

Take My Hand
Published by Mountain Brook Ink
White Salmon, WA U.S.A.

The website addresses shown in this book are not intended in any way to be or imply an endorsement on the part of Mountain Brook Ink, nor do we vouch for their content.

This story is a work of fiction. All characters and events are the product of the author's imagination. Any resemblance to any person, living or dead, is coincidental.

Scripture quotations are taken from the New King James Version of the Bible. Public domain.
ISBN 978-1-953957-22-1
© 2022 Kristen Hogrefe Parnell

The Team: Miralee Ferrell, Tim Pietz, Kristen Johnson, and Cindy Jackson
Cover Design: Indie Cover Design, Lynnette Bonner Designer

Mountain Brook Ink is an inspirational publisher offering fiction you can believe in.
Printed in the United States of America

Dedication

To James,
I am forever grateful
God gave me you.

Acknowledgments

Writing begins as a lonely labor of love, but I am so thankful a project doesn't stay that way. This story is no exception.

First, I am grateful to my Lord and Savior Jesus Christ who entrusted me with the stewardship of words. I believe stories are a powerful way of presenting truth, and I pray He finds me faithful with the ones He has given me.

I also could not have written this story without the love and support of my husband James. He never expected to marry an author, but I'm so glad he encourages me to pursue my calling. He has been my inspiration for this story in many ways. Finding him reading a rough draft on our porch rocking chair is a sweet sight imprinted on my memory.

My family and friends have been so gracious to ask and keep asking about this story. Thank you, Mom and Dad, for always loving me and believing in me. Thank you to my brothers David and Joe and their families for cheering me on along the way. Thank you to my Aunt Priscilla, who taught me to love books, and to my second mom Fran for being the best mother-in-love a girl could ask for.

My agent Stephanie Alton caught my vision for this project, and I am so blessed to partner with her in my publishing journey. Being part of The Blythe Daniel Agency feels like family.

Miralee Ferrell and the team at Mountain Brook Ink made it possible to put this book in my readers' hands, and I am so grateful. Finding the right home for a story is a process of much prayer and waiting, and I am honored to partner with this group.

Special thanks to my writing colleagues, Amberlyn Dwinnell, Ashley Jones, and my Page 5 Word Weavers. You saw some of the early drafts of this project and believed in it. Your words make a difference in my life.

There are too many fellow authors who have inspired me to list them here. Thank you for investing in other writers and leaving a legacy for us to follow.

I am also grateful to my church family and the single and married friends who have shared life with James and me over the last several years. Your community and friendship are so sweet to us.

And lastly, thank you, dear reader, for joining me here. I hope this story resonates with you and encourages you in whatever situation you are facing. As Kaley discovers, we may not have a choice in everything that happens to us, but we do get to choose our response.

Chapter One

If anyone needed a vacation, she did. Kaley massaged her jaw to unplaster the smile from her face and then focused on her laptop. Her last client of the day had left. Now, she just had to answer some emails and set her automatic replies before leaving the office.

She loved her work at TCS, Trauma Counseling Solutions, but everyone needed a break. In a few minutes, her Monday would be over, and she'd be off the rest of the week. Blissful thought.

A ski trip to the mountains of North Carolina should help her recharge. It didn't matter she'd never seen snow in her life. Skiing couldn't be that hard. And the twelve-hour van ride with a bunch of twenty-somethings wouldn't phase her either. She could sleep through a hurricane at this point. If not, she could distract herself with her never-ending master's thesis project.

The only rub was that Reef Mitchell would be going too.

Whatever. If she could counsel patients ranging from those with anxiety disorders to veterans diagnosed with PTSD, she could handle Reef.

Someone tapped on her office door.

"Come in," she called while typing an email reply.

Meg cracked open the door and stepped into the gap. "Hey, Kaley, Blake's on line one."

Kaley frowned. Why had their receptionist walked to her office when she could have simply transferred the call? "Is everything okay?"

Meg twisted her hands. "His client is in the waiting room."

Kaley's fingers froze on her keyboard. "But Blake left here hours ago for the hospital."

"That's just it."

A sinking feeling gnawed at her gut, but she forced a smile to her lips. "Please transfer him."

"Right away." Meg closed the door with a soft click.

The bottom right screen of her computer read five minutes after five. Kaley didn't have to be at the church until eight o'clock. Her church group planned to drive through the night, but she had hoped to get dinner and a shower first.

Taking an appointment for her boss might cancel those plans. Good thing her suitcase was packed and ready—and in the back seat of her car.

Her phone chirped, and Kaley grabbed it on the first ring. "Hey, Blake."

"Kaley." The edge in his voice did nothing to ease the tightening knot in her stomach. "I need a favor."

"Is everything okay with Gina and the baby?" She hoped the favor might involve dropping off something at the hospital and not something to do with the client in the waiting room.

"She's doing great. Contractions are about every five minutes." He hurried on. "Meg said Anthony Casale showed up in the office, demanding to see me. He doesn't have an appointment. Obviously, I canceled all my appointments to be with Gina."

Casale. The knot in her stomach doubled. Even though she was his junior partner, Blake confided in her about some of his more difficult clients during their staff meetings each week. Getting a second opinion and some distance often provided insights into tough cases, and the fact that her boss had the humility to ask her opinion made her respect him even more.

"You know I wouldn't ask this under any other circumstance, but I have to be with Gina right now."

She swallowed. "Of course. Do you have any idea why he might be here?"

Blake spoke to someone in the background and then sighed into the phone. "Sorry about that. Yes, I suspect it has to do with his family history to the Tampa underground. It usually does."

"But the mafia in our city is as extinct as Al Capone," Kaley said.

"Some say maybe not."

"Still, how does this constitute an emergency appointment?"

"I agree with you, Kaley, but you know our clients. It doesn't have to be a real emergency to be an emergency."

Kaley nodded, his words sinking in. Emergency or not, he was their patient. And with alleged ties to the Tampa mafia, however nonoperational, he was likely a sensitive case.

On her computer, she navigated to their shared hard drive and Casale's password-protected client file. She knew how to access it. Until now, she had never had a reason to do so.

"Anything I need to know before meeting him?" Kaley asked.

"Be alert for anything about Jack," Blake said. "Nightmares, imaginary meetings, blackmail—believe me, I've heard it all, and none of it makes sense. But it all gets darker when he mentions Jack's revenge."

Kaley tried to scan the pages of Blake's notes while focusing on the phone call. "Jack? Is that a person?"

"Who knows. Sometimes, it's a person. Sometimes, it's a possession. But it's always Jack that sends Anthony into a fit."

"What grounding technique works best for him—or how do you get him off this Jack rabbit trail?"

"The only safe place we've established is a local restaurant on the Hillsborough River." There was more mumbling in the background. "Ugh, I can't remember the name right now, but it's in my notes. Listen, the nurse called me back in. Don't hesitate to text if you need me."

Kaley forced a smile for her own benefit. Time to plaster on her professional face for one more meeting. "Tell Gina I'm praying for her."

"Thanks, I owe you big time."

"Sure thing."

"Chicken wing."

Kaley chuckled at their office joke. "See you next week."

As soon as the call ended, she dialed Meg's extension. "Tell Mr. Casale I'll see him in the conference room shortly."

"Thanks, I already saw him into the conference room. He was starting to make me nervous."

Kaley gripped the receiver. "Nervous? Are you okay?"

Meg's heavy breathing filled the phone. "Sorry, he just—I don't know—wouldn't stop pacing and asking to see Blake. He spilled all the business cards off the counter, emptied the paper cups at the water dispenser, and cursed at Monet's Self Portrait for a good five minutes."

"I'm coming, but please don't leave for the day until I see him out of the conference room."

Meg lowered her voice. "I wouldn't dream of leaving you alone with him. This is a red-button case if I've ever seen one."

Kaley grabbed her jacket off the chair and snatched her notebook. The last thing she wanted was to press the panic button concealed in the conference room for emergencies. If Meg had to call the police, Kaley might miss her eight o'clock bus.

"Help me, Jesus," she breathed and started down the hallway.

With a grunt, Reef grabbed another case of water from his Subaru and stacked it in the back of the church van. If he'd stuck with his original plan, he'd be half way to Jacksonville by now. Instead, he was at ground zero for starting this eleven-hour road trip—and some of the other class members hadn't even arrived.

"Thanks, bro, I couldn't have done this without you." TJ slapped Reef on the back. "Leaving Jenna with the kids is hard enough, and I didn't have time for a supply run."

"You got it, man." Reef nodded in return. He and TJ had been in high school together. It was still weird to think of TJ as his single group's pastor, but his friend had a wife and two kids now. Reef never thought he'd still be in this class, but his relationship attempts continued to crash and burn.

"Is there anything else you need before I head out?" he asked.

"Just the receipt so I can get you reimbursed." TJ ran a hand over his short black hair and offered his hallmark goofy grin. "You still going to drive yourself all the way there and back when you could enjoy the road trip with everyone else?"

"And listen to you and Matt dispute conspiracy theories the whole time? Not a chance."

TJ laughed. "You have a point. Guess the van does get loud, but hey, there's no chance of falling asleep at the wheel."

Reef loaded the last case and grinned. "I'll take my chances."

"Please tell me you at least downloaded the app."

"Um, there's a class app?"

"No, man." TJ face-palmed. "It's called Life360. It lets us keep track of everyone's locations if we get split up—or if anyone like you decides to drive by himself."

Reef quirked an eyebrow. "You want to babysit my every movement? Seriously, TJ, we're adults. This isn't children's church."

"I went over all this at the meeting where you clearly weren't paying attention. Your other option is to ride with us." TJ elbowed him in the ribs and nodded to a cluster of girls who were sitting on large suitcases. "You might even make some new friends."

Reef glanced at the girls. Macy was cool, but they were only friends. The blonde girl he didn't recognize, but she looked way too young for him. And the third was Olivia. If Matt had any say, she'd be off the market. She wasn't Reef's type anyway.

He shook his head and closed the van door on the side full of food and beverages purchased for the trip. "Fine, I'll download the app." He wanted to add that his friend should stick to pastoring the YA class instead of app-stalking and match-making.

Why it was called the YA class in the first place was beyond him. He and Matt were in their thirties with careers. Matt was a professional pilot, and even if people made fun of Reef's being an entrepreneur, he did well and loved his water sports business. Liam was probably the next oldest, in his late twenties, and he was already established in law enforcement. Most of the others were younger, but Macy, Olivia, and Kaley all had careers too. Some were fresh out of college, and he didn't know them too well—but still, "young adults" felt like a title that belonged to a youth group. Not a mismatched class of professional single adults.

"Just want to see you happy, bro." TJ turned to take a call, giving Reef a chance to slip away before anyone else caught him. They'd have plenty of time to hang out once they reached Beech Mountain—if this party ever got the show on the road.

A white Nissan sped around the corner, and his chest tightened. He'd recognize that car with the Ron Jon sticker he'd applied anywhere.

Kaley.

Her door shot open and heeled feet hit the pavement, followed by a pencil skirt and matching suit top. Really? She was leaving for the trip wearing that? Maybe he had dodged a bullet.

But in one hand, she clutched a Chick-fil-A® to-go bag like it was her only lifeline, and in the other, she pressed a cell phone tightly to her ear. The flush in her cheeks and messy bun on top of her head suggested it had been a day.

Whatever. She wasn't his concern anymore.

Somehow, she managed to pop open her trunk and drag out a suitcase equally as large as the other girls'. It would be a miracle if all that luggage fit in the van.

And then the CFA bag slipped. Waffle fries bounced onto the pavement, and Kaley let out a little cry. Her suitcase tipped over, crashing barely shy of the bag. She ended the call and bent down to collect the remnants of her dinner.

Something about her body language looked defeated. He should leave now and avoid a tangle with the girl who broke up with him without explanation. The girl who refused to answer his calls.

But he wasn't the kind of guy who could stand to see a woman cry. And if her swollen eyes were any indicator, Kaley was on the verge of a breakdown.

Squaring his shoulders, Reef strode over and righted her luggage. "Let me get that for you."

She glanced up at him from where she kneeled next to her to-go bag. Half a waffle fry hung from her lips, and she stuffed the rest in her mouth. "Oh!"

"Can I give you a hand?" He extended an open palm toward her.

"Thanks." She tucked a wavy strand of her dark blonde hair behind an ear and squeezed his hand.

Her touch sent an electric spark through him. Literally. She zapped him, as if he needed a reminder how crazy attractive he found her athletic build and wide green eyes.

She released his hand as soon as she was standing again and then placed a good three feet between them.

"You okay?"

She bit her lip. "Fine."

Why did girls say they were fine when they weren't? But Kaley wasn't his girlfriend anymore. He should just help her and get out of her way.

"I'll put your luggage with the others." He yanked the handle. "See you in the mountains."

Kaley took a step toward him again and tried to fix the messy bun that had collapsed onto the side of her face. "Thanks, Reef." She actually smiled.

He waved a hand and hurried away. The last thing he needed right now was her looking stupid sexy and sending mixed messages. She broke up with him. That was that.

If only his heart would agree.

Chapter Two

Kaley unwrapped her now cold chicken sandwich and curled against one of the back windows in the van. There was enough room in the passenger van for almost everyone to have a separate seat, and she preferred it that way. She needed time alone with her thoughts.

Where to start? The one day she had to work this week had turned into a disaster. The redeeming factor was that she hadn't lost all her dinner and had time to change into yoga pants, a pullover sweater, and fuzzy socks at church before TJ herded everyone into the van. Florida was typically cool in January, but the Beech Mountain forecast showed lows in the single digits, temperatures she'd never experienced before. She'd crawl into her ski jacket later, but this base layer was a comfortable start.

The van lurched forward, and Kaley missed colliding with the seat in front of her by inches. Guess she should buckle up. Macy had the first shift, and by her own confession, she hadn't driven a passenger van in "forever."

As if on cue, the passengers erupted into noise. Someone in the passenger seat started skimming through radio channels while at least three conversations competed for volume.

Setting her sandwich aside, Kaley fumbled in her bag. If she had forgotten to pack her earbuds, this trip would be torture.

Was that why Reef chose to drive separately?

She couldn't shake the image of his concerned hazel eyes and the feel of his strong grip on her hand as he helped her to her feet. But moments later, his clean-cut jaw had tensed, and he had practically jogged away with her suitcase in tow.

It wasn't like she had the flu or anything.

No, she had broken up with him and burned their bridges.

Her fingers grasped her earbud case and the tablet she'd thrown into her purse. She'd need that too, but for now, she closed her eyes and stuffed in her earbuds. Maybe she could have handled the break-up better. Okay, she definitely could have. But what was done was done, and it was safer this way. Reef was a wildcard with too many variables for her taste.

Plus, it had been over two months since they'd talked. He had to be over her by now and moved on to fresher waters.

Why did that thought make her stomach tighten?

When someone tugged on her earbuds, Kaley flashed her eyes open. Her friend Olivia's dark brown eyes sparkled from behind the seat in front of her. "Are you going to hibernate back there this whole ride?"

"We're barely out of the church parking lot." Kaley grabbed her sandwich to pick at it some more. "And it's been such a long day."

Olivia propped her elbows on the headrest. "What happened? Is that why you had to come straight from work?"

Kaley chewed her bite and forced herself to swallow. Thinking about her meeting with Anthony killed her appetite.

"Yeah, I'm not sure how much I can talk about it, though. It's one of our high-profile cases, and frankly, I don't even work with this client. But my boss is at the hospital with his wife, who's about to have a baby, so I was the only one free to meet with him."

"Him." Olivia pressed her lips together. "Did he try anything weird?"

Kaley forced a tight smile. Olivia had no idea the level of weird her job involved. But then, Olivia was a physical therapist, and her job had to have its share of interesting stories.

"Yes, everything about this client is strange. I put my earbuds in to try to process it and make some sense of my notes before logging them. I don't want Blake to think I didn't do a good job."

Olivia's gaze dropped to the tablet beside Kaley. "You did *not* bring work on this trip."

Kaley nudged the tablet under her leg. "I promise, once I type up these notes, I'm officially unplugged from work."

"I don't believe you."

"I mean it." Kaley leveled her gaze. "I'm not checking social media, emails, or even my phone except once a day. I need a break more than ever, and once I send these final notes to my boss, I'm reminding him we'll be in the mountains with no internet access or phone signal."

Olivia frowned. "We're not tent camping in the Appalachians. I'm sure there will be Wi-Fi at the cabin and cell reception in town."

"Doesn't matter," Kaley said. "He doesn't know that, and I'm not telling him."

"Okay, I believe you. But I'm giving you one hour before roping you into a road trip game."

"I might need two."

"You've got one—unless you want to talk about how totally ruffled Reef looked after he saw you?" Olivia arched a mischievous eyebrow.

Kaley sank lower into her seat and fumbled to stuff the earbuds back into her ears. "One will be fine."

"I'm telling you, Reef likes you." Olivia lowered her voice. "It's not every day girls our age find an attractive single guy who loves Jesus. I can't believe you're not snatching him up."

"My hour starts now." Kaley winked at her and retrieved her tablet.

"Fine. But I have a feeling this trip is going to make you believe I'm not wrong about you and Reef." Olivia spun around in her seat, and Kaley hoped she couldn't hear the pounding of her heart.

She'd been a poor friend not to tell Olivia about dating Reef, but they had agreed not to share their relationship status unless they decided to make it serious.

And it had been about to get serious, until she'd made that phone call.

But no one needed to know. She and Reef were both mature adults. This trip wouldn't change anything.

Kaley willed herself to focus on her tablet screen. She'd snapped a picture of her fragmented meeting notes so she could type and submit them during the road trip. She'd also sent the meeting recording to her drive so she could listen to it again. Maybe she'd start with that.

Could she really make sense of their conversation? It felt as if someone had dumped a thousand-piece puzzle onto a moving conveyor belt and asked her to assemble the pieces. She liked a good puzzle, but this client—he might be more than she could handle.

"The party's on Jack." Those were his first words as he practically lunged at her when she'd opened the door. Or had he meant, "The party's on, Jack"? Not two seconds into the recording, she was already pausing it. Who in the world was Jack?

Blake had warned her about "Jack's revenge," but Anthony had rambled about Jack's party or Jack's joke today. Was that the same thing? She pressed play again on the recording.

Big Eddie, he should have thought twice before messing with Jack. Yeah, Big Eddie and his fancy friends.

Kaley twisted her tablet sideways to enlarge the keyboard and help improve her typing accuracy. At her current rate, she'd need another hour to proofread her notes. She should've brought her laptop.

No, she'd promised herself a break. She'd listen to this meeting one more time, which might take her over Olivia's hour limit, and then get her notes in order for Blake. After that, her no-working, unplugged vacation would begin.

Tell me about Big Eddie. Kaley smiled at the level, calm tone of her voice in the recording. She might not enjoy client sessions like this one, but she was good at de-escalating situations. She could read her clients' emotional and mental states with a few decisive questions and observations—and then identify grounding techniques to calm them.

Yes, she was good at reading people.

Which is why Reef and she would never work.

Kaley bit her lip to refocus her attention. She had to get this done. Reef was a distraction she couldn't afford. Not now. Not ever.

Big Eddie, he thinks he's so big in the hood. Thinks little guys like me don't deserve a better cut. So that's why I make them myself. See, I deserve more.

The trembling in Anthony's voice sent a shiver down her spine. Anthony was afraid—deathly afraid—of this Big Eddie. He tried to pretend he wasn't, but his body language gave him away.

Was that why he sought out Blake's help—her help—today? Did their client legitimately fear for his life?

Unnerving as Anthony was, her heart went out to him. This poor man came to their office seeking help. Her own inadequacies to assess the situation weren't his fault.

Kaley started drafting her email to Blake while the recording continued playing. She didn't buy that Anthony actually worked for "the hood"—or mafia. The Tampa Underground died decades ago.

But there were enough other unsavory characters in Tampa. Depending on whom Anthony crossed, he might have a valid reason to be afraid. She would ask Blake to look into possible protection options for him.

An hour and a half later—and lots of glaring at Olivia to give her more time—Kaley finally powered down her tablet. She'd notified Blake, expressed her concerns, and even waited for him to acknowledge that he'd take the situation from here.

The man was a marvel, juggling new father stress and their client drama without batting an eye. He told her to enjoy her trip and that he'd catch up with her next week.

That was all the invitation she needed to log off, for good. Well, maybe. Her only other reason to power on the device would be to work on her thesis draft, and maybe she'd even take a break from that during this trip. Analyzing Viktor Frankl's theories from a biblical worldview might have to wait till next week.

"About time," Olivia said. "We just convinced Macy to pull over for coffee."

"But it's after nine o'clock, and you don't even drink coffee."

Olivia shrugged. "I told Matt I'd buy him coffee to keep him awake for his shift."

"Very good of you." Kaley unclipped her seatbelt as Macy pulled into a parking space.

Olivia batted her eyes. "Poor Reef has no one to buy him coffee."

"Like you, he doesn't drink coffee." As soon as the words left her mouth, Kaley wished she could retract them.

"Oh, and how do you know that?" Olivia smirked as if she had scored a mark.

"Observation." Kaley slipped past her out the now-open van door and offered a smug smile. "I'm good at reading people."

Chapter Three

Staring at the star-studded mirror, Val pressed on a generous coating of red lipstick. This might be her night to shine, and she had never felt more ready. Never before had a movie she directed been nominated for an Oscar, but *Hood* was special. She had this feeling in her gut.

Maybe because her history tangled too tightly with the fiction of her 1940s gang drama. Didn't every Hollywood icon have skeletons in her closet?

She hadn't been afraid to get dirty, and no one had worked harder to earn a spot on the red carpet than she had. Now, nothing stood in her way from making the next big step in her career.

Not her childhood spent begging on the street. Not her abusive father. Not the men who had manipulated her during her early years in Hollywood. Not her ex.

Not anybody who was still breathing.

A tap on her door pulled her thoughts to the present.

"Ms. Valentina, your limousine is here."

"Thank you," she called back. "I'll be down shortly."

Val pushed away from her vanity and carefully smoothed her black sequined mermaid-style ballgown. It accented her curves in just the right places. Maybe Brian would regret cheating on her when he saw her with her escort tonight.

"Have fun watching the Oscars from your couch." She laughed and inserted a pair of dangling diamond earrings.

But even as she surveyed herself, a pit formed in her stomach. Though she hid them well, forty years had left their mark. Her deep brunette hair, now dyed, didn't quite shine like it used to. Then there were those frightful bags under her eyes, though tonight, no one could see them. Thank her lucky stars for Botox and Guerlain.

There were the much deeper scars as well. Scars she could never erase.

Val pressed a thin smile to her lips. She didn't need to erase them. She had beat them.

Her phone buzzed, and she whirled to find it. Maybe it was in her clutch.

Was it someone wishing her good luck tonight? Was it Brian?

Val laughed as those ridiculous thoughts vanished. She didn't have many friends, and she had blocked Brian.

She retrieved the phone and glanced at the caller ID.

Her heart thudded into her heels. What did Eddie want now? Not more money. Maybe he had an update on their latest joint venture. But Eddie never called unless there was a problem. And tonight, she didn't want any problems.

For a split second, she thought about ignoring the call. After all, she could remind him later that tonight was her big night and she had been too busy to answer.

But she knew better. Eddie always knew when she lied to him.

"Hello, Eddie." She said his name as coolly as her pounding heart would allow.

"Val, it's the Cannoli Commission. We've got a rat."

Val pinched her nose. *Don't panic. Even if this enterprise failed, she still had enough in the bank to get through. Things would just be tight.*

"And the rat said he has insurance."

"Empty threat?"

"No, he was responsible for deposits. No telling how many emails he got copied on. My boys think he may also have cloned our server."

Her hand trembled. Money was one thing. Her reputation was another. She had worked too hard for anyone to demolish this dream. "What does he want?"

There was a low chuckle on the other line. "He wanted his life."

Eddie didn't use the past tense on accident. "Did—do we know where this insurance is?"

"No, he wouldn't talk—and the boys—well, he won't be talking to anyone now."

Val felt herself exhaling a cautious breath. "So we don't need to worry."

"Maybe, maybe not. He went and saw this shrink. But I've got a tracker on her."

"Tracker?" Val asked.

"Yeah, she's moving, going on a ski trip with her church group to a place called Beech Mountain. Ain't that nice."

Val's thoughts raced. If she could talk to this shrink before Eddie's boys got to her, maybe she could find out the truth about this insurance. "Is that out my way? Maybe I could arrange a visit."

Eddie stopped laughing. "It ain't nowhere near your hood, and keep your nose out of this. I'll handle the shrink in my own way."

Eddie only handled rats and their friends with a one-size-fits-all solution.

"But what if she can tell us where it is so we can destroy it? Otherwise, couldn't someone else find it?"

There was a long pause on the line. "Leave business to me. This will blow over. For now, you enjoy that red carpet." A slight pause. "But I will need your help offsetting expenses for extra muscle."

He wanted more money—to help pay for knocking off the rat and shrink. That didn't bother her half as much as him not caring that her interests were as deeply vested in this project as his were.

"Send me an invoice," Val said.

"Knock 'em dead, tonight."

Click.

Val stared at her phone, her mind swirling. Eddie may be the next closest thing to a Tampa godfather, but he was too cut and dry. In his world, there was only black and white, no gray.

An unsuspecting third party like this shrink was definitely a gray area, one that a diplomatic director like herself could better manage. At least, she could get the truth out of her before killing her. Eddie's gang didn't have that kind of tact.

She would have to do it in such a way that Eddie would never know. Otherwise, he wouldn't think twice before knocking her off along with the shrink.

But she had to have that insurance in her hand where she could burn it. Otherwise, she would forever be looking over her shoulder, waiting for her roots and her past to drag down the life she'd built for herself.

Val swept her clutch into her palm and twisted the door open, hurrying down the stairs of her uptown condo as quickly as her stilettos would allow. The place was slightly more than she could afford, but her motto had always been *fake it till you make it*. And make it, she would. Tonight at the Oscars could change everything.

Careful not to catch her heels on the carpet, she tugged out her cell phone. There would be no privacy in the limo, and her escort was probably waiting. The man was a hulk with no personality, so she couldn't risk revealing herself to him.

Instead, she texted Louis, her bodyguard who doubled as her own underground eyes and ears. "Beech Mountain. Everything I need to know and a slope-side rental property. Stat." She added. "Bonus for information on a church group from Tampa staying in the area."

Val smiled smugly and slid her phone into her clutch as the chauffer opened her limo door. Louis would have an update for her when she returned home.

And hopefully, she'd be holding a trophy in her hand.

Chapter Four

Someone had volunteered Kaley to be the navigator for the last leg on the drive, which was ironic. She could barely follow her smartphone's step-by-step directions in her hometown.

Now, it was barely six-thirty in the morning, and what little sleep she'd scored during the overnight drive had left a kink in her neck and what felt like toothpicks in her eyes.

But none of that mattered. Right now, she was more alert than even her morning coffee could make her.

The reason was simple. There was snow. Everywhere.

"Kaley, did you hear me?" Liam's question snapped her to the present. He was driving. Poor guy was probably running on less sleep than she'd had, and now, he was stuck with her borderline useless navigational skills.

"Um, one sec." Kaley shifted her gaze to the smart phone in her lap and pressed the screen back to life.

Liam sighed. "Is this my turn or not?"

Kaley grimaced as she saw her screen. "The good news is that this is not your turn."

"Okay then."

"The bad news is I think we were supposed to take the last exit. My phone signal keeps going in and out, but it currently just says 'rerouting.'"

Liam groaned and shoved one hand in his hoodie pocket while gripping the wheel with his other. "Here." He swung his arm toward her. "Use my phone."

Kaley frowned. "Is my phone not good enough?"

"If it doesn't have a signal, no."

"And how do you know yours will?"

"It's new and I have the best service anywhere."

Well then.

Kaley accepted his phone and pressed the screen. "It's asking for a password."

Liam sighed again. "Shelly513."

Kaley couldn't help herself. "Who's Shelly?"

It was Liam's turn to smirk. "My five-year-old niece whose picture is my wallpaper."

Kaley smiled at the girl's picture. Her strawberry blonde hair was tied up in a high pony tail, and she hung from Liam's neck with the biggest grin on her face. Liam must be a sweet uncle.

"No one for you to be jealous of."

She blinked. Was he still talking to her? Why would she be jealous? Did Liam think …?

Kaley cleared her throat. She liked Liam well enough, but it was too soon for her to think about dating anyone else. Or was it?

"Well, I—uh—say she's already got a pretty big stake on your heart," she teased back. That was casual enough, right?

"This heart's big enough for two."

What should she say to that?

"Oh, wait, I'm supposed to be giving you directions, right?" Kaley recovered and pulled up his maps app.

"Maybe you should just give the phone back to me."

She huffed and typed in the address for breakfast that Pastor TJ provided. "Definitely not. That's not being a safe driver."

"No offense, but I think we might actually get breakfast if you let me or someone else navigate."

"Turn here—*here!*" Kaley shrieked, and Liam yanked the wheel. Murmurs and grunts sounded from the back of the van.

She winced and glanced over her shoulder at the faces glaring at her from the back seat. "Sorry."

Liam snatched his phone from her hand. "I'm taking applications for a new navigator," he called to the back of the bus.

Pastor TJ raised a sluggish hand. "Here."

Kaley rolled her eyes and climbed out of the passenger seat to switch places with TJ. Liam gently touched her arm as she did. "No offense, Kaley."

"None taken."

She preferred a window seat with no responsibilities anyway. Her life was loaded enough. She pressed her face against the window and gasped in delight. "Would you look at all that snow? It's like someone dropped a puffy white blanket everywhere!"

"Haven't you seen snow before?" Pastor TJ laughed as he buckled himself into the passenger seat.

"No, I've lived in Florida all my life, and my family usually traveled during summer break when I was growing up." She sighed as a sense of delight washed over her. "I've seen pictures, but it's so much more shimmery in person."

Liam glanced at her in the rearview mirror and grinned. "It is stunning, especially with the sunrise."

"Right?" She smiled back. "It's clean—and fresh."

Fresh. She could use a fresh start this week, a break from all the burdens her clients had unloaded on her—and especially a break from her unnerving last meeting.

She sneaked another glance at Liam. Was he part of her fresh start? Something in her gut hesitated, and she didn't know why. Liam Bracken was handsome in a classic sort of way with smiling eyes and a muscular, thick build which suited his law enforcement career. His wavy ginger hair and beard had earned him an Ewan McGregor-Obi-Wan joke or two over the years. Reef said Liam and he sometimes worked out together at the gym, and she knew the two were friends.

Reef. Why couldn't she forget the way his grin made the corners of his hazel eyes crinkle? Or the way he had looked at her as though she were the only girl in the room?

She shook the thought away. Had Reef told Liam about *them*? Had he vented that she was the worst girlfriend and to steer clear of her?

She didn't think so, not with the way Liam kept snatching glances at her in the rearview mirror.

Kaley focused her gaze on the scenery. It was so much simpler than trying to untangle the mysteries of her heart.

20

An hour later, after winding through switchbacks that made Kaley thankful she wasn't navigating, the van pulled into a snow-covered parking lot belonging to perhaps the quaintest general store and restaurant she had seen in her life.

"Where are we?" she asked.

"Fred's," Liam said. "That's right, you've never been here before."

"No, but it's like a place that jumped out of a Norman Rockwell painting." Kaley tried to soak in the scene. The blue A-frame building had an old-fashioned *General Mercantile* sign gracing the front, while a fold-up sign by the street advertised the best breakfast in Beech Mountain. A sleigh with a stuffed Santa and snowmen lined one side, while snow-covered bird feeders dotted the other. White Christmas lights dangled from the roofline, and real icicles clung to them, suggesting that at least in Beech Mountain, Christmas didn't end in December. "It's adorable."

He snorted. "You girls and everything being adorable. But Fred's does have the best breakfast cinnamon roll you'll ever taste."

Pastor TJ hopped out and yanked the side door open. "Rise and shine! Breakfast time."

He didn't have to tell her twice. There was snow and cinnamon rolls. Beech Mountain was just what the doctor ordered for her—a place she could forget all the demands of real-life for a few days and enjoy the simplicity and beauty of a season she'd never experienced.

A ridiculous amount of childhood excitement bubbled up inside of her as she stuffed her arms into her thick white ski jacket. Well, she was going to use it as a ski jacket. She had bought it on Black Friday clearance, and the brand said Arctix. That had her convinced it was meant for skiing.

The rest of the passengers looked far less perky than she felt, but she waited for Olivia to crawl out. Her mascara streaked below her eyes.

"What?" Olivia growled at her. "While you were cooing about a winter wonderland, some of us were trying to sleep."

"Sorry." Kaley bit her lip. "I'm just so excited."

"Florida girl." Olivia cut her a sly smirk. "Or does Reef's car parked over there have anything to do with it?"

Kaley glanced to her right, and her stomach dropped. Of course, she knew Reef would be meeting up with them. She just wasn't expecting to see him so soon. And like this. A quick glance in the van window showed that she had the worst case of sleeping-in-a-car hair and her makeup was all smudged.

She looked away from her reflection and took a cold breath. It didn't matter. What Reef thought about her didn't matter.

"Let's go—I'm starving." Kaley linked arms with Olivia and hurried toward the entrance of Fred's where the others were filing inside.

A door chime welcomed them, and the warmth inside melted her nerves. Wooden tables filled the space where customers cupped hot mugs of coffee in their hands and devoured their breakfasts on still-steaming plates.

Along the whole side wall and part of the ceiling were windows where the light filtered through, making the smaller space seem bigger than it was. Local art adorned the walls, while beyond the restaurant, guests perused the store's goods and waited in line for ski rentals.

She could get used to a place like this, but her stomach encouraged her to find a place in line. It had been a long time since her dinner.

"I see you guys finally made it." The voice behind her shoulder made her freeze. She spun to find Reef sitting at one of the smaller tables with an empty plate in front of him.

The members of the group ahead of her turned back around to greet Reef, trapping her in place by the door.

Liam gave him a slap on the back. "Good to see you made it in one piece. How long have you been here?"

"Since they opened," Reef said. His glance grazed her and then returned to Liam. "I was sleeping in my car before then."

"You were sleeping in your car?" Brittany gasped and pushed past Kaley to join the conversation—or get a better look at the guy with the easy-going voice. She was the newest member of the group and clearly eager to make friends, especially with the guys.

"Of course," Reef said. "I'm not about to rent a hotel for two hours. I figured you all would make it eventually."

"Wait, didn't you leave about the same time we did?" Liam asked.

"Yep."

"And you got here two hours before we did?"

"Correct again."

"How is that even possible?" Liam ran a hand through his hair.

Kaley took the moment to nudge Olivia forward, but her friend only smirked at her in response, as if being in Reef's presence would somehow validate Olivia's theory that she and Reef were meant for each other. If she could only squeeze past her...

Reef rose and placed his empty plate above the trash can with some other dirty dishes. He rejoined the group and retrieved his half-full glass of OJ. "Well, you guys stopped how many times for bathroom breaks and to switch drivers? I stopped twice for gas."

"Oh, right, and you didn't have Kaley for a navigator." Liam turned to wink at her right as she finally managed to get around Olivia. *Groan*. Did he have to point her out?

But Reef seemed to ignore her. "My dad brought me up here every winter as a kid, and I haven't missed a ski season since then. I don't need a navigator."

Something about his words felt like ice, and Kaley stepped around Liam to finally get a place in line. Sure, she wasn't a good navigator, but everybody needed somebody, right?

Ugh. What did it matter? She didn't care what Reef thought.

Olivia caught up to her and offered a sympathetic smile, but Kaley pretended to study the menu even though she already knew what she was going to order. The last thing she wanted was her friend's pity about a relationship that had already failed to launch.

"What can I get you?" A waitress with purple hair asked her from behind the counter.

"One of your cinnamon rolls and coffee, please," Kaley said.

"Want the roll heated up?"

"Is there any other way?"

"Not really." The girl smirked and rang her up. "Here's your mug, and you can help yourself at the coffee counter. I'll bring your roll right out."

Kaley had no sooner filled her mug and stirred in a generous amount of cream and sugar than the purple-haired young woman handed her a warm plate with the biggest cinnamon roll Kaley had ever seen. It seemed to ooze cinnamon and brown sugar from every crevice, and Kaley could hardly wait to sink her teeth into it.

"Oh, my word!" Brittany's voice rang out from behind her.

"What's wrong?" Kaley asked.

"You're going to eat that?"

Kaley laughed and stared at her. "Um, absolutely."

"That roll does not belong in anyone's diet. I mean, I feel ten pounds fatter just looking at it."

Kaley offered a wry smile. Really? Brittany who might as well be a model was going to judge her? And how did she manage to tumble out of the van looking so absolutely perfect?

Reef caught her gaze and rose from his place. "You should give it a try, Brittany. A cinnamon roll from Fred's is worth breaking any diet."

Kaley's shoulders relaxed as she claimed a seat with Olivia and their friend Macy. At least Reef wasn't going to judge her eating habits.

But her heart sank into her shoes as he moved into the one empty seat right next to her across from Macy. Was there no escaping his presence?

"You ready to shred?" Reef propped his elbows onto the table.

"Totally," Macy took a gulp of her OJ. "As soon as we have breakfast, I'm asking TJ if we can get in line for our rentals."

Kaley stabbed a fork into her cinnamon roll and focused on the warm goodness touching her tongue. She had always envied

Macy's ability to be so at ease around the guys. Go figure she was a good skier too.

"How long have you been skiing?" she asked Macy.

"Oh, I don't ski." Macy set down her cup. "I snowboard."

"Snowboard," Kaley repeated. "Is that easier than skiing?"

"I'm not sure if it's easier or not, but it does take longer to learn." Reef jumped into the conversation. "I wouldn't recommend any of you newbies try learning to snowboard on such a short trip. It takes a good two to three days to get the hang of it."

"And you fall a lot," Macy grinned. "I should know."

"You were a great student."

"Wait, you taught Macy how to snowboard?" Olivia asked as the waitress appeared with her and Macy's orders

Macy thanked the girl and then turned back to Olivia. "Reef teaches all the newbies. He has the patience of a saint."

"I thought TJ signed us first timers up for a beginner class?" Kaley tried to hide the trembling she felt inside. She might die if she had to learn to ski from Reef.

He chuckled and glanced her way with something like mischief in his eyes. "Those beginner classes are all well and good, but with my teaching, you'll be skiing much better in way less time."

"Aren't you full of yourself!" Olivia said in a teasing voice.

"No, it's true." Macy came to Reef's defense. "The beginner classes are okay, but Reef is a good teacher. You get some one-on-one with him, and you'll be on your way in no time."

Kaley dropped her focus back to her cinnamon roll. One-on-one time with Reef was exactly what she needed to avoid on this trip.

"I'll be glad to help you learn, Kaley."

Kaley jerked her head to find him staring at her with the subtlest of smiles. Was he for real? After how she'd ended things, he was still offering to teach her?

He downed the last of his orange juice and rose. "There are what—two newbies on this trip?"

"Right—Brittany and me," Kaley found her voice.

"Great, then I'll see you on the slopes." He tugged on his beanie cap.

"You'll see us before then." Macy scooped a forkful of eggs. "I think Pastor TJ wants to get our rentals and then drop all our luggage off at the cabin. There's barely any room left in the van for gear, so it's going to be on our laps until we ditch the bags."

"Why don't you load the gear in the back of my Subaru?" Reef asked. "I packed light, so there's plenty of room."

Macy's face broke into the biggest smile. "That would be awesome."

"Perfect, I'll let TJ know." He paused and squinted at Kaley. "You better finish that cinnamon roll. You're going to need all those calories and then some for the slopes."

She offered a nervous chuckle. "Thanks?"

Her stomach tightened, and she stared hopelessly at the unfinished roll. Now there was no way she would be able to finish.

She had thought avoiding Reef would be easy on this trip, but if he made it his mission to be her personal ski instructor, that might be harder than planned.

Why would he volunteer for such a chore when he could simply enjoy the slopes with his friends? Why invest the time and energy into the new skiers—especially when one of them was her?

She couldn't find an answer that matched the profile she'd made for Reef, the profile of a self-sufficient Mr. Popular who worked hard so he could play hard. A dangerously attractive man who didn't seem to have any desire to commit or settle down.

He was unpredictable, nothing like the disciplined, dependable boyfriend she imagined she would date.

Reef was a high-risk and had triggered her flight coping mechanism that she'd perfected after several failed relationships. But had she gotten this guy all wrong? Did kindness and others-centeredness also belong on his profile?

"Are you going to finish that, Kaley?" Macy eyed her plate.

"I think I'm done."

"Good, then let me throw it away. I can't stand to watch the remains of your breakfast be played with."

Kaley dropped her fork. Playing with her food was a bad habit from childhood that resurfaced when she was nervous. "Sorry."

Olivia patted her hand. "You're going to do great out there. Skiing is so much fun."

"Says the girl who's been skiing since she was twelve."

Olivia gathered the rest of the plates and placed them on top of the trash can with the other used dishes. "Skiing is like riding a bike. Once you learn, it's a cinch."

Right, she just had to learn.

"And with Reef as your coach, you'll be shredding in no time," Macy said.

If only she could tell them that Reef being her coach was what had her terrified.

Chapter Five

Reef glanced at his phone and zoomed in on the Life360 app. It was coming in handy—not so TJ could track him but so that he could track TJ. Go figure his friend had forgotten to give him the directions to the cabin.

He was practically on top of the red dot now, and ahead of him was a snow-covered circular driveway leading to a two-story wooden cabin. If his dad were here to see it, he'd say that's the kind of cabin he'd like to have in the family someday.

The thought made him smile. He and his dad had taken a road trip to Beech Mountain to see the foliage last fall. It had been a good trip, just the two of them like it had been for so many years when he was growing up. Now that Dad had a new family with his step-mother Sherri and teenager step-sister Melissa, Reef was extra grateful for the opportunity.

Sure, he loved his extended family, but time alone with Dad was still special, even if Reef was thirty-five. An advantage of the years passing was no longer having to deal with his dad's awkward attempts at single parenting. The downside was getting to see his dad only a few times a year since he and Sherri now lived in Texas.

He parked his Subaru off the road. Who had been crazy enough to drive the van all the way down the steep driveway, still covered with snow? It was probably sleep-deprived TJ. Hopefully the man could get out of the driveway as easily as he had plowed into it.

The van doors opened, and the girls hopped out, one after another. Olivia and Brittany were all bundled up with their thick jackets, fuzzy snow boots, and colorful scarves, like a fashion parade.

Kaley was dressed simply in her snow-white jacket and yoga pants that hugged her curves in all the right places.

Shaking his head, he looked away. That girl could turn his head faster than anyone since ... well, since he was twenty-one. And he was a lot more stupid back then.

After retrieving his backpack, Reef strode toward the front and opened the door. Inside, several girls were squealing about the cabin and how perfectly "rustic" it was. He hoped it was their coffee and lack of sleep, because if this noise level was the normal inside the cabin, he might sleep in his Subaru again tonight.

TJ emerged from a room to his right, and his face lit up. "Hey, man! Glad you made it. Give me a hand with the food?"

"Sure." Reef slung his backpack onto a chair in the living room and went back into the cold. Not that it bothered him. He knew how to layer.

Freshly fallen snow covered everything in sight, giving the world the appearance of a fresh start. If only he could have that with Kaley.

What had gone wrong? Their dates had been the most fun he'd had with a girl, because Kaley didn't mind getting wet, dirty, or going out of her comfort zone. More important was that they both shared the same faith and core values. Even if she was more disciplined in her practice than him, he was sincere. Didn't his actions show that?

Plus, they had the same convictions. He had dated so many awesome girls, but none of them had seemed to understand why drinking was a deal-breaker. It wasn't that he looked down on them for drinking. Many of his best friends drank, and he didn't have a problem if their convictions were different.

But the girl he married had to share this conviction. His mother had broken his heart when she chose alcohol over him. No ten-year-old should have to lose a mother the way he had. He couldn't lose his future wife the same way.

That propensity ran in his blood. He needed the girl who would be his wife—and someday be the mom to their kids—to understand why they could never have beer in the fridge.

And Kaley had. She had her own reasons for not drinking.

So what had gone wrong? Maybe if he could figure that out, he could find a way to make it right. Or should he just keep his distance? But girls like Kaley didn't come around all the time. He had almost twenty years of dating to prove that.

Reef grabbed two cases of water and trudged back inside in search of the kitchen. Olivia and Kaley were already putting away orange juice, unloading breakfast muffins, and cramming snacks onto a shelf. He had to give TJ credit for buying enough food to feed an army.

Olivia must have noticed his load, because she pointed to a space behind a wooden table. "You can put the water in that corner."

He stole a glance at Kaley who seemed unnecessarily focused on organizing muffins. Maybe she was pretending he wasn't here.

"Kaley, can you hand that box to Reef to put on the shelf?" Olivia's words broke into his thoughts. "We don't need all of these on the counter, and we're too short to reach that shelf."

"Um, sure." Kaley swept up the box and stepped toward him. "Here."

Color flooded into her cheeks and made his own blood rush faster.

In his peripheral, TJ appeared at the doorway, and Reef tore his gaze off Kaley to meet his friend's worried expression. "Okay, Reef, so I need a favor."

"What's that?" Reef shelved the box and forced himself not to steal another look at Kaley. "More supplies to unload?"

"No, that was the last of them." TJ ran a hand through his hair. "It's the van."

"It's stuck?" Reef hated that he was right about the van's situation.

"Yeah, the snow is deeper than it looked. I can't get it out of the driveway, and we're already running late. The newbies are supposed to be at the slopes for their ski lessons in half an hour."

Reef smiled. The newbies included Kaley. "I can take them in my Subaru."

"I was hoping you'd say that," TJ said. "Liam and Matt are shoveling the driveway, so hopefully, the rest of us won't be far behind you."

TJ turned to Kaley. "Can you find Brittany, and let her know that you both need to be ready to leave in five minutes?"

Kaley blinked. "I don't even know where my suitcase ended up."

"Oh, I had Liam put it in the room with mine," Olivia said. "Hope you're cool with us being roomies."

Kaley's lips spread into a grin. "Of course! But where is our room?"

"Second floor, first door on the left."

Kaley edged past Reef and disappeared down the hallway. He would give more than a penny for her thoughts right now.

But soon, he'd have his chance to spend some time with her now that he was her ride. "I'll grab my gear and be ready to head out," he told TJ.

"I owe you," TJ said and then started talking to Olivia about meal plans.

"It's my pleasure." And really, it was. The last time Kaley had ridden in his Subaru had been their final date together, which definitely hadn't gone as planned. He had taken her down the Hillsborough River, and out of nowhere, his jet ski had died. Sam, his friend and colleague at the shop, had to close early so he could come pull them from the river. But she had stayed so calm the whole time. Had she really been upset?

"Get a grip, man," he muttered. He either had to accept that he wasn't ready to give up on Kaley or find a way to get her out of his mind.

Kaley was more than happy to let Brittany ride shot gun. The less eye contact and conversation with her ex-boyfriend, the better. Right?

"What kind of music is this?" Brittany asked as innocently as a cream puff. But surely even a girl like Brittany had to know Reef's music was ridiculous.

"It's keep-me-awake music." Reef threw an arm around the passenger seat and glanced over his shoulder to check the road.

The move sent his gaze her direction. Kaley squirmed and pretended to focus on the snow-covered scenery around them.

"It's—interesting."

Oh, Brittany. She was trying too hard.

"The only two words to the song are Cool and Beans," Kaley muttered.

"I see you remember this classic." Reef's voice held a teasing tone.

"Remember?" Brittany pounced. "You've heard this song before?"

"Hang around with the church group long enough, and you'll hear lots of things." Kaley forced a chuckle for Brittany's sake. "And trust me, once you've heard it once, you won't forget it."

"Funny, I've never heard anyone in our group play it …"

Kaley cleared her throat. It was time for a change of subject, even if she already knew the answer. "Reef, how long have you been coming to Beech?"

His gaze flitted to the rear-view mirror to catch her attention. It was as if he were questioning her intentions.

But they were on this church trip together, and as far as she was concerned, they needed to act normal—or as normal as this group could be.

"I've been coming since I was a boy." His tone was softer. "Like I said at Fred's, my dad taught me to ski here."

"Oh, that's so special!" Brittany squealed. "But if your parents like the snow so much, why did they name you Reef? It's kind of a strange name—no offense."

Kaley choked down a laugh. Leave it to Brittany to combine flirting and insults in the same sentence.

Maybe Reef was having a hard time not laughing either, because he cleared his throat before replying. "None taken. It was actually my mom's idea. Although my dad was from the mountains, she was a surfing hippie when he met and married her."

Biting her lip, Kaley dared to look in the rear-view mirror to glimpse Reef's expression. He wore a sad smile, and understandably so. She'd heard this story before.

"My parents were really young when they got married. Mom turned Dad's head around, but on the honeymoon, he realized she had been hiding a drinking problem. When they found out they were pregnant not long after that, Dad was worried for my safety and told my mother she could name me whatever she wanted as long as she promised not to drink during the pregnancy."

"And she picked *Reef* because she loved the water?" Brittany asked.

"She did—and I'm thankful to my dad and God that she kept her promise until I was born." Reef's jaw tensed, and he seemed extra focused on the road.

Kaley's eyes moistened. She was thankful too. She'd read about the irreversible effects of fetal alcohol syndrome. It was horrifying what those innocent babies suffered because their mothers drank.

Brittany checked her makeup in the passenger mirror. "So, what did she name your siblings?"

Closing her eyes, Kaley counted to ten. Brittany wasn't picking up on Reef's nonverbal cues that he'd rather not talk about this anymore.

Reef didn't answer right away. Instead, he took a deep breath and kept his eyes fixed straight ahead. "I don't have siblings. My mom died when I was ten."

"Oh, I'm sorry." At least Brittany had the decency to apologize before starting down another rabbit trail moments later.

The only benefit was that the girl's chatter left her alone with her thoughts. Kaley dropped her gaze to her gloved hands. Reef's dad meant the world to him, since he was all the blood family he had left. His mom's early death from liver failure had been a hard blow. When he had told her the tragic story of her descent into alcoholism, she had felt a bond with him. Her grandfather had been an alcoholic, and her dad had made her and her brother Zack promise never to touch the stuff.

Yes, she knew more about Reef and he knew more about her than a regular acquaintance should. How could she reverse the sense of intimacy and trust they had built? Well, she had broken it off after all. But still, something lingered between them, a sense that their breakup was too fresh and that the memory of what they had together might bring pain.

"Did you hear that, Kaley?" Brittany brought her attention back to the present.

"Sorry, what?"

"Reef was so young when he first came here that his dad actually used a leash-technique to help him learn how to ski!"

"That's sweet." Kaley couldn't help but smile. Toddler Reef must have been adorable. But even as a toddler, he'd missed having a mom in his life because of her regular visits to rehab. Her absence must have been so hard on him at an age when no child should have to wonder why mommy wasn't coming home.

Though Reef had come to grips with his past, she sensed perhaps underlying attachment issues. Did his sharing all this information reveal an anxious attachment style that would intrude into any future relationship? It had certainly crossed her mind and been one of the concerns she'd had.

She couldn't marry a case. Not that she didn't care about her patients—she did—but playing therapist to a husband would never work. She just hoped she hadn't added any more pain to his life.

Kaley never wanted to hurt another boyfriend again. Before she met Reef, she'd learned the hard way the pain that ending a serious relationship could bring. Her previous ex had become verbally abusive when she had asked for a time-out in their relationship, because he had started asking her for more intimacy than she was willing to give while dating.

When she had broken things off with Reef, she'd braced herself for another verbal berating, but he had surprised her. Though he seemed disappointed, he had respected her decision and even wished her the best. It wasn't what she had been expecting, and though she had been relieved, it had also made her wonder if she had him all wrong.

Maybe he now had a secure attachment style, despite his past. Or perhaps by being non-emotional, he actually revealed an avoidant attachment style?

Ugh, it didn't matter. She had analyzed the situation more times than she should have and still didn't have Reef figured out. Maybe that was her real problem: dealing with unknowns.

Whatever. The past was the past, and she wasn't going to let it ruin her day. She needed to let this go.

The next half hour was a blur of busyness. Once they reached the slopes, they lined up for their rental equipment and lift tickets. A young worker, probably high school or college age handed her the heaviest boots she'd ever worn.

But they weren't ordinary boots. They were ski boots–and they felt like weights on her legs. Lumbering up the entrance of the bunny hill while holding her skis and sticks was harder than she'd imagined. All her friends said skiing was so easy, but at this point, she could barely stand up straight in the boots—and she hadn't even locked them into her skis.

"Let me give you a hand." And with that, Reef took her skis and stomped a fresh path up the bunny hill.

"Thanks." But the cool breeze snatched her words away, and it was all she could do to follow his footsteps.

"Help!" Brittany shrieked from somewhere behind her, but Kaley didn't dare look back until she reached the top. Reef dropped her skis in front of her and rushed back down the snowy hill.

Reaching level ground, Kaley spun right as Brittany released all her skis and poles as if they were pieces in a game of Pick-Up-Sticks. Brittany's attempt to retrieve them while maneuvering her boots in the icy snow made her look like Goofy on ice. Kaley suppressed a giggle, but it died in her throat when Reef bent down to help Brittany and offered her a hand.

Kaley looked away. It shouldn't bother her if he took Brittany's hand. She couldn't begrudge him for being more than kind to the two klutzes in the group.

She squared her shoulders and hobbled toward a circle of other awkward skiers. Hopefully Reef would simply drop them off with the instructor and let them fumble without watching. She couldn't bear for Reef to see how cumbersome this learning curve felt for her. Maybe a ski trip wasn't the best plan for a relaxing weekend after all.

"You here for the beginner class?" A teenage boy to her left asked.

"Yes, is it that obvious?" Kaley laughed.

He grinned and adjusted the Beech Mountain logoed beanie. "Everyone has to start somewhere."

Says the local who probably could ski before he could walk.

"Circle up with the others—but don't put your skis on yet."

She wouldn't dream of it.

The kid offered a hand to steady another newbie and then called to a stray skier to rejoin the group. Go figure this teenager was her instructor.

Moments later, Brittany stomped next to her. "These boots are awful!"

Reef placed skis in front of her. "Yeah, they are. But you get used to them."

"Yours don't look nearly as restrictive," Brittany said.

"That's because I have snowboard boots."

She moaned. "I should have signed up for that instead."

"It's a lot harder." Reef pointed at a snowboarder on the bunny slope. Moments later, he face-planted in the snow.

Kaley chuckled, then winced. That would probably be her later today.

"You can learn the basics of skis in a day or two." Reef's tone was gentler again, and he seemed to be talking to her.

Kaley swallowed. Reef going out of his way to be nice added a whole new layer of awkward to this situation.

"Thanks for your help," she said. "I guess our ski class starts soon."

Reef frowned in the direction of the instructor. "I could teach you in half the time it's going to take him."

She stabbed her poles into the snow. "But at least you won't be tied down with us beginners." *You're welcome. Now go have fun without us.*

"It's no trouble," Reef said. "I like seeing people learn new things. I'll be back to check in with you in an hour after your class. Then the real ski lesson begins."

"I can't wait!" Brittany's laugh held a wobble. Maybe she was more nervous about skiing than she let on.

It was wrong of her, but Kaley felt a tinge of satisfaction knowing she wouldn't be the only uncoordinated newbie.

"Circle up!" The ski instructor called and swiped his beanie off to wave everyone to attention. Sans beanie, the teen's disheveled blonde hair spiked every which direction. His unkempt style and I-could-do-this-in-my-sleep confidence brought to mind the time Reef attempted to give her surfing lessons. If skiing was similar, she was going to be sore tonight, but at least this instructor wouldn't intrude into her dreams.

Get it together, girl.

As best as they could, the group of eight lumbered into a circle. Step by step, the teenage-instructor explained how to insert one boot into one ski, then the other.

He demonstrated "the pizza" or plowing method for slowing down. And if that failed, they should fall backward to stop. That shouldn't be too hard, right?

Wrong. Every movement was a struggle. If nothing else, skiing would provide an exercise in humility.

The one redeeming moment was the ride on the "magic carpet," or moving walkway, on the far side of the practice area that propelled them to the top of the bunny hill. Kaley had just glided onto it when the hair on the back of her neck prickled.

She jerked her head to see who was behind her. There was no one but another beginner student.

But she couldn't shake the feeling that she was being watched.

Chapter Six

Holding her breath to stay balanced, Kaley shoved her pole onto the clip securing her boots to the skis. Her instructor made this move look easy, but she kept sliding backwards into the fence outside the lodge.

"How was your class?" Liam caught her off guard, and she had to lean forward to keep from hitting the fence again. Kaley couldn't escape skiing enthusiasts.

"Tiring." At least she had managed to evade Reef since class let out, and Brittany was still practicing her heart out.

"You can't be quitting so soon." He readjusted his grip on a snowboard. "We just got here."

"It took that long to get the van out?" Kaley finally unclipped her boots and then leaned her skis against the fence. Now, she had to remember her number so she didn't accidentally take someone else's skis.

"Yeah, it was dicey. We shoveled the driveway, but the van kept sliding on the ice. A neighbor with a truck eventually towed us out."

That sounded almost as tiring as her bunny slope lesson. "Glad you finally made it. Have fun out there."

"Now wait a minute." Liam said. "You didn't come all the way from Florida to sit in a lodge."

"But there's hot chocolate in the lodge. Maybe I'll see you out there later."

Liam gave her a sideways smile. "Join me, and I'll buy you hot chocolate in a few."

A skier came up fast in her peripheral, and Kaley flinched. Getting plowed into by another novice skier was something she'd like to avoid.

But it was Reef. He unclipped his board and slapped Liam on the back. "Good to see you guys finally made it. There's some nice powder out there."

"I was trying to convince Kaley to come out with me." Liam nudged her with his elbow.

Reef's features seemed to freeze for a moment. "You might want to rethink that offer until she's had some real training."

"But didn't you take a class?" Liam turned to her.

"Yes ..."

"That was amateur hour." Reef told Kaley. "You ready for your real lesson now?"

She was ready for a cup of hot chocolate and to get out of these miserable boots.

"These your skis?" Reef nodded toward the ones she'd propped up on the fence.

"Yes, but ..."

He tossed them on the ground in front of her. "Come on, I'll take you up the green, and we'll go real slow."

Kaley glanced apologetically at Liam. "Guess hot chocolate will have to wait."

"My offer still stands." He clipped in to his board and saluted Reef. "Good luck, you guys."

"Ha, thanks," she muttered. Her stupid snow boots didn't want to clip in, and it didn't help that these guys made everything look so easy.

"You've got to get rid of the extra snow on the skis." Reef kicked it off. "Try again now."

Clipping in was still harder than it should be, but Kaley finally heard the snap. "Okay, I'm not very good at this. And didn't you want to help Brittany too?"

Reef shrugged. "She's still falling on the bunnies. You only fell twice that I saw. I'd say you're ready for the green."

He'd seen her fall twice. Great, so he'd been watching her. Then he should know the only reason she hadn't fallen more was that she was being too careful.

"You won't get better if you don't go for it." He nodded toward one of the chair lifts. "C'mon. Follow me."

Somehow, she propelled herself toward the lift line. That's when she noticed that most people were going in pairs, and Reef had positioned himself with room next to him. He waved her over.

There was no avoiding squishing beside him in the lift chair.

"We'll ski to the line when it's our turn. Then, sit back when the chair reaches us, and I'll pull down the bar."

"Okay." She gritted her teeth. *I can do this.*

They slid onto the chair lift seat without a hitch, and Kaley let her shoulders relax. The lift reminded her of riding the skyline at Tampa's Busch Gardens theme park. This part wasn't so bad.

"That's the blue trail over there." He pointed to her right. "We'll get you there soon enough."

"Uh-huh."

"And up there is the black diamond. Maybe next year, you'll be ready for that."

Today made her feel as if she were ready for nothing, but she wouldn't argue. She could handle Reef in his tour-guide persona. As long as he didn't get personal, this situation didn't have to be weird.

Never mind. It was definitely weird that her ex-boyfriend wanted to teach her to ski.

Too soon, the end of the lift came in sight. "Now getting off can be tricky, but all you have to do is stand up when we reach the end, and the chair will push you forward."

"Okay." Kaley gripped her poles.

Reef gave her a nervous glance. "Just do what I do."

But when their chair reached the bottom, she forgot everything. The next thing she knew, she was sprawled on the snowy ground underneath the chair lift.

Reef snow-boarded to her side and helped her slide out of the way so the next passengers could get off. "You jumped! Why?"

Kaley groaned and tried to right herself. "I don't know. I was trying to be ready."

"Never jump off the lift."

"I got that."

Reef's face lit into a smile. "I hope so. Here, give me your hand."

He squeezed her hand and helped her to her feet. "All right then. You ready?"

Ready for this endlessly awkward morning to be over.

But they had the whole mountain to ski down. Together. Awkward would be sticking around for a while longer.

She pasted on a smile. "Sure."

"This top section is a little steep in parts, but then it levels out. Follow me and do what I do."

Kaley still had her poles dug into the snow as Reef slid down the top looking completely relaxed.

"Follow him. Do what he does," she muttered to herself. Yet she didn't want to follow Reef or do life the way he did. His job seemed like a game to him. She viewed her work with seriousness and careful attention. He had no five-year-plan. She had goals.

He could ski down the mountain. She couldn't.

Kaley sighed and retracted her poles. "Just do what he does for now."

Somehow, she managed to get past the first steep section but then skied out of control into a snow mound beneath a blower. She gave Reef a thumbs up that she was fine, retracted her skis, clipped in, and tried again.

Could she possibly get down the mountain any slower? Kaley went from racing out of control to yard-sale wipeouts, Reef's phrase for when she lost all her skis and poles. When they finally reached the bottom, she was exhausted.

"That was awful." She moaned.

Reef's face was tight. "It wasn't awful, but you scare me."

She stared at him. "Scare you? You're not the one falling all the time."

"Everyone falls," Reef said. "The scary part is that you ski like you know what you're doing, but you don't have any control."

She glared at him. "Tell me something I don't know."

"Being out of control must be maddening for someone like you."

What was that supposed to mean?

"Thanks for the lesson." She bit her lip. "I think I'm going to take a break."

He shook his head. "No, we're going to do it again."

Kaley groaned and searched for anyone to rescue her. But none of her friends were in sight. There was only a tall man on the edge of the fence—and he was staring at her.

She shivered. Maybe he thought she was someone else. "I don't know if I can."

"Sure, you can. One more time, and then Liam can buy you hot chocolate." The edge to his voice was unmistakable.

"And then you can give Brittany her lesson," she shot back.

He took off for the chair lift. Did he expect her to follow him? Of course, he did.

With a sigh, she shoved off after him. This ski trip was turning out to be anything but rest and relaxation.

At this point, the best she could hope for were no broken bones—and no broken hearts.

She never wanted to leave this hard, uncomfortable seat. Ever.

Kaley propped her aching legs, boots and all, onto an adjacent chair in the lodge, not caring if any of the other skiers mulling about noticed she was occupying more than her share of valuable sitting space. But most were too busy eating over-priced cafeteria food or huddling around the giant fireplace in the one corner to care about her.

Except for that one guy who kept showing up everywhere she was today. Must be a weird coincidence.

Exhaling another pent-up breath, she glanced out the lodge window. The second time down the green slope, she had only fallen once, but the whole time, she felt like an accident waiting to happen.

She had excused herself when Brittany wobbled over and asked Reef for her ski lesson. How did that girl still look so perfect? Her straight blonde hair poked through a ponytail hole in her snow-princess-pink beanie cap and fell gracefully off one shoulder. Her glossy lips curled in a smile at Reef who taught her the "pizza" technique of forming a triangle with her skis to slow down.

If only Kaley could look that charming while skiing. Right now, her nose felt like Rudolph, and her hair was still damp with snow where her cap had come off during her last fall.

"Hot chocolate?" Liam appeared to her left, holding two steaming paper cups.

She smiled and accepted one. "How did you know I was here?"

"I spotted you coming down the green slope and guessed you'd beeline for the lodge." He blew on his cup and smiled at her.

"You weren't wrong." The heat from the cup warmed her hands and seemed to thaw something inside her.

"I see it's Brittany's turn for a lesson." Liam nodded toward the window. Sure enough, Reef was still helping Brittany with her form. She skidded toward Reef with her skis framed in a pizza shape but didn't stop. She ended up plowing into Reef, sending them both to the ground.

"Looks like she's having a good time anyway." Kaley snorted and cradled her cup more tightly.

"You jealous?" Liam arched an eyebrow at her, and there was a seriousness to his expression she didn't understand.

"Course not." She forced a lightness into her voice that she didn't feel. "I'm sipping hot chocolate in a heated lodge, and she's getting snow up her jacket."

"So, you don't have a thing for Reef?"

Kaley's lips stilled on the edge of her cup. What was he driving at? Maybe Reef told him they had dated, but if he hadn't, she'd rather not go there. Best to assume Liam was ignorant.

"No, I don't 'have a thing for Reef.'" She sipped at her drink, but it burned her throat.

She gasped for air. "Hot."

Liam's expression lightened. "Yeah, you might want to let that cool."

"Duly noted." She caught him studying her with something like ... interest? Oh, wait. Oh, no.

The last thing she wanted was to get asked out right now.

Kaley cleared her throat. "You know what's weird about ski slopes?"

Liam blinked. "What?"

"It's weird how people stare at you—at complete strangers. I mean, any other place it would be considered rude. But maybe they're trying to find someone, and everyone else is wearing the same gray, black, or white ski jackets."

"You've caught someone staring at you?" Liam asked.

The hair on the back of her neck prickled again. Kaley twisted in her seat to glance around the lodge.

She caught her breath. There, at the fireplace, was the same tall man in the black jacket who had been her shadow today. He turned away when he saw her.

A shiver crept up her spine, and she spun to face Liam again. "Yeah. That guy at the fireplace."

Liam slanted his eyes to focus behind her. "You mean the really big guy?"

"Right, I mean, do you think he's mistaken me for someone else?" Kaley forced her shoulders down. There was no need to get all panicky.

Refocusing his attention on her, Liam offered a crooked smile. "You can't fault a guy for staring at a pretty girl."

Heat rushed to her face, probably making her Rudolph nose glow brighter. "You're too kind."

"Well, it's true."

The double doors in the front swung open, and cold air rushed in, soon followed by Brittany and Reef. Brittany waved and hurried toward them as if she'd been separated from her best friends for years.

But who had cut the training session short: Reef or Brittany? Kaley might never know. It didn't matter anyway.

"Is that hot chocolate?" Brittany gasped. "I am so cold."

"They sell it over by the cafeteria." Liam nodded past the rows of tables.

"Oh, will you come get some with me?" Brittany rocked on her boots and cast her best baby face at Reef.

Kaley wanted to gag. Why did this girl annoy her so much?

Reef collapsed into a seat next to Liam. "I think I'll take a load off for a few minutes. Help yourself though."

"But I've never been to the cafeteria."

Liam kinked an eyebrow. "You won't get lost. It's right around the corner."

"Come with me, Kaley?" Brittany pleaded.

Brittany didn't need a chaperone to buy hot chocolate, but at least the errand would give her an escape from Reef's piercing eyes and Liam's subtle smiles. He was sending signals and clearly had no intention of buying Brittany hot chocolate.

"All right." Kaley winced as the tops of her boots bit into her shins. These stupid boots.

"You're the best!" Brittany clomped across the floor with all the grace of a lumbering bear. Not even she could make these ski boots look good.

Kaley felt the man's eyes on her again as they passed the fireplace. Maybe Tampa wasn't the only city with creepers. Once past him, she cast a glance back at Reef and Liam.

Their faces were serious, and they were both facing her but looking toward the fireplace. Had Liam told Reef about the guy who'd been watching her?

She shouldn't have said anything. One weird guy didn't warrant getting her over-protective ex-boyfriend involved or alarming the one member of their group who was a police officer.

"So which size did you get?" Brittany's voice interrupted her thoughts.

"Sorry, what?"

"Small or large hot chocolate?" Brittany said. "Your size looks about right."

Kaley's cheeks warmed. "I—um—Liam got this for me."

Brittany's eyes widened as a smirk formed on her face. "Oh, really? Are you guys …?"

"Just friends," Kaley hurried to add.

"That's the best place to start." Brittany winked. "Reef and I are just friends, too, but seriously, he is the absolute cutest human I've laid eyes on. I adore how sweet he is with us newbies."

The absolute cutest human. Kaley had no response for that.

Brittany ordered her hot chocolate and turned back to face her, concern etched on her expression. "You—you think I'm too young for him?"

"What? No, I mean, he's older than you for sure, but …"

"I know!" Brittany gushed. "He's thirteen years my senior, but stranger things have happened, right? I mean, I'm pretty sure my grandfather was almost fifteen years older than my grandmother, so age really makes no difference."

But maturity does. Kaley hid her lips on her cup. Nothing she said right now would come out right.

"I think he might like me, too," Brittany rushed on. "He reached for my hand several times to steady me today. Training the newbies is a smart way to meet pretty girls."

"Yeah …" They were nearly back to the guys. This conversation needed to end.

Brittany winked at her and lowered her voice. "And I hope things work out for you and Liam, too."

Kaley's jaw dropped, but she clamped it shut.

Liam rose as they arrived. "I'm getting ready to head out. Want to take the green with me, Kaley?"

The offer was so pointed, and he had bought her hot chocolate. Still, Brittany was going to get all the wrong ideas, and if she left now, that meant she'd be setting her up with Reef. Whatever. He was a big boy. He could handle her.

Kaley gulped down the last of her hot chocolate. "Sure. I guess I can survive a few more falls today."

"You got this." Reef offered her a tight smile.

Was it her imagination, or did he look extra stiff next to Brittany?

"Don't jump off the chair lift again."

Kaley laughed at the all-too-fresh memory. It felt good to laugh, even if this whole day had her on edge. "Never again."

She ignored Brittany's obvious wink and pulled her still-damp beanie cap further down on her ears. "See you kids on the slopes."

Chapter Seven

Did they have everyone? Did the whole group remember their gear? How many times had he asked TJ that this evening? Only half the crew had stayed for night skiing, but somehow, having the group split up made keeping track of people so much harder.

"See you back at the cabin!" TJ called from the bus, and Reef half-waved back. He had done more rounding up than their fearless leader, and he was beat.

Reef knocked the excess snow and ice from his boots and shoved his feet into his regular boots. Though snowboard boots weren't nearly as bad as the ones Kaley was wearing, getting his hiking boots back on felt good.

Dinner and a shower would feel even better. And hopefully, both were waiting for him back at the cabin. That was the only reason TJ had agreed to drop off Kaley, Olivia, and Brittany early. They had promised to have food ready for them.

Skiing with Liam and Macy had been much easier than teaching the newbies, but he'd be lying to himself if he pretended teaching Kaley wasn't the highlight of his day. She was so determined and such a fast learner. Why did she have to be so hard on herself?

Could it be their breakup was more about her than it was about him?

The question wouldn't leave him alone all afternoon. They had been so good working together on the slopes. They had been so good together, period.

But it was becoming apparent he'd have competition winning her back. Liam wasn't afraid to show how he felt about Kaley, and he couldn't blame his friend. It was his own fault. If he had simply told Liam they had dated and he still liked Kaley, Liam would have kept his distance. Now, he wondered if he could get her back without hurting his friend. If he could even get her back.

Dating was a messy business.

Reef cranked up his *Hot Rod* music. Kaley didn't get the nostalgia this CD held for him. She also didn't understand how it kept him awake while he was driving.

"Stop thinking about her," he muttered and turned the music louder. He was too tired for any more girl drama tonight. Brittany had worn him out with her flirting. He didn't want to hurt her, but she was not his type and too immature. It would be best if he could avoid both of them tonight.

After parking on the edge of the driveway to keep from being snowed in, Reef trudged to the front porch. He could hear laughter and music coming from the kitchen, because the girls had popped open the window. It must be toasty inside for them to do that.

But it was the smells that absorbed him. Garlic, pasta … dinner! He swung the front door open—and nearly barreled into Kaley.

Her eyes widened, and her hands flew to the towel wrapped around her hair like some kind of Arabian headdress.

"Sorry, it's cold out there." Reef stepped inside and closed the door. He rubbed his hands together to give his energy somewhere to go. So much for avoiding her all night.

She adjusted her headdress. "Yes—it is. But the heaters work really well. The bathroom feels like a sauna with that heater on."

"That's great." He shifted his gaze away from her fuzzy sweater, which looked extra cute on her. Where had that thought come from?

"Um, dinner's ready, I think." Hand still stationed on top of her head towel, Kaley retreated to the kitchen.

He followed her. The shower could wait, but his stomach was a different story. He no sooner stepped toward the kitchen entrance than Olivia emerged and reached for a metal bell attached to the wall.

"You want to ring the dinner bell?" she asked.

He grinned. "Does that mean I get to start the dinner line?"

She rolled her eyes. "What happened to ladies' first?"

"Chivalry is not dead. It's on vacation." The moment the words left his mouth, he regretted them. Olivia wasn't the best at picking up on his humor, and the last thing he needed was her feeding Kaley lies that he was a chauvinist.

"Just kidding," he added hastily and rang the bell before Olivia could argue.

He waited an appropriate amount of time for the girls who were present to go first, but he filed in after them. No one knew when the others would finish showers and waiting that long was ridiculous.

Reef scooped a heaping pile of spaghetti and two garlic bread slices. He had barely forked the first bite into his mouth when a hair-sopping Brittany ran through the dining doors. She wasn't wearing her make-up, a first for her, but even stranger was the wild look in her eyes.

"Has anyone seen my Fitbit?"

Reef swallowed and twisted more pasta around his fork, but a pit forming in his stomach warned him he might never get to eat it.

Brittany ran over to his place at the table. "Was I wearing it when we were skiing?"

He swiped a napkin over his lips and sighed. "I don't know. You were wearing a long-sleeve jacket."

"I know I was." She was so close her hair was dripping on to his shoulder. "I checked my calories on the green, so I must have taken it off when we took a break at the lodge. I was sweating, and everything on me felt gross."

Reef glanced at the clock. There was still another hour left of night skiing. If they left now, they could get to the lodge before it closed, and he could maybe finish a cold dinner around ten o'clock.

He pushed his chair back and stood. "I can take you back there and look for it, but we have to hurry." He paused and searched the girls' faces around him. "And someone else should come with us."

Chivalry was not dead, but his reputation would be if he drove twenty-something bombshell Brittany back to the ski resort alone.

His gaze stopped on Kaley. Would she volunteer to help? Or did she find Brittany as annoying as he did?

She frowned and adjusted her towel. Clearly, she didn't want to go anywhere tonight.

Just then, the front door opened, and TJ, Macy, and Liam filed in. Reef started forward, but Brittany ran ahead of him, blurting her sob story.

"I offered to go back and look for it if someone comes with us," he said after Brittany stopped for breath.

"I'll go," Macy said. "But ya'll had better save us some dinner, or trust me, there will be consequences."

Reef smiled. The world needed more girls like Macy.

"We will," Olivia piped up from the table. "Hope you find your Fitbit, Brittany."

"Thanks." Brittany sniffed and twirled her wet hair into a tight bun on her head. She yanked a hoodie over it and layered on her jacket.

Reef strode back to the table and grabbed one of his garlic bread slices. He winked at Kaley. "Save the rest for me?"

She avoided eye contact. "I'm sure Brittany would cook you up more if you asked."

He blinked. The edge to her words was unmistakable. What was going on here?

Reef stuffed the bread in his mouth, nodded goodbye, and followed Macy and Brittany out the door, wondering for the hundredth time if the girl he cared about would ever start making any sense.

"It was right here. It has to be!" Brittany's voice pitched so high that the remaining guests at the ski lodge jerked their faces to glare at them.

Great. The last thing Reef needed was a twenty-something having a meltdown and the lodge staff asking them to leave.

The frown on Macy's face suggested she might ask Brittany to leave herself. He owed her for coming along.

"Listen, you wait here, and Macy and I will walk around." Reef pointed to a chair and Brittany slumped in it. She clearly expected some knight in shining armor to find her watch without her having to lift a finger.

He was a nice guy, but he was not her knight. Still, having her sitting in one place waiting for rescue might be easier to deal with than her shadowing him.

"Yeah, maybe there's a lost and found or something," Macy said. "I'll go check by the cafeteria."

"I'll ask at the bar." The smell of liquor brought back memories he'd rather forget, but the bar was the only place still manned. Asking an employee there was his best option.

A lone man and a couple waited for service, so Reef would have to take his turn. The one man glanced his way and then seemed to catch the attention of someone behind him before paying the bar tender and swiping his gloves off the counter.

The couple ordered, and the bar tender left to make their drinks. Reef drummed his fingers on the counter, wishing he could find Brittany's stupid watch and get back to his dinner.

Five minutes going on forever later, the couple had their drinks, and he could finally get the bar tender's attention.

"What can I get you?" he asked.

"I'm looking for a Fitbit. My friend lost hers, and she thinks she might have left it on one of the tables."

The man nodded. "Someone did find a watch. Can you describe it?"

"I—uh, it's her watch. Let me get her. I'll be right back." Reef spun off the stool and started for Brittany's table.

He did a double take. She was talking to the man who had just left the bar. No, she was more than talking. She was flirting.

Yes, flirting. Fingers twirling her blonde hair, eyelashes batting, lips smiling, the whole nine yards.

Reef slowed his pace as he took a closer look at the guy. Tall, dark, but not handsome in the Hallmark sense of the word. He had the "bad guy" good looks some girls seemed to dig with a scratchy beard, rough edges, and a world-worn glint in his eyes.

The guy was grinning and leaning toward her as if sharing a secret.

Not on his watch. Brittany could flirt on her own time with sketchy characters but not when his dinner was getting cold.

He picked up his stride and tapped Brittany's shoulder. "Hey, sorry to interrupt, but the bar tender says they found a watch. He needs you to describe it."

She jumped a little at his touch. "Oh, Reef, you startled me."

"Well, I thought we came here to look for your watch."

Brittany still twirled her blonde ponytail around a finger. "Sorry, yes. I'm so rude. Reef, this is Derek. He's skiing at Beech this weekend too."

No, really? Because why else would he be hanging out at the ski resort lodge?

"Nice to meet you." Reef gave him a quick nod. "Sorry to cut you off, but this place is closing in a few minutes, so if you want your watch back …"

Derek straightened to a few inches taller than Reef's height and nodded back. "No problem. I'll see you guys around."

Reef pretended not to see the wink he sent Brittany before sauntering over to another table near the door.

"How'd you meet your new stalker friend?" Reef muttered as Brittany slid from her seat and started for the bar.

"He's not a stalker," she hissed back. "He's quite charming."

"Is his first name Prince?"

"What?"

"Never mind. Please describe your Fitbit to the bar tender so we can leave."

Brittany puckered her lips. "What's put you in such a foul mood? Wait, are you …?"

"Any luck?" Macy jogged over.

"We'll know soon." Reef waved to get the bar tender's attention. His eyes seemed to light up when he spotted Brittany.

Good grief. That girl was a man magnet.

"He has it!" Brittany clapped her hands as the bar tender dug around in a drawer. "He said my description matched what someone found to a tee. Isn't it wonderful to have such honest people here? This place is like a fairy tale."

"She even met Prince Charming." Reef rolled his eyes for Macy's benefit.

"Huh?" Macy asked.

"That hulk by the door who looks like he robbed a bank yesterday is Brittany's new man crush."

Macy wrinkled her nose. "Ew, he does look like he might have robbed a bank."

Brittany crossed her arms and huffed. "Cut it out, you two. He's drop-dead-handsome. You're just jealous."

Macy glanced at the man again. "Nope. Not in the least."

The bar tender cleared his throat. "Your watch, miss?"

Brittany spun back to face him. "Oh, thank you! You are a lifesaver."

Macy stepped farther away and sighed. "She'll probably give him her number too."

Reef faced her. "I hope she didn't give it to bank-robber man. They talked for only a few minutes."

"Don't underestimate her," Macy said. "Okay, now she's chatting with the bar tender."

Reef groaned. "We're never getting dinner at this rate."

"Intervention time," Macy muttered. "You get ready to intercept bank-robber Bill, and I'll take care of sweet-talking Harley."

Reef laughed and lowered his voice. "I guess we should stop judging these poor guys. They probably aren't the worst of the lot."

"No, they're keeping us from dinner, and for that reason, deserve their titles," Macy said. "I'll be right back."

She walked over to Brittany, hooked her arm in her elbow, smiled at so-called Harley, and started for the door. Reef followed and waved his thanks. Macy truly was the best.

But when they reached the door, bank-robber Bill jumped up and strode toward the girls. Macy immediately let go of Brittany's elbow and glanced over her shoulder at him. He couldn't tell if she was more annoyed or uncomfortable.

Reef reached her side as Brittany and "Bill" started talking again. He was not here to babysit.

"We'll meet you in the car, Brittany, but we're leaving in five minutes."

Brittany blushed. "I'll be right behind you."

He and Macy started down the steps, careful not to slip on the slush that was fast becoming ice.

"You can't leave her with bank-robber Bill."

"I'm not going to leave her with that guy," Reef said. "I only want her to take the hint that we're not waiting around for her to meet her next boyfriend."

Macy pulled her scarf higher around her neck. "I agree, but that guy isn't boyfriend material."

"Just please tell me she's following us." Reef stuffed his hands in his pockets to feel for his keys.

"See for yourself," Macy said as they reached the bottom of the stairs.

Reef craned his neck. There, still talking at the lodge entrance, was Brittany and "Bill." But they weren't simply talking. He was slipping something into her hand.

Then, as quickly as he'd touched her, the man backed away and walked the other direction.

Brittany waved at them and slowly started down the stairs, gripping the handrail to keep from sliding down to them.

Reef sighed. "At least she's coming."

"She can meet us at the car." It was now Macy's turn to lose her patience. "That girl needs a serious talking to."

He couldn't agree more.

A few minutes later, Brittany opened the passenger door and slipped inside. "Thanks for waiting for me."

Macy grunted and turned up the radio. She was clearly not looking for a conversation, and Reef didn't blame her. Still, as he pulled out of the parking lot, he found himself wondering what the man had given Brittany and if they hadn't seen the last of her secret admirer.

Chapter Eight

"You know you don't have to do those by hand. There is a dishwasher." Olivia's words broke into her daydream.

"Oh, right," Kaley said. "I thought I'd finish these up."

"I think you're washing more for your own benefit than for the benefit of the dishes." Olivia chuckled and pulled a pretzel snack bag off the shelf. "But do whatever brings you joy."

Kaley blew a strand of hair out of her face. "What do you mean?"

"It looks like you're stewing over there. Care to share?"

"I don't know what you mean. I'm fine."

"Right, because a perfectly fine girl chooses to do dishes by hand instead of use a dishwasher when she's on vacation."

Kaley sighed. "I just need sleep. I'll feel better in the morning."

Olivia popped a pretzel in her mouth. "This has nothing to do with Brittany stealing Reef away for the evening?"

"Nothing." Kaley rinsed the final cup and set it on the drying rack.

"Uh-huh." Olivia headed for the door. "Want to join the others and me in the dining room for games?"

"I think I'll pass, but thanks." Kaley kept her eyes on her sudsy hands and twisted the dishrag until all the water seeped out.

Olivia slipped out of the room, and Kaley draped the rag over the faucet. Who was she fooling? Yes, she was upset, but she hardly knew why. It was none of her business if Reef wanted to date an air-head.

That's not very nice. Her conscience pricked.

Still, it felt like the truth.

After pulling an extra-large mug from the shelf and adding water, she thrust it into the microwave and went in search of the hot chocolate packets she'd seen earlier while unpacking boxes.

Hot chocolate and time with Jesus were exactly what she needed.

An hour later, her hand cramped, and she set aside her Bible, journal, and paperback copy of Viktor Frankl's *Man's Search for Meaning*. Aside from her regular Scripture reading, she'd discovered that reading Frankl's book with her Bible open helped her keep his ideas in the proper perspective.

The man who had suffered so much in his life had reached some profound conclusions, such as the idea that people can't control what happens to them, but that they can choose how to respond to it. That truth was certainly biblical. Others sounded quite nice but weren't biblical. Of course, the man hadn't intended to write a Christian worldview on suffering, but that's where her thesis came in—to identify which of his theories aligned with Scripture and which didn't. It was a fascinating study to examine one of the most well-read books on compulsive behavior and existential psychology in light of biblical doctrine.

She should probably keep masters research separate from her personal quiet time, but since the two topics were closely related, it seemed to work.

As she reached for her phone with one hand, she wiped wetness off her forehead with the other. The remnants of her hot chocolate were cold, but her room was not. How could it be such an oven when there was snow on the ground outside?

Go figure. She had packed only long sleeves and sweatpants. But surely someone had a short-sleeve shirt she could borrow.

Shoving her hoodie to her elbows, she retrieved her mug and opened the door. The hallway felt twenty degrees cooler. Maybe she and Olivia should sleep with the door open.

Someone was in the bathroom showering, and Brittany's and Macy's room was empty, so she started down the stairs. Laughter drew her to the dining room, and she hesitated. Would asking for a favor automatically get her drawn into a never-ending board game?

"Hitler! I knew you were Hitler!" Pastor TJ screamed at the top of his lungs.

Eyes wide, Kaley peeked around the corner. Pastor TJ was standing and pointing at Liam as if he had sent his mother to a concentration camp. He dropped his hand when he noticed her standing there.

"Oh, hey, Kaley. You want to play the next round with us?" he asked.

All eyes turned to her—all eyes including Reef's. When did he get back? But that didn't matter.

She took a cautious step into the room. "Uh, no thanks. I wanted to ask if anyone has a t-shirt I can borrow? Olivia's and my room feels like an oven."

"Did you turn off the radiator in your room?" The corners of Reef's mouth twisted, as if he were trying to keep in a grin.

She bristled. "We don't have a radiator in our room."

"I bet you do."

Kaley shifted her attention back to the rest of the group. "Anyway, if no one has a t-shirt, no worries. Have fun with your game."

"I have an extra you can borrow," Liam said. He rose and pointed a finger at TJ. "See, I'm not always a Hitler."

"But you just were—and I knew it!" TJ's voice rose in pitch.

"I thought this was a Christian church trip?" Kaley quirked an eyebrow. "Why are ya'll name-calling each other?"

"It's a game called Secret Hitler," Olivia said. "It's complicated."

"I'll take your word for it."

"Be back with that shirt in a sec." Liam disappeared down the hall.

Pastor TJ and Olivia started reorganizing the game, and she glanced at Reef. He seemed to be absorbed in his phone. Good, she would simply wait for Liam.

"I could come find the radiator for you." His words took her by surprise.

"Uh, that's okay."

"A t-shirt is like putting a Band-Aid on an injury that's not bleeding."

At that moment, Liam returned with shirt in hand, rescuing her from the chore of untangling Reef's metaphor.

"Thanks," she said, accepting the shirt. "You guys take down Hitler—or whatever you're doing."

At the top of the stairs, the bathroom door was open. Maybe she would just change there, brush her teeth, and turn in for the night.

She glanced inside and wrinkled her nose. Brittany's clothes lay in a heap on the floor, and she'd left the shower curtain outside the tub during her shower. Everything was wet.

"Ugh!" She tiptoed around a puddle and safely reached the mat by the sink. Careful not to catch the clothes on the floor, she tapped the door shut.

Unbelievable. Apparently, not everyone old enough to be an adult acted like one.

After pulling her tooth brush from the case she had left on a shelf, she switched into Liam's extra-large t-shirt. It fit like a dress, but the lightweight cotton fabric felt like heaven on her warm skin.

As she reached to open the door, something on the floor caught her attention. A piece of paper stuck out of Brittany's hoodie pocket.

Kaley.

Why did it have her name on it? Frowning, she reached down. Her name was scrawled in thick letters that looked more like a man's handwriting.

"We know A.C. talked to you. Tell us where he put the insurance. Don't find us. We'll find you. Talk to the authorities, and it's game-over."

Pulse racing, she read the message again and again. Did A.C. mean Anthony Casale? Who were these people? What did they think she knew? And why not ask Anthony himself?

A sickening feeling twisted her gut. Clenching the note in her fist, she yanked open the door and hurried across the hallway to her sauna of a room. Despite the discomfort, she closed the door all the way. She needed to figure out what was going on in privacy.

Ignoring the grossly warm temperature, she fumbled in her backpack and pulled out her tablet. She had promised herself she wouldn't touch it for work for the rest of the trip, but all the warning bells sounding in her head made her recall her vow.

"C'mon, c'mon." She muttered as the tablet booted, and she entered her passcodes.

But there was no internet.

Wait, Olivia had said something about texting everyone the Wi-Fi password. Kaley dug deeper in her backpack for her cell phone and powered it on. She hadn't looked at it since shooting her parents a text that they had arrived safely that morning.

She held her breath as it powered on. Within moments, it was buzzing incessantly with texts and notifications.

No, no, no! What had happened in the one short day she had been gone?

Her texting icon showed over a dozen missed messages, and when she tapped on it, her eyes immediately found Blake's name.

Where are you?
Are you all right?
You might be in danger.
Please answer. This is urgent.
No one can reach you.
Casale is dead.
Listen, this is important. Please call me.
I need you to call me right away.
Are you getting these?
I'm sorry about your vacation, but this is urgent.
Hey, Kaley, can you call me asap?

Her throat tightened. Casale was dead? Poor Blake. He'd been trying to reach her all day. But she had warned him she was going offline.

She shot back a quick text. *Am just seeing these now. I'm fine, with the church group. Am so sorry. My phone was off.*

Kaley hesitated. Should she tell him about the note? Maybe not via text.

While waiting for his reply, she inputted the Wi-Fi password and connected to the internet, already dreading her inbox, which was bound to have the potentially gory details.

But she hadn't even logged in when she saw the blaring news headline.

Houseboat Suicide Disturbs Close-Knit Riverside Neighborhood

And there, with his mugshot to the left of the headline, was Anthony Casale's picture.

Kaley gasped and bit her lip. What had happened to this man? Even in his disturbed emotional state, she hadn't pegged him as a potential suicide case. More than anything, he had seemed like a frightened, caged animal.

Had he really killed himself?

She glanced at her phone, surprised Blake hadn't returned her text by now or tried calling her again. Sure, it was late, but the man all but slept with his phone attached to his ear. Maybe an infant would change that, but probably not under the circumstances.

Ugh, no. Her text had failed to send. Her cell reception was showing one bar.

Right then, the door creaked open, and Olivia walked inside. She stopped short when she saw Kaley's cell phone and tablet on the bed. "Hey, is everything okay?"

Kaley flipped her tablet over and forced a smile. "Uh, yeah, I forgot about something. Hey, is your phone working? I don't seem to have a signal."

Olivia scrunched her eyebrows. "No, none of us can get reception here—except for Pastor TJ." She paused. "Is there something you're not telling me?"

"Work-related." Kaley forced a laugh. "There's lots of stuff I'm not telling you. But thanks, I'll go check with TJ."

"It's past midnight. I think everyone's turning in, but he might still be in the dining room with the guys."

"Thanks." Kaley swung her legs off the bed, and Liam's t-shirt dangled to her knees. Whatever. She wasn't dressed to impress.

Taking the stairs by two, she hurried toward the dining room. The main living area and kitchen were dark, but there was still a light on in the dining room. But when she reached the doorway, no one was there.

Her heart sank. She was too late. Everyone must have turned in for the night.

But as she retraced her steps, something creaked in the living room. It was the slightest noise, just enough to tell her she wasn't alone.

Don't find us. We'll find you.

Chapter Nine

Kaley had walked right past them and now stood frozen in the dining room doorway.

Reef craned his neck from where he reclined on the couch, adjacent to the chair where Liam relaxed. "You okay?"

She squeaked and jumped three feet backwards, bumping into one of the wooden tables in the dining room.

Reef rolled off the couch to his feet, colliding with Liam.

"Gah!" Liam muttered and grabbed onto Reef's side to keep from wiping out.

"What are you guys doing?" Kaley's voice was still an octave too high. "You nearly scared me to death!"

Reef shrugged off Liam's grip and straightened his thick hoodie. "We were chilling."

"Chilling in the dark together? That's weird."

"Hey," Liam objected. "Guys can do nothing together, and it's not weird."

"Whatever." Kaley hugged herself. "Have you seen TJ?"

"He turned in a while ago," Reef said. "Why?"

"Nothing, I just need to talk to him." Her fingers worked nervously at the sleeves of Liam's shirt that hung to her elbows. "Guess it will wait until morning."

"Goodnight," Liam said, his voice a softer tone. "Sorry we frightened you."

Was Kaley shivering? Surely, they hadn't scared her that badly.

"Goodnight," she whispered and hurried up the stairs.

He and Liam looked after her for probably a second too long. Reef continued the silence by slumping back onto the couch and scrolling through pictures on his phone.

Liam sat in a nearby chair. "Man, she looks good in my t-shirt."

Reef felt something twist in his gut. "She looks good in anything."

Another long silence.

"Are we going to talk about the elephant in the room or not?" Liam said at last. His voice had lost his softness and now held an almost defensive edge.

"There's an elephant?" Reef pretended to joke. "I thought there were only two creepy guys—us."

"You know what I mean."

"Kaley?"

"Yes."

Reef sighed. He didn't want to tell Liam they had dated, but if he didn't, he would never understand how stinking complicated everything was right now.

"Okay." Reef sat up again and grasped his phone in his hands. "Kaley and I dated."

Liam stiffened, but he nodded for Reef to go on.

"There's not much to tell. We kept things on the down-low, because you know how much drama gets generated by this group."

Liam sighed. "Isn't that the truth."

Reef relaxed his shoulders. "It's been a few months since we broke up, and I thought this trip would be no big deal. Like, Kaley is a great girl, and we're both adults. I didn't think there would be any problems."

"Is there?" Liam rubbed his jaw as if choosing his words carefully.

"No—I mean, not between us, but …"

"But you still like her."

The truth of Liam's words hit him in the chest like cannon fire. He wanted to deny it, but he couldn't.

"Yes, I still like her."

"But she broke up with you?"

Why did admitting this make him feel so lousy? Maybe because he still didn't fully understand why she had.

Reef nodded. "Yeah."

A pause. "I'm sorry, man."

He nodded again. Why was there a stupid lump forming in the back of his throat? Reef swallowed hard. "But I get it, dude. You're interested in her, and I don't blame you one bit."

Liam waited as if not sure what to say.

Reef sucked in a deep breath. "So, what I'm trying to say is that no matter what happens, I want you to know I'm always going to be your friend. And if she's interested in you, I'll be happy for you, man."

Letting all the air out felt good. "And I'll get over her, if that's what she wants."

His friend offered a small smile. "Is it?"

Reef snorted. "You've seen the way she avoids me."

"Sometimes, a girl needs time to sort out her own heart."

When did Liam get to be so wise? For the first time in months, he felt something like hope flicker in his chest. Could Kaley be trying to sort out her feelings too? Would she give him a second chance?

Reef pushed the thoughts aside. False hope wasn't going to do him any good.

Liam leaned forward in his chair. "So, what are you going to do?"

"I—I don't know."

"Hmm."

"What are you going to do?" Reef turned the question around.

Liam pushed himself to his feet and slipped his phone in his pocket. "Pray about it. 'Night, man."

"Yeah, goodnight."

Alone in the room, Reef thought about what Liam said. He was a good friend, probably even a better man than he was. He couldn't fault Kaley if she liked him.

But did she?

He squeezed the phone in his hands and whispered, "God, you know how I feel, how Kaley feels, and how Liam feels. Sort this out for good, because I'm in over my head."

Reef still didn't know how to answer Liam's question, but tonight, he would follow his advice. He'd pray and trust God to lead the way.

And he would keep being kind to the girl who had the power to tear open his heart all over again.

With that, he pushed himself off the couch and started for the stairs. The door to Kaley and Olivia's room at the top of the stairs was closed, but he could hear muffled voices coming from inside and something else. Was that tapping?

He rapped on the door.

The tapping stopped.

"Who is it?" Kaley's voice called.

"It's Reef."

A pause. Maybe this was a mistake. No, he was doing the right thing.

"What do you need?"

He winced at her word choice. "I came to find your radiator."

Another pause, this one longer. Ugh, why did girls have to be so difficult when you were trying to help them?

The door cracked open, and a wave of heat slammed into his face. He coughed. "You do have a sauna in here."

Kaley frowned and planted a hand on her hip. "Yes, it's gross. But we already looked and—"

"It's probably behind one of the beds. May I come in?" He glanced behind her to her bed where her tablet, cell phone, Bible, and a book lay sprawled on the comforter. What was she working on this late at night?

"Yeah, sure," Olivia answered before Kaley did. "Ignore any mess. It's probably mine."

"Mess makes sense. You're on vacation. But unless you're reading, why are you on your tablet?" He left the question hovering in the air.

"You're right," Olivia agreed. "She's more of a mess than I am."

"Hey!" Kaley pushed the door open the rest of the way as he started the hunt. "I am working on a master's degree, you know."

Reef blinked. When they were dating, Kaley had talked about wanting to pursue another degree, but she had shared her worries that she wouldn't have time with how demanding her work was. But now, here she was, neck deep in research?

Olivia crossed her arms and glared at Kaley. "It's work, isn't it? And you promised you wouldn't work on this trip. At all. But you've been practically swearing at your phone for the last half hour because you have no coverage."

"Mumbling isn't the same as swearing."

"You broke a promise so that alone is a problem."

Reef focused on moving the first bed far enough away from the wall to see if there was anything behind it. He didn't need to insert himself into this argument and get shot at. Still, Olivia had a valid point. Was Kaley working? And why?

"I'm sorry." All the air seemed to deflate from Kaley's response. "I didn't expect ... this."

Something in her tone made his head shoot up. She sounded worried, almost scared.

"Everything okay?" he asked, then pointed behind the bed. "No radiator here."

"No, it's not okay." She shifted her gaze to the tablet. "And I told you there isn't a radiator."

"Oh, there's definitely a radiator in here—unless you girls figured out a way to pack Florida humidity into your suitcases."

Olivia hopped off her bed so he could inspect the wall behind hers. "Seriously, Kaley, what's going on?"

Kaley slumped onto the corner of her bed. "I can't talk about it."

"You're not a spy. It can't be classified," Olivia insisted.

"It's confidential and case-sensitive. I don't know what I can and can't say—and I can't get through to Blake."

Reef sneaked another look at Kaley. She had talked about Blake enough for him to remember he was her boss. This was a work situation, and Kaley wasn't one to exaggerate. "Is that why you wanted to see TJ? I think his phone gets reception."

Kaley massaged her temple. "That's what Olivia said. But he's asleep, so I'll have to wait until morning."

"At least it's not life or death." Olivia forced levity into her voice.

Kaley's face paled, and she didn't answer.

Reef's pulse quickened. Wait, was Kaley in some kind of trouble?

A moment later, she cleared her throat. "Anything behind that one?"

"Oh, um—" Had she caught him staring at her? Reef turned his attention to the headboard.

"Well?" Olivia asked.

"Aha!" He reached behind the mattress and switched off the radiator. "Found it."

"Thank goodness!" Olivia sighed. "Maybe we can sleep tonight after all. Thanks a bunch, Reef."

"You're welcome." He pushed the headboard back in place. "You'll need to move the bed some if it gets too cold in here."

Olivia laughed and wiped pretend perspiration off her forehead. "Are you kidding? I don't think penguins will be migrating to our bedroom anytime soon."

Reef strode toward the door but paused by Kaley's bed. "If there's anything I can do to help, let me know, okay?"

She forced a smile. "Thanks for finding the radiator. Sorry I didn't believe you earlier."

He hadn't been talking about the radiator. There was something bigger steaming in Kaley's work world right now, and he wanted her to trust him. He wanted to fix whatever her problem was. "No worries, it was hidden."

"Yeah." She tapped her phone again and sighed.

"Well, goodnight." Reef left the door open and slipped down the stairs, all the while wishing he had found an excuse to linger.

His gut told him that whatever was bothering Kaley wouldn't be as easy to fix as turning off a radiator.

When Val's small plane had landed on the private runway, Louis was waiting for her. Without a word, he took her suitcase and ushered her to his waiting Cadillac Escalade. The snow was falling steadily, but the vehicle's interior was warm and relaxing.

Unlike the last twenty-four hours. Big Eddie's revelation about the copied files overshadowed the triumph of her Oscar win. She had to personally find and destroy them before she could rest on her laurels.

Val shoved her annoyance aside and swept her mink coat clear of the passenger door. "Did you make contact?"

"Yes and no. I'll update you as we drive." Louis closed her door and yanked open the driver's door moments later.

He shifted into reverse and flicked on the windshield wipers as Val drummed her fingers on her thigh. He should know by now she was not a patient person.

"I spotted her on the slopes but was unable to make personal contact. But by a turn of luck, I met one of her friends. She's a pretty chick and about as smart as a brick, which made her the perfect delivery girl." He snorted. "I told her my name was Derek."

Val's fists clenched. "Delivery girl?"

"Yep, I gave her a message, the one you told me to tell her."

"The one I told you to tell her in person." Val ground her teeth. She couldn't trust anyone to do the job right unless she did it herself.

He tensed in the driver's seat. "Right, sorry. But this seemed like the next best move. Eddie's boys are watching her too, and unless we get to her first, you can forget any hope of seeing that insurance."

Of course, they were. After her last chat with Eddie, she wouldn't doubt Eddie had some hitmen assigned to her too.

Maybe that was a bit paranoid, but maybe not if Eddie suspected she was after the therapist as well. His threats might be threats for now, but if he found out she was interfering with his plans, that might change.

Val searched for her seat warmer and switched it on. "How's the joint look?"

"It's perfect for your plan. We can ski on and off the slope right from the backyard."

"Very good." She rubbed her hands together. "We have to move tomorrow. As soon as you see her or her group on the slopes, notify me at once."

Louis accelerated into a steep turn, and for a moment, she felt the wheels skid on ice. Switchback roads were sketchy, but her driver maneuvered expertly toward their cabin.

"You sure you don't want me to …"

"We'll stick to the plan. I just need you to be my eyes and ears—and then be ready to pack up and go once we have her."

Louis nodded. "And if Eddie's boys get her first?"

Val gritted her teeth. "We can't let them."

They continued up the incline in silence. She didn't need to explain to Louis everything riding on their success, her success. She could never fully enjoy the glory of her Oscar win until she had peace about the past—or the security that no one would dare open those pages.

Her home on the Hillsborough River made her traveling to Tampa justifiable to Eddie. He didn't need to know who was in her traveling party and if a certain therapist reluctantly joined them.

Kaley Colbert. She'd done her digging on the therapist. She was squeaky clean, even a church girl.

Her Hallmark-worthy backstory included salutatorian status, a senior trip to Disney, adoring family, and now a successful career. She had everything Val had only been able to dream of as a teenager.

Ironic. The tables were going to turn. Kaley's dream world would fast become a nightmare.

Part of Val felt sorry for her. The other part was ready to serve just desserts. Maybe Colbert hadn't realized the extent of her client's history, but that was her mistake for trying to help the snitch.

No one cheats the underground and gets away. Rest in pieces, Casale.

And no one helps a canary and keeps secrets. Get ready to sing, Colbert.

Chapter Ten

A vibration under her pillow jolted Kaley awake. The windows were still black, and Olivia was breathing softly in the other bed.

What time was it? And why was she sleeping with her phone under her pillow?

Eyes raw, she squinted at the screen.

It was Blake.

All the anxiety of the previous hours poured over her in fresh fury. Casale's death was labeled a suicide, but authorities wondered if foul play was involved. Blake's emails had said authorities wanted to talk to her since she and Meg may have been the last people to see him alive.

The thought made her shiver.

Had her text finally gone through? It appeared so, and Blake had sent a response, expressing relief she was fine and wanting to know when she could talk. For one glorious second, the snow clouds must have parted in time for her to have reception.

But she was back to none.

At least she had been able to use Wi-Fi to reply to the emails. Blake could tell the authorities she was on vacation in the mountains and hopefully they would understand.

But who was she kidding? Someone else seemed bent on robbing her of whatever vacation time she had planned.

That note still burned in her pocket. Who had given it to Brittany? And why had Brittany not bothered to tell her about it?

Kaley shivered again and reached for her comforter. Wait, their room was actually cold?

She poked her bare foot out from the sheets and quickly retracted it. Yes, yes it was.

All thanks to Reef.

She snuggled deeper under her comforter and placed her phone face down on the nightstand. If she did miraculously get signal again, she owed it to Olivia not to wake her with a cell phone light show.

Besides, there was no use staring at the screen. She needed sleep.

And an honest self-talk about Reef. The man kept going out of his way to be kind to her. First, there were the ski lessons, but he had helped Brittany too. He had also taken that girl all the way back to the lodge to find her phone, so maybe his kindness wasn't special to her.

But he had searched Olivia's and her room to find the radiator when he could have just gone to bed and let them sweat and suffer.

Did that mean he still liked her? Maybe. The flutter in her chest told her she hoped so?

Or maybe he was just a genuinely nice guy, and she was the last girl who told him to get lost.

She pulled the comforter above her head. She was a moron.

Why had she broken up with him again?

All her reasons were starting to feel empty.

1. Some of their views were different, and he wasn't as involved in church as much as she was. *But from what she was seeing, he was far more involved in caring for people without the window dressing of a "ministry."*

2. She wasn't sure where he stood in his personal relationship with God. Although he said he was a believer, he had confessed to not having a consistent quiet time. He'd said he wanted to read his Bible more, but finding time was hard. *Who was she to hold herself up as a standard?*

3. There were the potential attachment issues resulting from his childhood trauma. But now, he seemed confident in who he was. He was either a great actor or the real deal. Either way, his mom's poor choices weren't his fault.

4. He didn't have career goals like she did. From her relationship studies, his lack of personal drive could be a major area for conflict, because she was so goal-driven. He liked his job,

but it seemed less like a job and more of a way for him to do something he loved. *What was wrong with that? Maybe another goal-oriented, driven person was not who she needed. Maybe she needed someone who would complement, not compete with her.*

Another thought made her blush. All this time, she was thinking about the kind of guy she needed. But was she the kind of girl he needed? When had she become this selfish in her search for a spouse?

"God, I'm sorry," she whispered. "Have I been wrong?"

There was no audible answer, but the conviction she felt in her spirit rang loud and clear. She needed to apologize to him, to say she was sorry for misjudging him. She needed to thank him for the lessons and turning off the stupid radiator. She could ask for another chance, but that felt like opening herself up for disappointment and rejection.

If she could get past the first two, maybe she would be at peace. But after how she felt seeing him with Brittany, something told her she wouldn't be until she knew if his feelings for her had changed or not.

Was now even the time for this? Her mind jumped back to the Casale case and note. Poor Anthony. If only she could have done more for him. But she had asked Blake to consider protection services for him. She couldn't have known how urgently he needed them.

Now, did she need them? How could this be happening to her?

You can't control what happens to you, but you can choose how you respond to it. She'd penned that paraphrase of Frankl's principle in her journal mere hours ago. Somehow, those words were a lot harder to swallow right now.

She wouldn't panic. She would call Blake as soon as she could and figure out what the next right step was for her to take.

But what if she was endangering her group? That thought sent a pang of fear through her heart.

"God, what am I supposed to do?" She closed her eyes. All she could do now was pray and get some sleep. In the morning, she would tell Pastor TJ and borrow his phone.

Be still and know that I am God.

The verse from the Psalms soothed her racing mind. Even with her relational life in shambles and with a possible murder investigation clouding her nearly perfect career, God was still on His throne and He was still in control.

She didn't have answers, but she could go to sleep trusting the One who did.

Freezing.

She was sleeping in an igloo. The Abominable snowman had just found her.

Something crashed, and she bounced upright.

But instead of an igloo, the wooden walls of the cabin came into focus. There was no Abominable, but the room was crazy cold.

Sunlight peeked through the curtain edges, and she felt for her phone. 7:30 am. Why hadn't her alarm gone off?

Olivia's bed was already empty, and she groaned. She had told her friend she would help make breakfast.

Gritting her teeth, she pried off her comforter, wormed her feet into a pair of socks, shrugged into a hoodie and started downstairs.

Voices came from the kitchen, but the living room was empty. Maybe she had beat most of the group, and there was still time to help Olivia.

Kaley padded around the corner to the kitchen and met Olivia's grinning face. She was scrambling eggs while Brittany was microwaving bacon. Was that even a thing?

"Morning, sleeping beauty," Olivia said. "How'd you sleep?"

"Too long." She slumped into a wooden chair. "My alarm didn't go off. I'm sorry I wasn't down sooner."

Olivia lowered the burner heat. "I switched it off, so there's no need to apologize."

Kaley blinked. "You what?"

"Yeah, after how much you checked that crazy phone of yours, the minute you actually let it out of your sight on the nightstand, I turned off your alarm."

Brittany covered another paper plate of bacon with a paper towel and placed it in the microwave. "You might want to think about password protecting your phone or something."

Kaley felt her mouth hanging open and forced her lips to work. "I never had a need for a password, until now apparently."

"You're welcome," Olivia said.

"I—I just can't believe you went into my phone." Kaley felt her face flush. Had Olivia seen Blake's emails and text?

"I only went to your clock, so don't get all paranoid that I'm reading your secret texts or whatever. You needed to sleep."

"What secret texts?" Brittany asked.

Kaley wanted to ask her about secret notes, but maybe now wasn't the time. She would need to catch her alone if she hoped for an honest answer.

"Is there anything left for me to help with breakfast?" Kaley changed the subject.

Olivia salted her freshly scrambled eggs. "Liam was going to start the blueberry bake, but he received some important work email, so that job is yours if you want it."

"Liam bakes?" That news was a revelation.

"Ooh," Brittany winked at her.

Olivia rolled her eyes. "Yes, he's quite good at cooking in general, but he doesn't seem to understand the work-life balance any better than you. Anyway, you can follow the recipe off my phone." She reached into her back pocket and handed Kaley her phone. "See, I share mine too."

"Yes, but you're giving it to me."

"Nuance. Anyway, go to Notes, and you should see the recipe."

Kaley didn't argue. Olivia was the baker in their friendship, and Kaley could sure use the practice if she hoped to cook a decent meal one day.

"Can I help?" Brittany asked. "This is the last of the bacon."

"Perfect, you two can work together," Olivia said. "The kids can start with eggs and bacon, and your blueberry bake will be for the latecomers."

Brittany giggled. "Kids? Aren't we all kids?"

Kaley smiled but didn't reply. She wasn't about to tell Brittany she was probably a decade younger than her.

"You can mix the blueberries with a light coating of flour while I get the other ingredients." Kaley hit the preheat button on the oven.

"On it." Brittany rinsed the berries and then dumped all of them into a mixing bowl.

Well, the directions didn't say how many berries, so Olivia must have bought the right amount.

But when she and Brittany mixed them into the rest of the batter, there seemed to be an overabundance of blueberries. Still, was there such a thing as too many blueberries?

"How long should I set my timer?" Brittany pulled out her phone as Olivia grabbed a pile of paper plates for the dining room.

Kaley skimmed Olivia's note. "Thirty-five minutes."

"Done," Brittany said.

Olivia disappeared around the corner, and Kaley recognized her chance. "Thanks, Brittany. Hey, this is kind of random, but do you know how a note with my name on it came to be on the bathroom floor?"

Kaley left off the part about having to pull it out of Brittany's pant pocket.

Brittany seemed to tense. "A note?"

"Yeah, I found it on the bathroom floor and was wondering who wrote it?"

She pretended to scroll on her phone. "Sorry, this guy at the lodge asked about you. I was going to give it to you but forgot."

Why was Brittany avoiding eye contact? What was she not telling her?

"Do you know this guy?" Kaley asked. "Because his note was …"

A sharp ringing cut her off mid-sentence. "Wakey, wakey, eggs and bacon!" Reef's voice bellowed from the hallway. Moments later, he peeked his head into the kitchen. "Morning! Something smells good in here, but Olivia said it's off limits for now."

Brittany giggled, seeming to have completely forgotten Kaley's question. "We're making a blueberry bake."

Reef's gaze drifted to hers. "Well, good morning to you too." He surveyed her sleep pants and hoodie. "Looks like you're nice and cold."

Kaley readjusted her pony tail and lowered her gaze to her plush socks. "Thanks to you."

Brittany started chatting again, and Kaley turned away to scrub a random dish in the sink. She hadn't had the chance to even glance in a mirror yet, and Brittany looked like she'd walked off the winter edition of a fashion magazine cover.

"Well, thanks for breakfast," he said. "Leave those dishes alone. We guys should clean up after we finish. For now, come join us while everything's hot."

As Brittany followed him to the dining room, Kaley darted back up the stairs the minute they left. She would at least look presentable—and then find Pastor TJ.

But when she returned a few minutes later, Pastor TJ wasn't in the dining room, and Brittany had claimed the seat next to Reef.

Swallowing hard, Kaley grabbed a plate and tried to rehash her pep talk from last night. She would not eat in the kitchen alone like a coward. She would pick the seat right across from Reef and join the conversation.

Still, her hand shook a little when she set down her orange juice and paper plate across from him.

Reef glanced at her, but she couldn't read his expression.

"Mind if I join you?"

"Go right ahead." He turned his attention back to his plate.

Was that displeasure? Annoyance? Should she leave? She stabbed some eggs with her fork but didn't take the bite.

If she wasn't careful, she would choke. The kitchen seemed awfully friendly right now.

"You ready for your next set of lessons?"

Her head shot up. "Lessons? I thought we only got lessons on the first day."

Reef waved a hand. "Those were cookie cutter lessons from a high schooler who works for minimum wage. Today, I'm your instructor."

Brittany clapped her hands. "Eee! This is going to be so fun."

Kaley stared at him. She wasn't going to gush all over him like Brittany, but she could do this. She could be nice.

"That's very good of you, but I'll only slow you down. You could be having fun on the harder slopes."

"Or I could be having fun with you."

His words knocked the fork from her hand. It fell to the floor, eggs and all.

"Sorry," she mumbled and retrieved it. Why did she have to be so clumsy?

"When do we leave?" Brittany asked.

For once, Kaley was grateful Brittany took the attention off her.

"Not till this afternoon," Reef said. "We're doing night skiing tonight. This afternoon, I think the plan is to hang out here, or—"

Brittany's phone alarm started beeping. "Oh, our blueberry bake! I'll go check on it." She exited the dining room with the air of one on an important errand.

Kaley smiled at Brittany's enthusiasm. She wasn't overly optimistic the bake would turn out well since they had been missing a few ingredients, but she hoped it would at least be edible.

"—or I was thinking of getting a sled from Fred's and hitting the community sledding hill," Reef finished his sentence.

"Sledding? Really?" Kaley hesitated. "I've never been sledding."

"You've never been sledding?" The grin tugging at Reef's lips grew bigger. "Well then, I think we need to fix that."

"How much do sleds cost?"

"Fred's sells plastic ones for about fifteen bucks. A few of us could share one."

Kaley's smile faltered for just a second. Of course, he meant Brittany. Still, there was no reason she couldn't have fun. "I'm in, if you have room in your group."

"Absolutely."

Brittany returned, proudly holding the cookware with two hot mitts. She set it down on the table and beamed. "It looks good, doesn't it?"

Kaley bit her lip. Blueberry oozed out of every corner of what otherwise resembled a cake.

Olivia strode over from her seat and glanced at it. "How many blueberries did you girls put in that thing?"

"All of them?" Brittany faltered.

"You guys, it only needs two cups."

Kaley felt the sudden need to defend their creation. "The recipe didn't say."

Brittany shot her an appreciative look and tentatively sliced a piece.

Olivia burst out laughing. "Well, you two sure do put the blueberry in blueberry bake. I'm sure it will taste—very blueberry."

Brittany put the slice on Reef's plate. "You can tell us how bad it is."

"You can't mess up blueberries." Reef poked his fork in a piece and stuffed it in his mouth.

His eyes grew wide.

Brittany covered her face with her hands. "It's awful! I knew it."

"Hot!" Reef grabbed the closest glass of orange juice. He gulped, then groaned in relief before his gaze settled on the glass. "Oh wait, was that yours, Kaley?"

"It's okay. You clearly needed it more than I did."

He smeared on a smile. "Clearly."

"So, is it really awful?" Brittany peeked between her fingers.

"No, it's just really hot!"

They shared a laugh, and Brittany eagerly began cutting pieces for everyone. For one short moment, Kaley's heart felt light. This group might be ridiculous, but they were enjoying themselves.

"Smells good." Pastor TJ emerged from the basement stairs. "You guys save any for me?"

"Of course!" Brittany beamed and scooped him an oozing piece. Pastor TJ raised an eyebrow.

"It's good," Reef said.

Kaley's stomach twisted. Pastor TJ reminded her of everything she couldn't avoid for much longer.

"Do you mind if I borrow your phone?" she asked. "Olivia said you have signal."

"Oh, sure." He pulled it from his hoodie. "Help yourself."

"Thanks." She scooted her chair back and started to leave.

"You haven't finished your cake yet," Brittany called after her.

"It's—cooling." Kaley paused at the doorway. "I'll be back in a bit."

But the half-hour conversation with Blake left her head spinning. He wanted her back as soon as possible, but she wasn't supposed to return to the office until Monday, and the church group wouldn't even be back until late Thursday night. But he had warned her that with the investigation into Casale's death underway, someone had even suggested that her vacation looked like fleeing the scene.

"That's ridiculous!" She wanted to scream into the phone but kept her voice down. "I'm on a church ski trip for crying out loud."

"The authorities need your statement," Blake assured her. "You not being here is making things more complicated."

"Blake, I haven't had a vacation since—"

"I know, this timing is awful. I'm sorry. Can you at least call Detective Reynolds and explain?"

Kaley balled her fists. She was going to be on the phone all day at this rate. "Yes, what's his number?"

"*Her* number," Blake said and rattled it off.

She saved it to a note on her tablet.

"Stay in touch, and keep your eyes open. There's been a threat against the office, but we're not sure if it's valid or not."

"Will do. Thanks, Blake."

Kaley hung up and dialed the number before she lost her nerve.

To her relief, it went to voicemail. She left a brief message and explained she had no signal on her phone and that she was using her pastor's phone. She asked the detective to call back if she needed her.

She ended the call and sighed. Now, she had to explain everything to TJ, or else he would wonder why a detective was calling her about a man's murder.

So much for unplugging on this ski trip.

When she returned downstairs, most of the group, including Pastor TJ, were huddled in the living room playing games.

Kaley held out the phone to Pastor TJ and then lowered her voice. "Pastor TJ, can I talk to you for a minute?"

There must have been a warning in her voice, because not only TJ but also Reef and Liam glanced up at her in surprise. "Sure," TJ said.

"In private?" She nodded to the kitchen. "I'll meet you there."

She avoided Reef's curious stare and slipped into the kitchen. She helped herself to a clean mug and emptied the dregs of the coffee pot into it.

"What's up?" Pastor TJ arrived as she was stirring in some cream.

Kaley nodded to the wooden table and chairs. "Take a seat? This is going to be more than a minute."

Keeping her voice down, Kaley briefly explained the situation.

"Wow, I'm sorry. Do you need to get back home? The Asheville or Charlotte airports are about two hours away."

"Thanks, I don't know yet. I don't want to miss out on the trip, but if you think I'm endangering the group …"

"You really feel like you're being watched?"

Kaley nodded, and her gut twisted again. She had to be completely honest with him. "Yes, and someone gave Brittany a note for me. It was somewhat concerning, about someone wanting to find me."

"There are plenty of guys wanting to find pretty girls," Pastor TJ said. "It could be nothing, or it could be something. Did you tell the detective?"

"No, she didn't answer. That's why I'm telling you now. She's probably going to call back."

"I'll keep the phone on me," Pastor TJ said. "If she calls, I'll let you know."

"Thanks." She hesitated. "Reef was talking about some of us going sledding. I'd like to go, but—"

"You can't sit around all day waiting for a call. If she hasn't called back in an hour, then you're probably not an emergency."

Relief seeped through her core. Maybe Pastor TJ was right. "Okay, I'll let Reef know I'll be free in an hour if he still wants to go out."

Pastor TJ stood. "Sounds good. Thanks for telling me what's going on. And if you need anything, let me know."

"I really appreciate that."

After TJ returned to his game, Kaley busied herself in the kitchen, drying the dishes the boys had apparently cleaned. Then, she scooped a fresh spoonful of blueberry goodness onto a clean plate since someone had thrown away her other one.

Matt appeared a moment later. "I told Olivia I'd take out the trash," he said, "even though she kicked me out earlier while you were making breakfast."

Kaley nodded but didn't try to talk with her mouth full. She also didn't know how to respond to Matt's complaint. Her friend's mind about Matt was anything but clear, and she didn't want to get caught in the confusion.

"I see you're sneaking seconds." Reef's voice made her jump.

She gulped. "Hey, I helped make it."

"You're within your rights."

Matt glanced between them and tied the trash bag. "Do you know where Olivia put the trash bags?"

"They're on the shelf above you." Kaley pointed.

"I'll get a new one, thanks," Reef said.

As Matt disappeared, Reef slowly inserted a new bag as if using it as an excuse to stall. "You still want to go sledding today?"

"If you're still planning to go." Kaley licked the spoon. "I have cash for the sled too."

She couldn't have him thinking she expected him to buy it for her.

"I'm not worried about it, but it will only be a few bucks if we split it three ways."

"Nice." She swallowed hard. Yes, it rubbed her the wrong way that he'd invited Brittany too. She needed to accept that she wasn't the only girl in his life.

"Everything okay? You and Pastor TJ were talking for a while in here."

Kaley rinsed off her spoon to buy time. She'd like nothing more than to tell him what was going on, but they weren't in a relationship, and the whole case was technically confidential.

"There's a situation with work." She chose her words carefully. "I had to tell Pastor TJ, because someone might be calling for me."

Reef frowned, causing deep creases between his eyes. "Are you okay?"

"Yeah—I'm fine." She forced a lightness she didn't feel into her voice. "Guess it was wishful thinking I could escape work on this trip."

"I know you're good at what you do, but your job shouldn't pull a stunt like that. I wouldn't answer calls on vacation. Maybe you shouldn't either."

A retort formed in her throat, but she swallowed it. His job would never require him taking calls on vacation, because his job was vacations. More than likely, he'd never be dealing with dead bodies.

But then again, she'd never thought this situation would cross her desk either.

"I can leave in an hour," she offered. "Just let me know what works for you."

"Sure, I'll let—"

A loud crash sounded outside the kitchen window. They exchanged glances and ran to look outside.

All they could see was a pile of snow—and Matt's body crumpled on top of it.

Chapter Eleven

Reef shoved the front door open and darted outside. The cold morning air nipped at his exposed skin, but there was no time to find gloves or his heavy jacket.

The image of Matt's limp body seemed imprinted on his brain. Surely there had to be some explanation.

"Matt!" He cried and slid into the snow next to him. "Matt, can you hear me?" But his friend didn't respond.

Reef examined him for injuries. His body wasn't unnaturally angled, so he didn't suspect any spinal injuries. There was no blood and nothing in the snow—except footprints.

Someone had run away from his body?

Reef's skin prickled from more than just the cold now. His senses on heightened alert, he scanned the perimeter for any signs of movement.

"Is he okay?" Voices behind him intruded into the now suspect scene.

"Stay back," Reef called. "I think someone else is—was—here." There was no time to tell them all the possible ramifications of this fact.

"Yes, stay back, everyone." Liam spread his hands to herd the rest of the group toward the porch. As a cop, he understood the importance of keeping a crime scene clear.

Yet how could this possibly be a crime scene? They were on vacation in the mountains of North Carolina for crying out loud.

"Should I call 9-1-1?" Brittany's voice sounded shrill and scared, like a screech owl.

He wouldn't answer that. She should already know none of their phones worked except TJ's.

"Can I help?" It was a whisper behind his shoulder that caught him off guard. Somehow, Liam had missed Kaley in his herding efforts—or maybe she had been standing behind him all this time.

"Get Pastor TJ." Reef checked for a pulse. It was sluggish but there. Kaley took off back toward the cabin.

Matt groaned and rolled toward him.

"Can you hear me, man?" Reef gripped his shoulders.

Another groan.

Reef waved Liam over. "He's coming to. Help me get him inside."

Liam hurried to support Matt's other side. "Hey, Reef, did you see those footprints?"

"Uh-huh." Reef grunted. For a gangly guy, Matt sure was solid.

Liam helped him carry Matt inside and lower him to the couch. "You take care of Matt," Liam said. "I want a closer look at those prints. Holler if you need me."

Kaley and Olivia appeared with a bottle of water and damp dish towel.

Hesitantly, Olivia pressed it against Matt's forehead. "I thought maybe something cold would help him come to? I don't know. What do you think is wrong with him?"

"Did he fall?" Brittany asked. "That driveway is so slippery."

"Maybe." Reef bit his lip. Those footprints didn't indicate an accident.

Kaley reappeared with Pastor TJ behind her. Her face was ghostly pale, almost the same color as Matt's. Had she seen the prints too? What else could have gotten her so scared?

Pastor TJ's features were tight with concern. "What's going on here? Kaley said something about calling 9-1-1?"

"Matt had an accident," Brittany rushed to say.

Another moan escaped Matt's lips, and his eyes flickered open. "Re-ef?" His voice quivered.

Reef clasped his hand. "It's me, dude. Are you okay?"

"I—I don't know. What happened?"

Relief washed over Reef. "We found you in the snow. Did you fall, or did something hit you?"

Matt tried to sit up but winced. "Man, my head!"

"Take it easy." Olivia helped him edge to a reclined position.

"Are you my guardian angel?" Matt forced a smile and locked eyes on her.

Olivia rolled her eyes. "He must have hit his head really hard." But there was a new softness to her tone.

"There's a clinic in Boone." Pastor TJ scrolled on his phone. "Should we take him there?"

"I'm fine." Matt grumbled.

"Clearly, you're not." Olivia's take-charge voice came out. "Now hold still. I want to see if your eyes are dilated."

"What for?"

"You might have a concussion. How's your vision?" She stretched one eyelid open, then the next.

"They're blurry when you do that." The teasing in Matt's voice was a good sign.

Olivia huffed. "How about when I stop?"

Matt rubbed his eyes. "Everything seems on the level, but I have a headache."

Olivia looked past him to TJ. "His eyes don't appear to be dilated, but it's your call. He could still have a concussion, though. I'm not a nurse, only a physical therapist."

"Thanks, Olivia," TJ said and turned to Matt. "How are you feeling? Do you want to get checked out?"

Matt relaxed into the couch. "I think I'll be okay if someone can spare me an Aspirin or something."

"Oh, I've got drugs!" Brittany darted up the stairs.

Reef winced. He hoped she meant that in the over-the-counter sense of the word, or they had more problems than a potential concussion.

Maybe he should stick to planning his own road trips and inviting just his own people.

His gaze drifted to Kaley. She still stood rigidly at the foot of the couch, staring at Matt as if she were somehow—guilty?

"Did you see anyone, Matt?" Her voice was barely above a whisper.

Reef's pulse quickened. She must have seen the footprints, but why should she look guilty about that? He had been right next to her in the kitchen when they heard the crash.

Something was off here. What had Kaley been talking with TJ about earlier? And why had she needed his phone right away this morning? And then there was the fact that she'd been on her tablet last night.

"I—I don't think so?" Matt stammered. "I don't remember. I only took out the trash."

Reef squinted his eyes at Kaley. Was she in some kind of trouble, and had that trouble found them here?

Right then, the front door swung open. "Reef."

Liam's broad frame silhouetted the doorway. When he saw the others staring at him, he relaxed his features and waved toward the couch. "How's the patient?"

Matt managed a thumb's up.

"Never say that taking the trash out is easy." Liam offered a grin.

Reef stepped toward him. Liam was trying to make everyone feel comfortable, but he could tell his friend wanted to show him something.

Reef jammed his hands in his pockets. "Think I left something outside. I'll be right back."

Without a word, Liam followed him.

"What'd you find?" Reef asked as they stepped outside the porch.

"There's a trail of footprints from the woods to the garbage cans. It looks like someone was waiting behind the vehicle and then must have jumped Matt. I don't like this at all."

"Where did the prints lead?"

"I followed them through the woods. There's a new construction site down the road. Looks like someone staged a vehicle there and then took off. The tracks in the snow are fresh."

Reef raked his hand through his hair. "I don't get it. Why would someone want to ambush Matt?"

"Right? Matt's not the kind of guy who has enemies. And it's not like a church group is a prime target for theft."

"Wait." Reef sucked in a breath. "There's no way this person knew Matt would be the one taking out the trash. It could have been any one of us."

"What's your point?" Liam crossed his arms.

"My point is Matt wasn't a specific target. Someone is targeting our group—in general."

"But why?"

Reef sucked in another deep breath of cold air. That was the burning question. There was no clear answer, but his mind kept going back to Kaley and the way she'd been acting. But until he knew what was going on in her life, he wouldn't say anything.

"Do you think we should call the police?" Reef asked instead.

"I'm going to make a few calls and get acquainted with the local force," Liam said. "Maybe this was a teen prank or something, but I still want to report it. Perhaps there are similar incidents going on around here—the local force would know. Maybe you're right that Matt as the target was purely random."

Reef nodded and didn't say anything more. Everything in him wanted to believe their theories were correct.

"Let's talk to TJ and let him know," Reef said. "And let's get back inside. It's freezing out here."

He cast one last look at the surrounding forest. At a glance, this place was a winter wonderland. But he feared something deeper was about to surface, and his gut cried out that Kaley knew something about it.

He would just have to get her to trust him and talk to him again. Before something else happened.

Half an hour later, Reef shrugged on his jacket and quietly closed the door to the room he shared with Liam. His friend was still on the phone with the local force and nodded goodbye to Reef.

As he started up the basement stairs, he quickened his steps. It was now or never to get Kaley away from the group. It was almost lunchtime, and in a few short hours, everyone would start getting ready for night skiing.

Everyone, except Matt.

In the dining room, Macy and Kaley were playing a game of Farkle that neither seemed especially interested in.

"I'm going to run out and get more ibuprofen for Matt since he took the last of Brittany's," he told them. "Want to come with?"

"Yeah, I'm getting cabin fever," Macy said.

Kaley dumped the dice back in the cup. "I'm in. Maybe I'll actually get signal at Fred's."

Macy shook her head. "I thought you were going to disconnect on this trip? From what you were telling us on the bus, you need a serious vacation."

"Yeah, I tried." Kaley hesitated as if she wanted to tell them something more. "But there are some things I can't escape."

Macy didn't seem convinced. "You're a therapist, not an on-call doctor. I'd tell my office to get lost."

"I—" Kaley closed her mouth and shrugged.

Yes, there was more. Something was wrong, but she wasn't telling them what it was. Whether or not it related to Matt's accident, Reef didn't know. But he needed to find out.

The girls grabbed their jackets while he told TJ they were making a Fred's run.

"Can you pick up more coffee filters too?" TJ asked. "We're out."

"Sure thing." He hoped he'd remember. Shopping lists were the girls' strength, not his.

Kaley met him at the base of the stairs. Her pony tail poked outside of a baby blue beanie, and her lips shimmered with a glossy coat.

His pulse quickened. What did her lips taste like? He shook off the thought. He could forget about lips if she refused to trust him with her problems.

But he should tell her she looked nice. Giving compliments wasn't a crime, was it? He opened his mouth to say something, but his tongue seemed glued in place. He cleared his throat and tried again.

"Coffee filters."

Kaley arched an eyebrow. "Coffee filters?"

"Yeah." Reef tugged on a beanie cap, hoping to hide the color he felt creeping up his neck. "And you look really nice."

"Uh, thanks." Kaley stuffed her hands in her coat pockets. "I look like a nice coffee filter?"

"No—no." Reef waved a hand, hoping to help clear the air space between them. "TJ asked us to pick up coffee filters, and I thought maybe you can help me remember."

"Okay, sure."

"And I like your beanie hat, but sorry, there was no transition between those two thoughts."

Kaley smiled. "No, there wasn't. Guess I still have yet to figure out the workings of a man's mind."

Reef grinned back. "Well, that's good, because I haven't figured out a girl's either. But I'd like to, if she'll give me a chance."

Kaley dropped her gaze. Was that discomfort or just a blush? Did he dare push harder?

"Are you kids ready to go, or are you too busy studying the floor?" Macy's voice broke into his thoughts.

Kaley shot him an unreadable look and yanked open the door. "Ready."

The trip to Fred's took a grand total of five minutes, which was a blessing. No one seemed very talkative, and he kept the CD player off since his music seemed to antagonize Kaley.

The girl needed a music education, but he had to prioritize here.

"I'll find the coffee filters," Kaley said as he parked the car.

Macy popped open the passenger door. "I'm grabbing a movie for Matt. Poor guy isn't going to be skiing tonight, and he needs something to do at the cabin. Fred's has rentals, right?"

"Yep." Reef locked the car and followed them to the entrance. A few hours ago, he wouldn't have bothered. Beech had seemed like a little piece of paradise where people respected others and their property.

But someone had just clubbed Matt over the head, so there went that illusion.

The three parted ways inside, each on a mission. Reef found the ibuprofen and went in search of coffee filters—and Kaley.

He found her studying a small selection on a shelf. "You find some that will work?"

Kaley jumped. "Oh, hey. Yes, I think these will work." She snatched a package off the shelf. "We should go find Macy."

"Wait, can I ask you something first?" Reef leaned across the aisle, blocking her exit.

She frowned. "What?"

"What we were talking about before we left—a chance."

"A chance for what?" She shifted her weight to one hip. She was trying to look casual, but she didn't play stupid well.

He swallowed and softened his voice. "Another chance for us—and for you to actually tell me what's troubling you."

Emotions flickered across her face. For a moment, she looked hopeful but then her miss-independent mask fell over her features again. "I don't know what you mean."

He straightened. "Kaley, you don't have to pretend with me. You haven't been acting yourself. You've been staying up late working when you told the group you'd be taking a break. And you looked worried when you weren't able to use TJ's phone last night. I'm not a detective, but I can tell something's wrong, and I want to help."

She frowned. "You're right. You're not a detective, but maybe I should talk to someone else."

"Someone else?"

"I told Pastor TJ, because he's my pastor and in charge of our group. He had a right to know."

"To know what?" Reef forced himself not to cross his arms. People always told him he looked angry when he did. He had to keep his cool for Kaley to trust him.

When Kaley didn't reply right away, he tried another approach. "You just said you should talk to someone else. I'm someone else, and I care."

Shoot, Kaley was the one crossing her arms now. "Liam's a cop. Maybe I should talk to him."

"Wait, so you trust Liam but not me?" Reef couldn't keep the frustration from his voice.

"I trust Liam's position."

So much for not crossing his arms. "But you'd be wasting your breath to trust an entrepreneur like me, is that it?"

Kaley's cheeks blazed. "You can't begin to understand."

"Because you won't give me a chance."

"Hey, guys?" Macy rounded the corner, carrying something big and plastic under her arm. "Look what I found!"

Reef spun to face Macy. "Oh, yeah! That's a Fred's sled all right."

"Weren't you talking about getting one earlier?" Macy asked. "It's only fifteen bucks. And the community sledding hill is right down the street."

"But what about Matt?" Kaley stepped next to him but avoided eye contact. "We said we were getting ibuprofen for him—and coffee filters."

Macy shrugged. "No one would miss us for five extra minutes. Besides, he can't take more pain meds for a few hours."

"I agree." Reef offered to carry the sled and started toward the check-out counter. Over his shoulder, he called, "But since you don't trust my opinion, we'll tell anyone who asks that it was Macy's idea."

"Fine by me." Macy grinned.

Kaley didn't respond, and Reef didn't bother looking back. Caring made her sting of rejection and distrust hurt worse. If only he could convince his heart to move on.

Chapter Twelve

Kaley watched as Reef pulled his gangly legs inside the plastic sled and nodded to Macy to shove him down the hill. His broad, boyish grin suggested he didn't have a care in the world.

And yet she had seen the way his smile faded, and his eyes lost their glow when she mentioned telling Liam and not him. She had hurt him. Again.

Macy pushed until his momentum took over, and he sped down the slope past children and their own sleds.

There may or may not have been a sign that read the sledding hill was for twelve and under. But everyone here was having enough fun of their own to bother enforcing it. Besides, snow was snow and channeled every adult's inner child. A dad next to her settled onto a sled with his toddler on his lap and scooted off the hill—looking every bit as excited as his little one.

"You're up next." Macy slapped her shoulder, jolting her to the present. Reef had just reached the bottom and nearly barreled into the fence.

"It's not my sled. And like you said, we can't stay here long."

Macy shook her head. "Stop overthinking everything and enjoy the moment, okay?"

The truth to her words stung. Yes, she did overanalyze. It was part of who she was. She was not a risk taker, and she didn't like borrowing the sled belonging to a man whose heart she kept wounding.

But when Reef reached the top of the hill, dragging the sled behind him, there wasn't a trace of ill-will on his face. Instead, he had the most genuine smile as he handed her the sled. "Your turn."

Hesitating only a moment, she accepted the sled. "Thanks."

Kaley pushed her worries aside for one moment. She had always wanted to sled, and here was her chance—on a small community hill reserved for twelve-year-olds.

It was now —or maybe never. She curled herself into the sled and gripped the sides.

"Ready!" Her heart pounded as Reef gave her a running start.

She squealed in delight at the rush of cool air on her face and the crunch of snow beneath her. When she came to a stop right before the slush pile, she grabbed the sled and started running back up the hill with only one thought in mind.

"Can I go again?" She gasped for breath. "That was the best thing ever."

"Told ya." Macy smirked. "This time, we double up. Reef, think you can push both of us down that hill?"

"Piece of cake!" He pretended to flex his muscles. "Get in your chariot, girls."

For half an hour, Kaley felt like a twelve-year-old again. She and Macy doubled up, and then Macy finally dared Reef to squeeze in behind them both. It was a ridiculously tight fit, and Kaley ended up falling off the front, but they had more fun than even the kids appeared to be having.

Her pants were soaked through with snow, but Kaley didn't care. She lay where she'd rolled to a stop in the snow, trying to catch her breath. Reef appeared above her and extended a hand.

She accepted it and got to her feet. For a moment, her world swirled. How far had she rolled after tumbling out the sled?

"Whoa, steady." Reef planted a firm hand on the small of her back.

"I'm good." Kaley blinked hard and brushed some of the snow off her pants. "This has been the best thing ever."

"Second best thing ever," Reef said.

"Hmm?" Kaley couldn't focus with his hand on her back. She slowly stepped away so she could face him. "What's the best thing then?"

Reef nodded across the street. "Brick Oven Pizza."

"Oh, pizza is in a category of its own."

"Brick Oven is the best you'll have anywhere." Reef tugged the sled behind him as they started back up the hill toward Macy. "Their crust tastes kind of like a pretzel. I tried to bribe the cashier for a secret recipe, but it didn't work."

Kaley laughed, imagining Reef cranking up the charm on a young cashier. She was surprised it didn't work. "Well, it sounds amazing anyway."

"Want to try some? We could go for a late lunch."

"Yes." The word sprang from her lips before she could think her response through. She'd taken Macy's advice to stop overanalyzing, but wait, had she accepted a lunch date invitation from Reef?

She shook her head, trying to clear the fog as they reached Macy. "But wait, we need to get the medicine and coffee filters back to the cabin."

"Of course, we'll drop those off first."

"But …"

"Two more minutes!" Reef called and went barreling down the hill head first. He plowed through the slush and hit the fence.

Kaley gasped, but his thumbs up and wobbly smile a minute later assured her he was fine.

She, however, was not.

"I think I just agreed to a lunch date with Reef," she mumbled.

"Good." Macy nodded her approval.

"Good? I'm not sure it's good at all."

Macy rolled her eyes. "Stop over-thinking everything."

"But …"

Macy held up a hand. "Reef is an awesome guy. He loves Jesus, and he loves people. And apparently, he likes you. Those are all in your favor."

Kaley felt her jaw hanging open. How could Macy put everything into perspective like that so easily? But relationships weren't that easy. They were complicated. And hers and Reef's had already failed to launch once. She had little faith a second attempt would go much better.

She pulled her gloved hands to her mouth to warm them. "Well, it's only a pizza date."

"In my experience, good things often start with pizza," Macy said and then jogged over toward where Reef was dragging the sled back up the hill. Apparently, she wanted another turn.

Why did life seem so black and white for people like Macy, and from where she was standing, everything looked gray?

A little girl in a bright pink tube drew her focus to the present. Her face expressed sheer delight as she barreled toward the arms of a smiling man at the base of the hill.

She trusted her daddy to catch her and keep her safe.

Kaley needed to do a better job trusting her heavenly Father to do the same.

To the left of the little girl and her daddy, another man caught her attention. His gloved hand held a phone, and he lifted it as if to snap a picture.

And it was pointed right at her.

"Macy's taking the sled for one last run." Reef's breathless voice came from behind her. "Do you want to take it down once more too?"

Kaley shivered and turned to face him. "No, I think we should get going. The others will wonder what's taking us so long."

"Right, and I don't know about you, but pizza sounds good right now." He waved at Macy, now at the bottom of the hill, and pointed toward the sidewalk along the edge of the hill. She gave a thumb's up that she understood to wait for them there.

"Yeah, it does." Kaley followed in his footsteps down the snowy ledge toward the sidewalk.

"Careful, it's slippery." Reef held out a hand below her.

"Thanks." She took it. His grasp was firm and warm, inviting her to lean in to his strength and trust him.

Maybe she should, or at least admit there was a situation at work that was following her here. There was no harm that could come of it, other than Reef thinking she was paranoid.

They reached the parking lot at the bottom of the sledding hill, and as Reef slid their sled into the back of his Subaru, she glanced back at the hill one more time. The man she'd seen moments before was gone.

Could it be a coincidence that he had left when they did?

Maybe. But Kaley couldn't shake the feeling that someone was watching her, someone with an interest in the Casale case. She prayed Matt's accident was unrelated, because otherwise, her presence in the group might be placing them all in danger.

"It took you an hour to get coffee filters, ibuprofen, and a Tom Cruise movie rental?" Olivia placed her hands on her hips, cornering Kaley in the kitchen.

Kaley tore the packaging on the coffee filters and pulled one out to make a fresh pot. She was sure Pastor TJ wanted some, and if not, she could definitely use another cup herself. "Well, we did get a little side-tracked."

"A little side-tracked?"

"Oh, c'mon, Olivia, there's snow everywhere, and Fred's sells cheap sleds. When Macy found one, we couldn't tell her no." Kaley smiled at the memory of Macy's excitement and her own childlike enthusiasm. "Sledding down a hill is quite possibly my new favorite thing."

Olivia smirked and studied her fingernails. "Sledding down a hill with Reef, you mean."

"I don't know what you mean."

"Oh? Is that why you're now going on a date with him to get pizza for lunch?"

Kaley cringed. She would need to remember that Macy couldn't keep secrets. "It's not a date. He was just telling me about this local pizza place and then asked if I'd like to try it."

Olivia walked over to her and took the coffee filter from her hands. "Here, I'll make coffee. Clearly, you can't talk, think about Reef, and make coffee at the same time."

With a huff, Kaley stepped back. "It's not a date."

"It is too a date when a guy invites only one girl to go with him."

She had to get a grip on this conversation before Olivia blew it out of proportion. "We're two friends going to grab some lunch."

"Ah, so you admit that you're finally friends! That's a start." Olivia added the coffee grounds to the filter and then started the percolator.

"I never said we were enemies," Kaley shot back.

"You don't have to get all defensive." Olivia held up her hands. "I'm very happy for you and your pizza date."

"You're impossible." Kaley reached for two clean mugs from a cabinet. "While we're on the topic of dates, how was your time with Matt while we were gone?"

Olivia slanted her eyes. "Staying at our group's cabin with an invalid does not qualify as a date."

Kaley squeezed some honey into the bottom of her mug and filled the second with water before placing it in the microwave. "Brittany told me you stayed by his side the whole time, made him hot tea, and even helped him send texts to his family."

"I would have done the same for anyone in our group." Olivia leaned against the counter and crossed her arms. "Well, maybe anyone except you at this point."

She couldn't stop the laughter from bubbling up in her throat. "Oh, Olivia, you know Matt's got it for you bad. I'm sure you're the best medicine for him."

"Stop it!" Olivia pretended to scowl, but she couldn't hide a smile. "You're ridiculous. In return, I expect you to rehash all the juicy details of your pizza date before we go night skiing."

"Well then I'm sorry in advance for disappointing you, but I'm sure there will be no juicy details." Kaley pulled the mug from the microwave and stirred in a packet of Swiss Miss. Then, she checked the percolator, which was close enough to being done. She removed the coffee pot, added coffee to her mug, and reinserted the pot into the percolator.

She pulled open the refrigerator door to grab the French vanilla creamer. "You want me to add a splash of creamer to your hot chocolate?"

"I didn't ask for hot chocolate."

"Well, I made you some, and you're welcome." Kaley slid the mug toward her friend across the counter. "It would be simpler if you just drank coffee, you know."

"You're a brat, and I love you. Now don't keep Reef waiting too long for his pizza." She winked and disappeared around the kitchen entryway with her mug in hand.

Kaley cupped her own steaming mug and inhaled the vanilla flavoring. If only she could fix everything in her life as perfectly as her coffee.

Chapter Thirteen

In the kitchen silence, Kaley moved to perch on a wooden chair by the window and savored her coffee. Reef could easily find her here after checking in on Matt.

No sooner had she taken her first sip than the floor behind her creaked. She spun on her seat and cocked her head to see who it was.

Liam appeared, his head tucked toward his shoulder, pinning his cell phone firmly in place. "On hold," he mouthed.

"Need coffee?" She whispered and pointed toward the percolator.

He nodded and readjusted his phone. "You're an angel." There was a tired, worn look in his expression she hadn't seen earlier.

Wait, why was he on the phone—and was that his phone? Did his cell phone work too? Liam had bragged about having the best cell coverage, but in that case, why hadn't he offered to let her use his phone last night? Sure, he was a cop, but his phone couldn't be *that* classified—or could it? Olivia had mentioned something about his work contacting him.

She scooted off her seat and moved toward the coffee pot. She could make very little in this world right, but she could help keep the people she cared about caffeinated.

The self-confession hit her as she held up creamer options for Liam to make his preference. Yes, she did care about him. He was her friend. But did she want to date him? Did his presence confuse, excite, and terrify her the way Reef's did? No.

While she felt safe and enjoyed being around him, she did not feel attraction. Would Macy call this realization progress?

Liam shaking his head drew her attention back to focus. "Black," he mouthed.

"Oh." She handed him the coffee mug and returned the rejected creamers to a shelf in the refrigerator.

As she closed the door, Reef slid into the kitchen. Yes, slid. All of them left their boots at the door to keep from tracking in snow and mud. So their choices were barefoot, socked feet, or, for those smart enough to plan ahead, fuzzy slippers.

Thankfully, Reef did not have fuzzy slippers, but he seemed to be enjoying his wool socks.

"Ready to go?" He grinned at her. "We have about two hours. I told Matt I'd be back by four o'clock so the rest of you can go to the slopes, and I'll hang out with him."

"That's good of you," she said, "but I thought you were planning to ski?"

"Sorry, I was going to give you another lesson, but TJ can't stay back since he has to drive the van. And despite what Matt says, I'm not comfortable leaving him alone."

She swallowed the disappointment she felt. Wait, disappointment? She really was in for trouble here.

"Anyway, you ready to go?" Reef glanced from her to Liam who was now talking into the cell phone again.

"Yeah, I just need to get my boots." She gulped most of her coffee and then rinsed out the mug.

Out of the corner of her eye, she caught Liam give Reef a strange look. "Where are you going?"

Did Reef hesitate? "Brick Oven Pizza, right down the road from Fred's."

"Oh." Liam shifted the phone to his other ear.

"We'll be back soon." Kaley waved at Liam, feeling almost guilty. Why? Sure, he had been nice to her, but he'd never asked her out.

"See ya." He offered a tight smile as she followed Reef from the kitchen.

Kaley shook out her boots on the porch and stuffed her feet inside. "I hope this pizza place is as good as you say it is. Breakfast was a while ago, and I didn't get a chance to eat lunch."

"Me neither." Reef opened the passenger door, and Kaley warmed at the attention. After he closed the door after her, she slipped her fingers in her jacket pocket to find her lip balm.

Kaley slathered Burt's Bees® on her chapped lips and hoped her heart wasn't nearly as vulnerable as it had been a few months ago.

Reef slid in the driver's seat and started the engine. "So, what do you like on your pizza?" He glanced over his shoulder to back out the driveway.

Her heart deflated a little. He didn't remember how she liked her pizza. Surely that was something important an ex-boyfriend should remember.

"Oh, wait." He braked and craned his neck to see through his semi-defrosted windshield.

"Yes?" She hesitated. Was he talking about her pizza or something outside?

"Hand me a napkin from the glove compartment?"

"Uh, sure."

She popped it open and passed him a few.

He accepted them and rubbed at his windshield to get better visibility. "There, do you see all the deer?"

She tilted her head to the side "Oh, yes! They're right in front of that new construction."

"Yeah." Reef chewed on his lip and continued driving.

"What is it?" Kaley asked. "What's wrong?"

He seemed extra focused on the road. "Liam followed footprints away from where we found Matt in the snow. They traced back to that place."

Chills crept up her spine. Why was he telling her this?

"You saw them too, didn't you?" Reef glanced her direction.

Wow, this conversation had spiraled quickly from pizza to Matt's attack.

She dropped her gaze to her fingers and picked at the chapstick still in her hand. "Yes, I did. I hoped—I had hoped they didn't mean anything."

"Listen, I'm going to level with you, and I'd really appreciate if you'd level with me," Reef said. His tone wasn't angry. It was almost—pleading?

"Liam is reaching out to local law enforcement to find out if other people have reported similar attacks. We're hoping it was simply a matter of Matt being in the wrong place at the wrong time, but still, it seems like a random attack."

Kaley swallowed. "Yes, it does."

"But you don't think it is."

Could he read her that clearly? And why did she have a hard time telling him what was going on in her life? Why was it so hard to trust someone who clearly seemed to care about her?

"Cheese pizza is my favorite." She forced a smile. "I thought you might remember that from our pizza date on the beach."

Reef's body went stiff. "Wait, we just jumped from Matt's accident to pizza?"

"You asked me what pizza I liked," she shot back.

"Yes, I did—like two minutes ago."

"Anyway, I remember that you like pretty much everything on your pizza." She sighed. "Even with something as basic as pizza, our tastes are totally different."

"Listen, Kaley." Reef chanced another glance her way and offered a kind, though guarded, smile. "I know you girls can multi-task and carry-on multiple conversations at once, but guys' brains don't work that way. I'd like to talk about Matt's accident with you, and I would also like to talk about our pizza date, but I can't do them at the same time. So, which would you like to talk about first?"

She stuffed her chapstick back in her pocket. "Matt's accident, I guess."

"Okay," Reef exhaled as if he'd been holding his breath. "What's your take?"

Kaley shrugged and adjusted her seatbelt strap. "What you said makes sense. I guess we'll have to wait and see what Liam finds out."

"But what's your take? You've been jumpy lately. Are you worried about something?" Reef pulled into the last open space in a parking lot, decorated by a snow-covered sign advertising "Brick Oven Pizza."

"Place looks busy." Kaley unbuckled and reached for her door handle.

Reef pressed the door lock button, and she jumped. "Kaley, you're avoiding my question. Please, I want to help, but you have to talk to me."

She frowned at him but couldn't hide the smile that his persistence tugged out of her. "Okay, I'll tell you once you order me the cheesiest of cheese pizzas."

He unlocked the doors and grinned. "Deal."

Kaley tore off paper towel napkins from a chunky roll on the table to give her nervous energy something to do. Reef was at the counter ordering, and she had grabbed a vacant table for them.

Apparently, dates with Reef still made her insides roil. She hoped she could enjoy the pizza.

"Relax," she muttered and gazed around her table. All along the wall next to the tables were drawings that guests had made about Brick Oven's pizza. She smiled as she read one titled "Bigfoot loves Brick Oven Pizza."

She was still studying the drawings when Reef slid across the wooden table from her and pushed a plastic cup toward her. Whatever it was still fizzed.

"You ever had Cheerwine?" he asked.

"Cheerwine?" She quirked an eyebrow. "But I thought …"

"No, no, it's not wine. It's North Carolina's version of cherry Dr. Pepper—but even better."

She smiled. "Sounds good." And it was.

Reef took a generous sip from his own cup and then folded his hands on the table, as if waiting for her.

"Okay." She sat up a little straighter and mirrored his clasped hands. "Just don't call me crazy."

"Kaley." He reached for her hands and covered them with his own. "I would never. Please tell me so I can help."

"I don't know if anyone can." She pulled her hands back. There was no way she could get through this with his touch searing her skin. "But here's the gist of it: The day we left Florida, I met with one of my boss's clients. The man was—disturbed, even deranged—and seemingly scared of something. He claimed the mafia was after him, which seemed ridiculous at the time. I was able to calm him down, and he eventually left in a somewhat more stable frame of mind, but that's why I was so late to meet the bus."

Reef frowned. "Yeah, I remember. You were still dressed in your work clothes."

"Yes, that's right." Kaley nodded. "I planned to wrap up the report, send it to my boss, and enjoy a completely unplugged vacation."

"What happened?" Reef asked softly.

Kaley bit her lip, trying to keep her emotions out of this. "Authorities found him dead on his houseboat that night."

"What?" Reef's voice rose.

"Shh, keep it down." Kaley sank lower in her seat and gazed around the neighboring tables. A child at the table behind them was tacking a new drawing on the wall, but his attention was focused on the wall. His parents seemed to be leaving, and at least no one appeared to notice Reef's outburst.

"Sorry." Reef lowered his voice. "Wait, so is that why you needed TJ's phone?"

"Yes, I had to contact my boss. Apparently, the local authorities need to interview me as soon as I get back since our receptionist and I were the last two known people to see him alive."

Reef folded his arms and leaned closer. "Was it a suicide, or was it—the mafia?"

"Order for Reef!" A worker shouted.

Reef sighed. "Hold on, I'll be right back. Don't go anywhere."

She forced a smile and stared after him, but something at the table behind them caught her eye. There was a new bright red drawing. The crude scribblings of a pepperoni pizza made her wince. Why were there so many pepperonis? And why was the marinara sauce running like ... blood?

Her heart skipped a beat as her eyes followed the marinara sauce to the bottom of the picture. It read, "We'll find you ... at Brick Oven Pizza."

Chapter Fourteen

The steaming pizza in his hands sent Reef's stomach rumbling. He maneuvered away from the kitchen window, carefully guarding his pizza pan from anyone who might bump into it.

It was the most ridiculous looking pizza, half plain cheese, half supreme. But hey, if it made his girl happy, he was happy.

But he couldn't call Kaley his girl yet. Still, she was finally opening up to him, and that seemed like a good sign.

"Check out this beaut—" But Reef stopped short when he saw Kaley's face. It was sheet white, like someone had scared her out of her wits.

"Kaley?" Reef slid the pizza pan onto the table and then scooted into his seat. "Kaley, what's wrong?"

She gulped and dropped her gaze to the pizza. "I—I think maybe we should go."

"Go?" Reef asked. "But our pizza is hot out of the oven. I thought you were hungry?"

"I—I just …" But she didn't finish her sentence. Was she trembling?

Reef took a deep breath. Being hangry right now wasn't going to help. He ignored the growling in his stomach and reached for her hands again. "Kaley, what's wrong?"

She stared at him, tears pooling in her eyes. "I think someone is after me."

He blinked. That was not at all what he had expected her to say. Hadn't they been discussing her client's suicide? Had she said that it was a suicide? No, she hadn't.

A knot started forming in his stomach. He leaned closer. "Why do you say that?"

"Come here," she mouthed and patted the seat next to her. Then, she cast an anxious glance around the room before offering him a wobbly smile.

"Okay." He scooted out of his seat and briefly surveyed the room as well.

That's when he saw him. He was walking into the bar room, but it was impossible to miss that profile. He'd spent too many minutes staring at the man as he sweet-talked Brittany in the lodge.

Reef sank into the seat next to Kaley and wrapped his arm around her shoulder. It would look casual, like they were on a date.

Whether she understood his intention or not, she didn't push him off but rather seemed to sink into him.

"Did you see someone?" he whispered.

She shook her head, staring straight ahead. "No, I saw that— that drawing. It has the same message as the one Brittany gave me, and it wasn't there when we first arrived."

Reef's head spun. Message? What message had Brittany given her?

But then he remembered. The man at the lodge had pressed something into her hand. Had it been a message for Kaley? And if so, why hadn't Brittany said anything?

He wanted to give that girl a good talking to, but he willed himself to focus on the present problem. Following Kaley's gaze, he saw the red pepperoni drawing and the words scrawled below it.

Could that man walking in to the bar be responsible? And what exactly did he intend to do now that he'd "found" Kaley?

"You're right," he said softly. "Let's go back to the cabin. I'll get a box for the pizza."

He hesitated as he stood up next to the table. "Why don't you come with me?"

Kaley grabbed her purse and was by his side in a flash. "I think that's a good idea."

Reef squeezed her hand and then grabbed the pizza pan. It would probably be cold when they reached the cabin, but he didn't care about that right now. Right now, all he could sense was Kaley's very real fear and the growing dread in his own gut.

He didn't know the rest of her client's story, but whatever this case was, it must be big. Why else would someone be tracking Kaley in the sleepy ski town of Beech Mountain?

After asking for a box, he slid the pizza into it, thanked the waiter, and handed it to Kaley. Carrying pizza would at least give her fidgety fingers something to do.

There was no further sign of the man from the lodge, and Reef wasn't going to wait around for a closer encounter. Keys ready, he hurried to his Subaru ahead of Kaley and unlocked her door.

"Thanks," she said and slipped inside with the pizza.

He cast one look over his shoulder and hopped inside. As they left the parking lot behind, his anxiety lessoned. Maybe the man being there was a coincidence. But what about the note Kaley saw on the wall? Could that really have been for her?

Beside him, Kaley popped open the pizza box lid. "Remember on our second date when we were so hungry, we didn't even wait to get to the beach before helping ourselves to a slice?"

That was a good memory. He'd been happy to find the girl he was dating didn't mind eating pizza in the car on the way to their sunset date.

"Yeah," he grinned. "Should I confess now that I eat pizza in the car all the time?"

"I'm okay with that."

Kaley seemed to be savoring the aroma—and perhaps their beach memory too?

"Wasn't that the date where you tried to teach me self-defense or something?" She offered a wobbly smile.

He laughed and smacked his hand on the steering wheel. "Oh, right, it was. Hey, every girl ought to know how to break out of an arm lock and the right way to punch someone, but if I recall, you weren't all that excited to learn."

"I can't focus well when I'm hungry."

"I'll remember that for next time." He held his breath. Would Kaley let there be a next time?

But Kaley didn't seem to pick up on his hint. Instead, she held out a supreme piece to him. "It's a bit messy though."

He couldn't help but smile at her offering to hand him a piece but quickly returned his gaze to the road. The ice and snow made driving conditions extra slippery, and even though the Subaru had four-wheel drive, he didn't want to take any risks.

"I'm good for now," he said. "These roads demand I keep both hands on the wheel, but you should go ahead and try yours while it's still hot. Let me know if it's as good as I worked it up to be."

"I'm willing to take one for the team." Kaley replaced the slice with one of her own. She took a bite off the end and closed her eyes.

"Well?" He accelerated into a turn to keep his momentum going.

"This is amazing." She groaned and wiped a strand of cheese off her chin. "You were definitely right about—"

A loud bang cut her off mid-sentence, and Reef felt the Subaru shift its weight. He yanked the wheel to keep from hitting a boulder on the other side of the sharp turn.

"Hang on!" He aimed for the closest driveway that was level and off the narrow road. The Subaru skidded to a stop inches from another car.

Reef parked and looked at Kaley. "You okay?"

Part of her pizza was on her jacket, and the rest of the slice had splattered against the window. Somehow, she had kept the box from flying off her lap.

"I'm—fine." She took a shaky breath.

He squeezed her hand. "Stay here. I think we blew a tire."

She nodded and turned away to scrape the pizza off herself and the window. He could tell she was shaken, but he didn't want to add to her already frayed nerves by telling her he'd replaced all his tires before this road trip.

There was no reason any one of them should have blown, unless someone had tampered with it.

Fragments of his tire still hung to the rim, but he didn't have time to access the remains. He needed to get the spare on ASAP before whoever was responsible came to see how they had fared.

He sucked the cold air and scanned the area. No one was in sight—probably because everyone here was out on the slopes. They could have easily slid off the edge of the road, hit the boulder, and ...

"Thank you, God," he breathed and popped open the back of his Subaru. Within minutes, he had jacked up the frame, removed the old tire, and slipped on the spare. It wasn't ideal for these driving conditions, but at least it was on the back left and not a front tire that was most responsible for gripping the road.

"That was fast," Kaley said when he returned to the driver's seat.

"Didn't want to keep you waiting with that pizza." He forced a teasing tone into his voice.

"I had another piece." It was spoken like a confession.

"Good." He backed out of the driveway and resumed navigating the switchbacks. "I'm glad your first Brick Oven pizza didn't disappoint."

"Thanks, Reef," she said. "I'm sorry I spoiled lunch."

"You didn't spoil lunch." A flood of relief washed over him as the cabin's driveway came into sight. "One day, we'll go back and have a proper sit-down Brick Oven meal."

She smiled. "I'd like that."

His gut twisted again as he parked the car and they walked much more quickly than usual to the front porch. So much for a lunch date to talk about a second chance for Kaley and him.

That would have to wait. Right now, they needed to talk to Liam about what just happened and see if he could coax Kaley to share more about that note from Brittany.

He clenched his fists thinking about what a fool that girl must be but then took a deep breath. "Can I get a slice of that pizza?" he asked as they waited for someone to unlock the front door. At least

Liam was on top of his game for keeping out any unwelcome visitors.

Kaley lifted the lid. Half the pizza toppings had rubbed off the top, but Reef didn't care. He scraped off a slice and stuffed it partway in his mouth.

Even cold, dismembered pizza had a way of making problems seem farther away.

Kaley followed his example and passed him the box. "Last piece for me," she mouthed between bites.

He laughed. "Glad you're enjoying it. I hope Liam doesn't let us freeze out here."

Seconds later, there was a scraping sound and the door opened. Olivia's eyes widened. "What happened to you guys? Why do you have pizza all over your jacket?"

"It's complicated," Kaley said and slipped past her. She cast a look over her shoulder at Reef. "I'll be down in a minute. I want to clean up."

While Olivia continued to stare, Reef stepped inside the cabin and locked the door behind him.

"Where's Liam?" he asked, kicking off his muddy boots in the entryway.

"I don't know, probably in his room," she said. "What's wrong with Kaley?"

"We had a tire blow out," he said and tried to keep his voice level. "When she comes back down, would you tell her to meet me in Liam's room?"

Olivia quirked an eyebrow. "I don't think Kaley will want to hang out in a guy's room. It's—weird."

He sighed. They didn't have time for formalities here, but he didn't want more questions from Olivia. "Then tell her we'll meet her in the dining room."

With that, he darted down the hallway toward Liam's room with the mangled pizza box in hand.

To his relief, Liam answered on the first knock. "Hey, man, you're the person I wanted to see. C'mon in."

"Thanks." Reef stepped inside and slumped against the wall. "Man, this trip."

Liam's expression tensed. He closed the door partway and then stepped closer to Reef. "Wait, what's going on?"

Reef briefly recounted recognizing the man from the lodge at Brick Oven, Kaley's paranoia at a strange note displayed on the wall, her reference to a note Brittany delivered, and then their blowout. He also shared what Kaley had told him about her client's death and hoped she wouldn't be angry later that he'd told Liam.

"I tried to play it cool, but Liam, our accident might not have been minor if I weren't a skilled driver. Someone not used to driving on icy roads could have easily panicked and plummeted off the side of the switchbacks—or simply run into something."

"Glad you two are okay." Liam pulled out his phone and scrolled through something. "But now, I don't know what to think."

"What do you mean?" Reef shifted from the cold wall to an old chair in the corner. It wasn't much more comfortable. He lifted the pizza box lid for another slice and motioned to Liam to help himself.

His friend waved his no-thanks. "The local force said Matt's attack sounds like one of many in a string of incidents in this area. They think it's a group of teens trying to take advantage of tourists. A lot of them forget to lock up their cabins while they're skiing. There have been several thefts and a few incidents similar to what happened to Matt."

Reef shifted his weight on the lumpy chair. "So you think Matt was in the wrong place at the wrong time—and his attack didn't have anything to do with Kaley?"

"Yes, but that doesn't explain the strange notes Kaley has received." Liam frowned. "I suppose the most plausible explanation is she has an admirer who's turned stalker. It does seem like a stretch to think work problems could have followed her here."

"Right, but what if the man's death wasn't a suicide, and someone thinks Kaley knows something?" Reef asked. "I can't shake the feeling we're dealing with a deeper problem here. Like I said earlier, I just put brand new tires on my car. Icy roads shouldn't have been a problem, and I don't remember hitting anything in the road."

"You could have run over a nail and hit a rough patch," Liam said. "That might be enough to mess up your tire. But I agree that we should continue to be cautious."

Reef rose. The chair was far too uncomfortable, and Kaley might be down soon. "I told Olivia to tell Kaley we'd meet her in the dining room. Maybe you can share what you told me and then get your take on her story. She's pretty tight-lipped about the whole thing, but I don't think she'd mind you knowing."

"That's because it's confidential." Kaley's voice made him jump. She stood in the doorway, now fully open, with her arms crossed. "And I would appreciate you remembering that."

Reef stepped toward her to narrow the space between them, but she slipped further into the hallway, increasing the distance.

From behind her, TJ appeared from his room and held out his cell phone. "Kaley, call for you."

"Thanks." She gave Reef one parting frown, accepted the cell phone, and then retreated up the basement stairs toward the dining room.

TJ shuffled toward him and Liam. "Everything okay?"

Reef didn't answer. Everything was definitely not okay. Forget his tire blow-out and a possible stalker. The afternoon he'd planned to focus on Kaley and their relationship had become a disaster—and now she was upset with him for talking with Liam.

Liam answered for him. "The local force thinks Matt's attack might be one in a string of neighborhood incidents. We need to make sure we lock up anytime we leave—and stay more alert."

TJ sighed. "Guess that's what I get for renting the cheapest big cabin I could find."

"But this isn't like Beech Mountain," Reef cut in. "This place has always felt like a little piece of heaven where people respect each other."

"The world creeps in everywhere," TJ said and turned back toward his room. "I'm going to get changed for night skiing. You guys coming tonight?"

Reef shook his head. "I told Matt I'd stay with him."

"I'm going," Liam said. He glanced at Reef. "I'll keep an eye on Kaley and the other girls. I'm sure they'll be fine."

"Yeah." Reef wished he felt the same confidence.

Chapter Fifteen

Kaley stepped inside her bedroom door. At least Olivia wasn't here. "I can talk now, Blake," she said into the cell phone. "Sorry, I needed to get somewhere quiet."

"No problem," Blake said. "Listen, I have good news."

Kaley slid onto her bed and lay back on a pillow. "I could sure use some of that."

"The police detective has arranged to meet with you in the office on Tuesday," he said. "She no longer seems too impatient that you're not here either."

"Why is that?"

"They have a suspect in custody."

"Really?" Kaley closed her eyes in relief. "They've ruled out suicide?"

"Yes, the marks on the victim could not have been self-inflicted." The tone of Blake's voice made her shiver. She hoped never to see a picture of how they found the poor man hung in his own houseboat.

Her own imagination more than filled in the gaps.

"They've taken the man who reported finding him into custody," Blake continued. "The man lives on a houseboat as well, and they were currently docked beside each other. When they boarded his boat to question the man, they found drugs on him."

"What does the neighbor say for himself?" Kaley asked.

"Of course, he denies any illegal activity and swears he doesn't know how the drugs got on his boat. Authorities found some of the same narcotics on Casale's boat. They think the two may have gotten into a disagreement and things turned nasty."

"How awful." Kaley placed her arm over her forehead.

"But at least they found the guy who did it," Blake said. "I'm just glad that the detective decided it was safe to remove the bodyguards assigned to Meg and me. It's been weird—and with a newborn and no sleep, it's added an extra layer of stress seeing him follow us everywhere."

"How are Gina and the baby?" Kaley realized she didn't even know Blake's son's name.

"Gina and Elliot are great." His tone brightened. "We all came home last night, and even though no one's getting much sleep, it's much better getting no sleep at home than in a hospital."

Kaley smiled. "So true. Well, try to get some rest, and if you need anything, text this number. Otherwise, I'll see you Monday."

"Thanks, see you then."

Kaley ended the call and sighed with relief. At least she could ski in peace tonight and try to enjoy the last few hours of the trip before they started the long drive home bright and early tomorrow.

She should go tell the guys the good news, if she could even call it that. At least she didn't have a reason anymore to be so jumpy. The last few days showed that she suffered from both work fatigue and an overactive imagination.

But the relief made her feel more exhausted than anything else. She was tired. Reaching around her pillow, she hugged it to herself and rolled so she could stare out the frosted window. Outside, untouched snow formed a perfect covering over tree branches. How she wished nothing could mar her time here. At least now she could breathe a little easier, knowing that the case back home was being taken care of.

Even so, it had still been a long day. First there was Matt's attack and then the tire blow-out. She needed some quiet and rest.

"Only a few minutes," she murmured and closed her eyes. For this one moment, everything seemed perfect.

What felt like seconds later, something bumped against the wall, jolting her eyes back open. Olivia stood in the doorway, staring at her with a confused expression. "You okay, girl?"

Kaley pushed herself up to a seated position. "Yeah, I'm fine. Just dozed off, I guess."

Olivia arched an eyebrow. "Just dozed off? You've been asleep over an hour. We're leaving in fifteen minutes for skiing. Are you coming?"

"What?" Kaley sprang to her feet, sending Pastor TJ's cell phone tumbling to the floor.

Olivia reached down to retrieve it. "I'll return this to TJ." She poked a finger at Kaley. "You need to get dressed if you're going to join us."

Kaley glanced to her ski pants and jacket hanging in the open closet. "Thanks, I'll meet you downstairs in a minute." As soon as Olivia left, she wiggled into her extra layers, stuffed her beanie cap on her head, and wrapped a scarf around her neck. She wasn't about to miss her last chance to practice skiing.

Only Olivia and the guys were waiting downstairs. The other girls must still be in their rooms getting ready.

Kaley dropped into a chair across from Pastor TJ. "Sorry about keeping the phone so long, but I have good news from my boss."

Reef glanced her way from his seat next to the couch where Matt was resting. She ignored his curious expression and focused on TJ, recounting what Blake had told her about the investigation.

Liam leaned forward in his seat, adjacent to TJ. "Then it's like I was telling Reef earlier. Matt's attack is probably linked to that gang the local force has been tracking. We still need to be alert, but it was random."

"But what about the notes Kaley received?" Reef still sounded worried.

"It was only the one note, really." Kaley felt her neck warming. She should have waited to add the scarf until they were outside in the cold. "Maybe the one at Brick Oven was a weird coincidence."

"Or you have a secret admirer," Liam said. "He could be harmless, but tonight, stay with a group to play safe. You can hang with me since Reef won't be there."

Was there an edge to Liam's words? He couldn't be—jealous of Reef? Whew, it really was getting too hot in here.

121

Kaley smiled at Liam and willed herself not to look at Reef. "Thanks, I'd like that."

"There's still my tire blow-out," Reef pointed out.

"Wait, tire blow-out? And did you guys say Kaley has a stalker? What are you guys talking about?" Olivia moved from where she'd been putting on her boots to Kaley's chair.

"I'll fill you in later," Kaley said. "Everything's fine."

Olivia snorted. "It doesn't sound fine."

"I agree," Reef said and looked as if he had more on his mind, but at that moment, Brittany and Macy appeared.

Pastor TJ stood. "Ya'll ready?"

"Oh yeah," Macy said. "Let's do this."

Kaley was more than glad for the attention to be off her. She hurried over to her boots and stuffed one foot in the cold fabric and then the other.

"You promise to fill me in on what that was all about?" Olivia whispered beside her.

"Yeah, how about on the ride home tomorrow?" Kaley asked. "I want to enjoy the rest of our time here without dwelling on the drama."

"Deal."

"You guys have fun." Reef offered Pastor TJ a tight-lipped smile and sank deeper into his chair. Their whole group had assembled in the living room to gear up for night skiing.

Maybe a quiet evening in—away from the girls—was just what he needed.

But the restlessness he felt brooding inside him challenged his bluff. Still, Matt shouldn't be left alone, and no one else had volunteered to stay.

"You really don't have to stay on my account." Matt glanced at him from reading his tablet. "If I were you, I'd want to night ski with the others."

"Thanks, man, but that's okay. It's been a day."

Matt grunted. "You can say that again. Still, if you change your mind and want to join them, that's fine with me. I'm gonna catch up on the news and maybe listen to a podcast."

Olivia rolled her eyes and muttered something to Kaley. Reef groaned for his friend. If Matt wanted to attract Olivia, he really needed to start talking about things that might interest her. Newsfeeds and podcasts clearly weren't on that list.

"You should totally join, Reef!" Brittany clapped her gloved hands. "Then you can help me on my technique some more."

More time with Brittany was the last thing he wanted. "You got this." Reef offered a thumb's up and then glanced past her to where Olivia and Kaley were following Liam out the door.

Kaley didn't look back, and even if she had, Brittany might have blocked her from view.

Reef dropped his gaze to his phone and pretended to study something on it—anything to avoid more conversation with Brittany, anything to hide how he really felt about staying behind.

But who was he kidding? The afternoon that started out so promising had crashed and burned. Kaley seemed closed off again. He was glad everything at work had sorted itself, but still, something wasn't right. His blow-out wasn't an accident, couldn't have been. And even though Liam had written off the strange notes as a secret admirer, they were still creepy nonetheless.

He hoped he wasn't making a mistake staying behind. Liam had seemed more than eager to invite Kaley to stay by his side all evening.

Reef reminded himself he had his chance with her this afternoon. All Liam had to do was keep the evening from becoming a total disaster, and he improved his chances with Kaley exponentially. Still, Liam deserved a happy ending, probably more than he did. If only his friend would find another girl to write his story with.

The cabin seemed eerily quiet once everyone had left. Reef stretched before moving to the front door. No one had thought to lock it.

It was a good thing he'd stayed.

"I'm going to check the back door too," Reef told Matt. "Then, we can just relax for the evening. Want me to get you anything?"

Matt looked up from his reading and grinned. "Hot chocolate sounds real good right now. Olivia has a whole box of individual packs in the pantry."

"On it."

After checking the back door, Reef helped himself to the kitchen. Why not make it two cups of cocoa? He had nothing to kill but time. Maybe they could watch the Tom Cruise movie Macy had rented, or if Matt was too busy with his newsfeed, he could watch it himself. At least she had good taste in movies.

Reef had just stirred in the two packets of hot chocolate when Matt called his name.

"Yeah?" he poked his head out of the kitchen. "Everything okay?"

Matt had swung his legs off the couch and sat hunched over his tablet. "Reef, you've got to see this."

"Coming." Reef grabbed a warm mug in each hand and hurried back to Matt as quickly as he dared. Cleaning hot cocoa off the floor was not his idea of a fun evening.

He placed a mug in front of Matt, but his friend didn't even glance at it. Instead, he shoved his tablet into Reef's free hand.

"What?" Reef gripped his own mug more tightly to keep from spilling it and lowered himself next to Matt.

"That headline." Matt's voice held an urgency that sent Reef's senses on high alert. "Isn't that where Kaley works?"

"Murder investigation reopens after suspect is cleared of blame." Reef jerked at the title, spilling cocoa on his pants. "Ugh." He set the mug on the table and studied the article more.

"Trauma Counseling Solutions," Reef said. "That's her agency all right. Where did you find this?"

"I was going through the Tampa news online," Matt said. "You know, bored. I didn't read past the first paragraph. What else does it say?"

Reef scrolled through the article, his pulse quickening with each line.

Suspect cleared ... released ... hours later, struck down in a hit and run... Investigators have called for witness protection for others involved, who will remain unnamed for safety.

Reef inhaled a sharp breath. "Kaley. Kaley needs witness protection."

"What?" Matt asked.

Reef handed him back his tablet and stood. "You can read the rest yourself. I've got to find Kaley."

Matt pushed himself from the couch and winced. "Hold on a sec." He took a deep breath and then continued. "I'm coming with you."

"No, man, you need to get better," Reef said.

Matt shook his head. "I'm better off than our girls who could be skiing with thugs. Olivia and I may not be where I'd like us to be, but I'm not about to let anyone touch her. I'll take a few more ibuprofen and will be good to go."

Reef couldn't argue. He would appreciate the help and extra set of eyes. And since Matt felt about Olivia the way he did about Kaley, he couldn't tell him no.

"Okay, I'll meet you back here in two minutes." Reef raced toward his bedroom for his gear. He stuffed a knife and flashlight in his snowboard pants. The gear seemed lame, but it also seemed better than nothing.

He hadn't exactly packed for a rescue trip.

Maybe they were overreacting, but he didn't think so. Something wasn't right in Beech Mountain, and he had to make sure nothing happened to Kaley or anyone else in their group.

He shoved his phone in another pocket, even though at the moment, he couldn't do anything with it. Stupid reception. It would be so much easier if he could call TJ, but he didn't have time for what ifs.

Matt met him geared up and ready at the front door. Without another word, they headed out. Matt locked the cabin door while he scanned the darkening woods with his flashlight and unlocked his Subaru.

He just hoped for no more "accidents." That little donut tire needed to see him through the night and until he could get to a bigger town with a Walmart or something.

"God, watch over us," Matt whispered as they started down the road. "Keep our girls safe."

"Amen." Reef clutched the wheel harder. He had to keep a level head. This was no time to panic.

But he would never forgive himself if anything happened to Kaley and he never got to tell her how he felt about her.

Chapter Sixteen

Kaley gasped in delight. She made it down the green for the first time without falling. Feeling somewhat wobbly from her success, she spotted Brittany's baby blue jacket near a fence and skied toward it. Liam, Macy, and Pastor TJ had circled up around her.

"Hey, guys." Kaley barely skidded to a stop before reaching the fence. She still needed some serious practice, but at least she hadn't taken anyone out yet.

Liam placed a steadying hand on her shoulder. "Feeling more confident?"

"Yeah, I'm better than yesterday." Kaley laughed and glanced at Brittany. She knew so little about this girl who often rubbed her the wrong way, but there was no time like the present to start trying. "You looked really strong on that run."

Brittany adjusted her scarf and smiled. "Thanks."

"Who's ready for the black?" Macy nodded toward a ski lift Kaley hadn't ridden yet. If it took people to the most difficult run, that was probably why.

"I'm down for that," Liam said but looked at her. "Do you want to try?"

Her heart pounded. Reef had told her the black was much steeper. She didn't really want to fall down the whole thing.

"I'm good with green for this year," Kaley said, "but you guys should go ahead. I'll be fine."

Liam hesitated. "That's all right. I don't really need to ski the black. I'll stick with you on the green."

Brittany rolled her eyes. "Seriously, you guys, we don't need a babysitter. I may be improving, but I'm not going on black either, not without Reef. I'll stick with Kaley on this round."

Kaley didn't know whether to feel flattered or annoyed. Brittany wanted to stay with her, but the only reason was Reef's absence. If he were here, she'd dump her in a heartbeat.

Think kind thoughts.

She took a breath and nodded at Brittany. "Yeah, we'll be fine together on the green. You all can meet us back at the lodge after a few runs for hot chocolate or something."

"Sounds like a plan!" Macy turned to ski toward the chair lift and called over her shoulder. "See you guys at the top."

"Okay, just stay together," Liam said.

Brittany made a face. "Yes, Daaaad."

Liam glanced to Pastor TJ who seemed to hesitate.

Kaley offered a reassuring smile. "We'll be fine." Hadn't they all heard her tell them that her work threat was no longer an issue? And surely a stalker who'd only seen her from a distance a few times couldn't be that taken with her. After all, Brittany's odds of getting sex-trafficked seemed much higher than her own. She was younger—and a beautiful blonde.

"Okay, we'll meet you at the lodge in a few," Pastor TJ said as he and Liam slowly slid toward the lift line.

"What is up with these guys?" Brittany muttered. "I didn't sign up for a bodyguard. I was just hoping for a boyfriend."

Kaley's throat squeezed. Brittany had no qualms stating her current goals, and she didn't want to get into a boyfriend discussion with her, one where Reef's name would likely come up. "Ready to take the green again?" she asked instead.

"Sure." Brittany pressed her poles into the snow and pushed off toward the ski lift for the green.

Kaley took a steadying breath and followed her. When their lift chair arrived, she and Brittany eased into it like old pros, lowered the foot rest rail, and settled in for the ride in silence. Yet the moment seemed too short, and she might not get another chance to talk to Brittany one-on-one. As much as the girl annoyed her, Kaley hadn't exactly tried that hard to get to know her.

"You been enjoying the trip so far?" she asked.

Brittany kept her gaze on the scenery. "Mostly."

128

"Yeah, it has been a little intense this year, with Matt's accident and all."

"Oh, right."

Silence.

Kaley hesitated. "Is something else bothering you?"

Brittany cut her eyes back to Kaley. "I don't know. It just feels like we should all have been invited for pizza."

It felt like Brittany had punched her in the stomach. "Well, it was—was kind of last minute."

"If you have designs on Reef, you might as well tell me. And know I'm not giving up without a fight." The edge to Brittany's voice was unmistakable.

"Whoa!" Kaley wished she had a hand to hold up, but both were clutching her poles. "Reef's my friend, and he's yours too."

"Just a friend?"

She gulped. It would be a lie to say otherwise, under the current situation. "Just a friend."

"Sure he is." Her words dripped sarcasm.

Kaley sighed. "I was hoping we could be friends too."

Brittany straightened in her seat. "Looks like we're almost to the end. Better put up the foot rest."

"Right, yes." Kaley moved her skis off the metal railing. Brittany was right. Their ride was coming to an end, but there was so much she wanted to talk to her about. She still didn't have a clear story of who gave Brittany the note for her, but clearly, now was not the time to get answers.

She wasn't even sure if the girl wanted to be friends.

They lowered their skis to the snow bank and let the lift push them forward. Kaley released a breath when she stayed standing. She'd fallen getting off the lift only once today, and she wanted to keep it that way.

The moment they cleared the landing area, Brittany dug her poles into the snow and sped forward. "See you at the bottom!" With that, she disappeared among the skiers.

"Yeah, see you," Kaley muttered. So much for staying together.

She started to push off herself when someone screamed behind her. Kaley dug her ski into the snow to stop her momentum and spun around. A woman lay in a heap at the base of the ski lift. She must have fallen when she was trying to get off—a scary experience as Kaley well knew.

No one else was around to help, so Kaley shoved toward her. "Ma'am! Are you okay?"

The dark-haired woman cringed. "My foot! I must have twisted it."

Kaley drew closer. "We've got to get you clear of the lift before the next chair gets here. Can you at least push yourself away from the lift?"

She bit her lip and kicked with her good leg until she was clear of the next chair, which arrived moments later. A tall, thick man skied past without so much as a glance their direction.

Big help he was.

The woman collapsed onto her back and groaned. For the first time, Kaley got a close look at her. She was a middle-aged woman with olive-colored skin and exotically beautiful features. Surely, she wasn't skiing by herself?

"I'll get help," Kaley told her. "Someone at the bottom can send the ski patrol and a sled. We'll get you taken care of."

"No, no!" The woman protested. "If you can help me out of my skis, my cabin is on the other side of this slope. I can actually see it from here."

Kaley peered across the snow to an enclave of cabins. They were close enough on skis, but a good distance for someone with an ankle injury.

"I think ski patrol is a better idea," Kaley said.

"I'll be fine. Just please, give me a hand."

Kaley sighed and unclipped from her skis. The woman kicked off her own pair and then held out a hand for her to take.

"I'm Val," the woman said. "You're an angel."

"I'm Kaley." She clasped the woman's hand and started at the firm grasp. The woman pushed herself up with her good leg and wobbled next to Kaley. Val stood a few inches taller than her, sporting the build of an athletic model.

Without warning, the woman wrapped an arm around Kaley's shoulder. "See, if you help me to that cabin there, I'll be fine."

"But we'll have to leave our skis and poles," Kaley said.

"Who's going to take them?" she asked. "Besides, they're numbered to us. We can always reclaim them later."

"Okay, but ..."

"It's not far. I promise."

Her grip seemed to tighten as Val limped forward, giving Kaley no choice but to follow. It seemed like the good Samaritan thing to do, and yet this beauty pageant queen made her uncomfortable.

"You from around here?" Val asked.

"No, I'm from Florida," Kaley said.

"No kidding, I have a place in Florida too." Her casual tone seemed forced, but then, the poor woman did have a sprained ankle.

"Yeah, I'm out of my element here, but the snow is beautiful." Kaley swiped perspiration off her forehead. Shouldering a taller woman's weight was a workout.

"When are you going back?"

"Soon." Kaley said.

Val actually laughed. Kaley jerked her head to see if something were wrong. What had she said that was so funny?

A smile twisted on Val's face as they neared the cabin door. They had descended from the ski slope to the cabin's porch.

"Don't mind me. It's the pain. I'd rather laugh than cry."

Kaley chuckled nervously as Val pulled on the door handle. Apparently, she hadn't heard about the string of attacks in the area.

Once inside, she helped her shuffle toward a sofa chair, and Val sank into it with a sigh of relief. "You really are an angel."

Kaley massaged her tired shoulder. "Glad to help. Is there someone I can call for you?"

Val waved off the question. "My boyfriend should be here soon. If you could help me get these ski boots off, I'll be fine."

Her own ski boots were cutting into her shins. They were awful to walk in.

"Okay." Kaley kneeled next to Val and unfastened her first boot. But something moved in her peripheral.

The door. They'd left it open. And the same tall, thick man who had skied past them on the slopes now filled the frame.

"Oh!" Kaley fell backwards in surprise. "Is that your …?"

"Shut up!" The words fired from Val's mouth faster than a bullet.

Fear prickled through Kaley as she swung her gaze back to Val who now stood above her.

She crawled backward. "What …?"

Val nodded toward the man. "Lock the door."

Kaley searched for another door. There, on the other side of the room, a sliding door led to the porch. She jumped to her feet, but her boots slowed her down. Someone grabbed her from behind, and she screamed as giant arms seemed to squeeze the air out of her lungs.

What was happening? Is this how girls were trafficked? But why had they chosen her and not Brittany?

Goliath yanked her away from the door, still holding her in his death grip.

"Ple—ease," Kaley gasped. "What do you want?"

Val sashayed toward her with alley-cat attitude. "You're coming back to Tampa with me, and then you're going to tell me everything you know about Casale's insurance."

Kaley froze. The room seemed to shatter into tiny shards of glass that stabbed her with the undeniable truth. Nothing that had happened the last twenty-four hours had been an accident or a freak mistake, including Matt's attack. Her nightmare was coming true.

Bile rose in her throat. "I—I don't know anything."

Val snatched her chin. Her eyes were so black and filled with an emotion Kaley feared to guess. "For your sake, I hope you do."

Chapter Seventeen

Reef skidded into the closest parking spot he could find and popped his door open. His adrenaline urged him into a jog, but the strained look on Matt's face tempered him into a brisk walk.

"I'll check for her at the lodge." Matt pointed that direction. "Meet me there when you finish looking around?"

Reef nodded and forced a smile. "Yeah, thanks." His friend didn't need to tell him he still wasn't feeling well, but leaving him behind at the cabin wasn't an option. At least Matt could rest and wait for him at the lodge.

After climbing the icy steps to the bottom of the slope, Reef scanned the lines of skiers waiting for the lifts.

Thank goodness Kaley was wearing a white ski jacket. She should stand out in the middle of the sea of black jackets.

But she would also blend in well with the snow and spot lights illuminating the slopes. He trudged closer to the line waiting for the ski lift to green. She seemed to be getting more comfortable on that run, unless someone had dared her to try blue.

"Reef?" A high-pitched voice made him spin.

Brittany skied up to him with the biggest smile on her face. She seemed overjoyed to see him, and for once, he was glad to see her too.

Her lips seemed to curl up at him like the Cheshire cat. "You miss me too much to stay away?"

He didn't have time for flirting. "Have you seen Kaley? It's urgent that I find her."

Brittany's face fell. "What do you need her for?"

It wasn't Brittany's business, but she might close him off if he didn't scare her a little. "I think she's in trouble—like, real trouble."

Her eyes widened. "Trouble? Did her credit card get stolen?"

Reef gaped. If that was the worst trouble Brittany could imagine, she really was sheltered.

"Uh—no—bad guys are looking for her."

"What for?"

He didn't have time for this. "When is the last time you saw her?"

She swiveled on her skis and pointed up the green. "We rode the lift together—maybe twenty minutes ago? I haven't seen her since."

Reef frowned. "Weren't the others with you? I thought everyone was staying together."

"TJ and the others wanted to ski the black, but Kaley and I didn't feel ready for it. So I told them we'd stay together."

He clenched his fists, trying to maintain his calm. "And you didn't?"

Brittany suddenly seemed very interested in the snow beneath her. "She's slower than I am—and I think she may have stopped to help someone who fell off the chair lift."

Of course, Kaley would stop. She'd fallen off the lift herself. "But you didn't stop?"

Brittany glanced up, eyes narrow. "I'm not her babysitter."

That wasn't his question, and she knew it. Reef waved her off. "Matt's back at the lodge waiting to regroup. If I were you, I'd go there. I don't need you to go missing."

Her face blanched. "Missing? You think Kaley's missing?"

"I don't know what to think until I find her." He motioned for her to move on. "Now hurry, and don't let anyone stop you."

She hesitated, as if wanting to say more, but closed her mouth. Casting one last confused, frightened glance his way, she dug her poles in the snow and muscled toward the lodge.

Reef avoided a skier who was out of control and trudged closer to the lift lines. The snow grabbed at his boots, and he wished for his snowboard. He could move so much faster on it, but he'd left it in his Subaru. He hated to go back, but if he wanted to do a thorough job searching for Kaley on the slopes, maybe he should retrieve it.

"Hey, man!" Liam waved at him and came to a stop mere feet away. "I thought that was you, but what are you doing here?"

Reef briefed him on the news story Matt had found and glanced toward the green. "Brittany said that was the last place she saw Kaley."

Liam scowled. "I can't believe she left her. They promised to stay together."

Reef crossed his arms. "You really thought she'd stay with Kaley? Brittany only cares about herself."

"I'm sure she's fine." But Liam wasn't smiling. "I'll go up the green, see if she's stuck somewhere. You stay here at the base. Between the two of us, we can't miss her."

"Yeah, I'm sure you're right."

But as Liam skied off and more skiers came off the slope, Reef couldn't shake a growing sense of dread. If Kaley were on the slopes, she shouldn't have taken this long to get down, even if she'd fallen a few times.

Something was wrong.

And all he could do was stand there, watching and waiting, as his boots sunk deeper into the snow. He'd never felt more helpless.

Was it possible to pray with your eyes wide open and your heart squeezing to death?

God, please help her be safe. Help her be fine. Help us find her.

All he could manage were simple pleas. A child could pray better than him right now. But God knew his heart. The thought both comforted and convicted. God knew, yes. He also knew Reef could be a better man.

Minutes later, Liam returned from the green.

Alone.

Reef's heart sank. *No, no, no! Where was she?*

Liam's countenance did little to ease his anxiety. "She's nowhere on the slopes, but—"

"But what?" Reef held his breath.

Liam pulled his phone from his jacket. "Do you remember the number on her skis? I found two pairs of skis off to the side of the ski lift exit."

His heart rate quickened. "Brittany said Kaley stopped to help someone who had fallen off the lift."

"Here." Liam held his phone out to Reef who snatched it.

"Thirty-nine," he muttered. "Those are hers all right. But if she helped the woman, where are they now?"

Liam's face brightened. "Maybe a ski patrol brought them back. I'll go find out."

"Okay, meet me back at the lodge. There's a chance Kaley's there too." But even as he said the words, he didn't believe them.

Even if the woman was hurt, why had Kaley left her skis on the slope? She could have waited with the woman until help arrived and then continued skiing.

Something was wrong, very wrong.

Every second waiting for answers was taking him further away from where he needed to be: finding Kaley.

But he'd told Liam to meet him at the lodge. He would do as he said... after he retrieved his own gear from the Subaru.

If Kaley wasn't with ski patrol or at the lodge, he would spend the night scouring every last inch of the slopes until he found her.

Reef leaned forward at the table where everyone had gathered. Everyone but Kaley.

Across from him, Brittany ducked her nose into a cup of hot chocolate. More than anything, she looked guilty.

"I should never have left the girls for the black." Pastor TJ ran a hand over his face and stared hopelessly at his cell phone. "And now Kaley is missing, and I missed a dozen calls and two voicemails from the case detective."

None of the news was good. Not only had their former suspect been murdered, but an arsonist had also targeted Kaley's office. Firefighters were still putting out the building fire, and reports were too preliminary to know how much damage had been done.

At least no one had been hurt.

Liam stood at the edge of the rectangular table, repeating the information he'd already told Reef. "Ski patrol said no one notified them of an injury on the green. They examined the other pair of skis next to Kaley's and said it isn't one of theirs—but are probably privately owned. There's no way to trace the owner unless someone claims them."

"We're wasting time." Reef pushed his chair back. "I've got to start searching for her."

"Ski patrol already is," Liam said. "If anyone will find her, it's them."

Reef shook his head. "Ski patrol is great, but they don't know what we know—that some deranged person wants information Kaley has. We've got to find her and fast."

Olivia's breath hitched. "Wait, who's this deranged person? Is that what she was going to tell me on the ride home?"

"It's a client she helped who appears to have been a target. Right now, he's dead along with a former suspect. The police want to put anyone involved in the case—like Kaley—in witness protection." Reef stared out the windows toward the darkening slopes. "I'm worried we're too late."

Brittany planted her head in her arms on the table and let out a stuttering sob. "This is all my fault."

Reef bit his lip. He wanted to tell her it was, but that wouldn't be entirely true.

She sniffed and lifted her face. "When that man gave me a note for her, I thought he was being fun and flirty. He said his buddy was interested in Kaley, but he only had eyes for me."

A tear streaked down her cheek. "But I haven't seen him since. And I should never have left her today ..." She choked on more sobs, and Olivia reached for her shoulder.

Brittany's confession did little to soothe his nerves. If anything, they reaffirmed his fear–that someone had been watching for the perfect moment to get Kaley alone.

"The slopes close in an hour." TJ interrupted his thoughts. "You and Liam can stay here, and I'll take the others back to the cabin. We don't need any other girls going missing."

Macy stood straighter. "I'd like to help. No one can catch me on this snowboard."

"Me too." Olivia nodded. "Kaley's my best friend."

Brittany seemed about to chime in, so Reef cut off the chance for any more volunteers. "I know you're both good skiers, but it's easy to get separated out there."

"Wish I could be of more use," Matt mumbled and massaged his head again. "But as the night goes on, I'm feeling more and more useless."

Reef patted him on the back. "You're not useless, man. You're the one who found that newspaper article."

Matt offered a wry smile and turned his gaze toward Olivia. "But I promise that migraine-level pain or not, I wouldn't let anything happen to the girls."

Olivia actually seemed to meet Matt's gaze. "I'll go back with you, TJ. But Macy is the best snowboarder I know, second to Reef. She can really help the guys."

Reef nodded. "Let's go."

"Here." TJ pressed the cell phone into his hands. "If you find anything, you'll need this more than we will."

Find anything. The words thudded in his chest. What would they find? He just wanted to find Kaley.

"Thanks, man."

Liam held open the lodge door for Macy and fell in step with Reef. "I say we take the green and then spread out by the cabins on the slopes. If Kaley and this injured woman walked, they couldn't have gone far."

"Good plan."

The lift seemed extra sluggish. With each pause of the chairs, precious moments slipped away. All he could do was stare at the back of Liam's head in the chair ahead of them and wait.

"Did you and Kaley have an argument?" Macy broke the silence next to him.

Had they argued? Reef thought for a moment before answering. No, they hadn't. They never had argued when they were dating either. That's why her sudden break-up had taken him by surprise.

He took a deep breath. "No."

"That's a loaded sigh."

"We really didn't," Reef said. "I just—I didn't get to tell her some things I wanted to say."

It was Macy's turn to sigh. "You men. I don't get why telling a girl how you feel is so hard."

"I tried." The words rushed out before he could check them.

"And she turned you down?" Although he couldn't see through Macy's ski goggles, her tone revealed her surprise.

"Yes and no."

"Oh." Macy cleared her throat, probably not sure how to respond to that. "Well hopefully, we'll find her soon, and then you can clear the air between you."

Ever practical Macy. If only clearing the air were that simple. But when they did find her, he would tell her how he felt, regardless.

The ski lift dropped them off at the top of the green, and they skied to the edge of the slope by the cabins. At least the blowers for making snow were down a little further, so no fake snow would hide someone's tracks.

Liam was already there and motioned them closer to him. "Look!" Macy unclipped from her snowboard and kneeled next to where he was pointing.

Reef followed her example. Sure enough, there were two pairs of tracks, though one seemed to be dragging a foot.

"Maybe that was the injured woman," Macy said. "If so, perhaps Kaley is waiting with her in one of these cabins and unable to call us."

Hope lit in his chest. Could all his anxiety be for nothing? Could the solution be that simple?

They followed the tracks to one cabin's back porch. Reef glanced to the sliding door beyond, and his hope fell. The cabin looked dark.

"Let's go around front." Liam led the way.

The driveway was empty, but fresh tire marks dug into the snow. Someone had been here recently.

"I'll try the doorbell," Reef said. Liam was too busy looking up at the power lines and light pole to answer.

Macy followed him to the door, and they both held their breath while he rang the bell. It echoed inside the cabin, but no lights came on—that they could see through the small vertical glass pane next to the door.

"Can I see TJ's phone?" Macy asked.

"Sure." He handed it to her and tried to come up with reasons they wouldn't be here—other than ones involving Kaley being kidnapped. Maybe the woman was too injured to drive, so Kaley drove her to a medical clinic. They should look up a list of the closest ones and call.

Macy turned on the cell's flashlight app and was shining the light through the glass. This girl was worth keeping around. "Can you see anything?"

"I think there's a pair of ski boots in the entryway, but I can't be sure." She handed him the cell phone.

He imitated her efforts. Sure enough, there looked to be ski boots on the floor near the door. But who was to say those belonged to Kaley?

"Hey, you guys." Liam's voice behind them made them jump. "Stop acting like you're about to break in. I don't want to explain what you were doing when the police review security cameras."

Reef switched off the flashlight app and faced him. "What security cameras?"

Liam seemed to ignore his question. "Can I have the phone for a sec?"

"Sure." Reef passed it to him.

Liam pointed it at the street light and snapped a picture. "Rental properties use outside security cameras to keep track of their properties." He paused, then slipped the cell phone into his pocket. "If you're done attempting to see through the front window, I'd like to call the local force to see if they can find Kaley in any of the footage."

"Brilliant!" Macy hooted.

Liam looked at him with an unreadable expression. "I'll need a picture of her to send them."

Reef's lip twitched. Yes, of course he still had a picture of Kaley on his phone. "My phone's in the car," he told Liam. "If you can get me to the lodge's Wi-Fi, I can email you one."

Liam nodded. "Then we should get going."

Macy shot him a curious glance, but to his relief, made no comment about him having Kaley's picture on his phone.

Back on the slopes, they clipped back into the snowboards and skis. "Do you guys want me to keep looking while you go to the lodge?" Macy asked. "The slopes are going to close soon, and if those security cameras turn out to be a dead end, I might be able to find something else along the slopes."

"We're not leaving you alone," Liam said, his voice sterner than seemed necessary.

Reef shot him a look and hurried to add, "It's not that you're not capable. It's just that the three of us are sticking together."

Macy frowned. "I totally get what you're saying, but the fact is we're running out of time."

Her words felt like a brick to the face. Reef was well aware that time wasn't on their side.

"I looked along the edges while waiting for your chair to get here," Liam said. "Those were the only tracks I saw. I think we should head back and get on this lead as soon as possible."

Reef frowned at his friend. Sure, his lift chair had arrived a few moments before theirs, but there was no way he'd had time to scan the whole perimeter.

But Macy seemed to accept his answer. "Okay," she said and slid onto the more even snow. "Then let's go."

When she turned her back, Liam gave Reef a worried look which only caused the knot in his stomach to double in size.

So that was it.

That was why Liam wanted to hurry back. That was why he had snapped at Macy. That was why he said he'd searched the whole perimeter when he hadn't.

Because Liam had found something back at the cabin that he and Macy had missed.

And whatever it was, it wasn't good.

Chapter Eighteen

Val pressed her back against the leather airplane seat and sighed. That had been so easy she almost felt guilty. Stealing candy from a baby couldn't be simpler.

The engine of the small private jet purred to life, and she settled in for a smooth ride. It wouldn't be so smooth for the woman who was now unconscious in a body-sized duffle bag on the floor behind her.

She had reminded Louis to give her breathing holes. It seemed generous, after her annoying outburst in the SUV.

How that girl could plead. But Val was immune to sob stories. She'd tried telling the one of her childhood a few times, and it never got her anywhere. The only way to get what you wanted in life was to suck it up and step on anyone who got in your path.

Poor little Buttercup in the back hadn't learned that lesson yet.

She smirked and closed her eyes. The girl would talk. Despite her protests, she and Louis had pried from her that she had indeed met with Casale before this trip, confirming Big Eddie's report.

She would use any persuasive methods necessary to help her remember every little detail Casale said until that pesky insurance of his was safely in her keeping.

A thud next to her in the cabin made her eyes flash open. Louis had climbed into the cabin with her bag in one hand and his cell phone in the other. He handed it to her.

"What's this?" She couldn't keep the irritation from her voice.

His eyebrows almost met in a giant black unibrow. "Big Eddie," he mouthed.

Val shot up in her chair. How in the world had Big Eddie gotten hold of her bodyguard's private cell number?

She willed her voice to stay level. "Yes?"

"Valentina, you have gone too far."

"Hello to you too, Eddie." She forced levity into her voice. "To what do I owe the honor of your call?"

"You weren't answering your phone," he accused, "but at least your bodyguard is more attentive to answering calls from his boss than you are to yours."

Her heart thudded. Big Eddie had cloaked his phone number to look like hers so he could get through to her henchman?

"What do you want?" Val cooled her tone.

"You're playing a dangerous game with me. I told you to stay out of my way and that I'd take care of the Casale situation."

"I'm sure you will," Val cooed. "What does that have to do with me?"

Big Eddie paused. "Don't lie to me. What are you doing in Beech Mountain?"

Of course, he had tracked her.

"I needed a vacation from the spotlight." She yawned into the phone. "I thought a little ski town might be exactly what the doctor ordered."

"So you have nothing to do with the girl's disappearance."

"Oh dear, someone disappeared? How dreadful."

"I like you, Val, but don't play with me." There was poison in Big Eddie's tone.

"Tell you what, Eddie. If I find her, I'll see that she's safely delivered to you."

The line went silent, and for a moment, Val thought he might have hung up.

But then his voice returned, low and lethal. "You're a baller, Val. I like that about you, but don't push me."

"I wouldn't dream of it. Now please let me enjoy the rest of my trip."

Big Eddie snorted. "Yeah, enjoy that private jet of yours. And give my regards to the poor soul in the body bag."

The call disconnected, and a shiver raced up Val's spine. Big Eddie knew. He knew she'd stolen the girl he'd been trying to knock off.

She would have to race against the clock to prove her move was merited, or she might end up in a body bag herself.

One without air holes.

Chapter Nineteen

The ride back to the cabin felt painfully long. The only distraction to the question burning a hole in his head was listening to Liam's phone calls to the local force and then to area emergency clinics.

The police would pull security camera footage of the area. They would put out a missing person's alert. They would even contact the Tampa force in case her disappearance was somehow linked to the Casale case.

None of that seemed enough.

Especially since none of the clinics had treated any woman matching the general description Brittany provided of the woman Kaley had helped on the slopes for ski-related injuries.

The only reason Reef held his tongue was because of Macy. She had been listening to Liam's conversations too, and she was no dummy. Her long face revealed she was starting to understand the seriousness of this situation.

As soon as he parked the car, Macy popped open her door and hurried inside, as if on a mission. Reef didn't try to find out what was bothering her.

Instead, he turned to Liam who sat next to him in the passenger's seat. "Spill, man. What did you see back there?"

Liam sighed and slipped TJ's phone into his jacket. "You mean at the cabin?"

Reef crossed his arms. "Yes, at the cabin."

His friend gazed after Macy who disappeared around the front porch. "The closest security camera looked like it had been shot out. Whoever took Kaley isn't an amateur. They know how to cover their tracks. I'm hoping another camera will have been close enough to give us some clues."

Reef's mouth went dry as he let go any last hope that somehow, this was all one big misunderstanding.

Shooting out security cameras spelled premeditation.

"Let's get inside." Liam opened his door and stepped onto the driveway. "We need to find Kaley's phone and contact her employer. He might be able to shed more light on the ongoing investigation."

Reef followed, but his legs felt like lead. They also needed to call Kaley's family.

The cabin held no respite from the anxiety building in his chest. The group seemed to be in an uproar. Brittany was attempting to make dinner, but something was burning. She was shouting Olivia's name, but Olivia was nowhere in sight.

TJ was trying to help Matt get comfortable on the couch, because his pale face suggested his headache had returned with a vengeance.

Reef met TJ's gaze and the unspoken question it held. "No, we didn't find her." He choked at the tightness in his throat.

"We will," Liam added, "but we need to find her phone."

"It's probably with her things in her room," TJ said. "Olivia might be up there, so knock before you go in."

"Will do," Liam said.

"Do you still have my phone?" TJ asked. "I need to call Jenna—and Kaley's family."

Liam handed him back his phone and started up the stairs. Reef followed him, feeling like a dog with its tail between its legs. Relief and remorse vied for his emotions. He didn't want to be the one to have to call Kaley's parents, and yet, part of him wished he had a reason to be the one.

But he didn't know what Kaley had told them about him. It was just as well Pastor TJ offered to make the call.

Liam rapped on the door belonging to the bedroom Olivia and Kaley shared. "Olivia? You in there? We need Kaley's phone to get her boss's number."

The door swung open, and Reef blinked. It was Macy.

She waved them inside. "Welcome to the escape room."

"The what?" Liam asked.

Macy shrugged. "That's what Olivia and I have started calling it. We're not leaving until we figure out the password on Kaley's cell phone."

Beyond her on one of the queen beds, Olivia sat with her legs crossed and fingers tapping against Kaley's touch screen.

Liam cracked a grin. "And I thought I was the investigator here."

"I've tried everything—her birthday, her birth year, the year she graduated from high school and college." Olivia huffed. "She must have added a password after I told her I'd turned off her alarm. I shouldn't have said anything."

"Try JK22." The passcode spilled from his lips before he could catch himself.

Olivia's mouth gaped open. Macy arched an eyebrow.

"Well, try it." Liam motioned impatiently toward Olivia.

She tapped in the code. "I'm in!"

Macy's gaze still fixed on him. "And how did you know that?"

"It's the last part of her Wi-Fi password at home." He cleared his throat. "Doesn't matter how I know."

"Blake's her boss, right?" Olivia asked. "He looks like the most recent person she's called."

"Yes, that's him," Reef said.

Olivia nodded. "Right, I remember her talking about him a few times. But we'll have to use TJ's phone, because hers still doesn't have reception."

"We can use mine," Liam said.

"What?" Macy asked. "I thought TJ's was the only one working."

"My job-issued one works fine," Liam said. "I brought it in case there was an investigation alert. I'll go get it."

He disappeared, and Olivia handed Reef the phone. "So you're a psychic, and Liam is more than your neighborhood cop like he's led us to believe all these years."

"I'm not a psychic," Reef said, "but I agree that it looks as though Liam's been holding out on us."

"So JK22," Macy chirped. "What does it mean?"

"JK is a type of Wrangler," Reef said. "It's Kaley's dream vehicle."

"And 22?"

The memory tugged a smile out of his tight lips. "It's the amount of money she's willing to spend on a used one someday."

Olivia narrowed her eyes at him. "I'm her best friend, and I don't even have her passcode memorized."

Reef shrugged and slipped toward the door. "Cars are more of a guy thing, you know?" Before they could answer, he hit the stairs.

Downstairs, he danced around an impatient Brittany who kept repeating that their spaghetti dinner was ready and dodged TJ who was pacing the floor while talking on the phone. Down the hallway from the dining room, Liam's door was cracked open, which was all the invitation Reef needed.

He tapped and nudged it open. "Hey, man."

Liam sat on the floor next to his duffle bag and seemed to be charging a black-cased phone. "Hey."

Reef slouched across from him on the floor. "Are you James Bond or something?"

Liam snorted and pressed his charging cable into the wall. "Sorry to disappoint you on that."

"Liam, we've been friends for years. Most cops don't carry around a job-issued phone while they're on vacation."

His friend didn't respond right away. Instead, he seemed to forget Reef's presence while authenticating his identity for a laptop login using the cell phone.

"I'm an undercover narcotics cop," Liam said without looking up. "Some cases are dormant for a while but escalate quickly. I'm basically always on call for emergencies. It's easier for my cover if I let people think I'm a regular police officer—not that any position with a badge is less important than another or should ever be taken lightly."

"Agreed." Reef rocked and stared at a picture of Beech Mountain on the wall. "But does this mean you can help us find Kaley?"

"Yes and no," Liam said. "There's going to be a lead detective on the case, but I can work with him as much as he'll let me—and at least get the right people notified of the situation. That's why I need to talk to Kaley's boss and get more details."

Reef jumped to his feet. "Let's go get that number from Olivia."

But Liam didn't budge. Instead, he narrowed his eyes to read something on his phone.

"What is it?"

"Just got a notification from Hudson."

"Hudson?" Reef repeated.

"The local officer I talked to about the security cameras." Liam turned his focus to the laptop and pulled up an email account. "He offered to send the footage to my work email once he verified my position."

Reef sucked in a breath. "Did you get it?"

"Yeah."

"Am I allowed to see?"

Liam grinned. "Off the record."

Reef circled behind Liam to peer over his shoulder at the screen. The footage was grainy, at best. "Where is that camera even located?"

Liam opened another tab and pulled up Google Earth. He narrowed down to the chalets next to the slope and adjusted the street view to get some perspective.

"Looks to be across the street, kitty corner."

"Can we see the driveway?" Reef hated the whine in his own voice but felt the impatience rising in his chest.

Liam didn't seem phased but kept toggling between screens to get a better perspective.

"Okay, top right corner should give us the best view of the end of the driveway and street belonging to our cabin."

Reef chewed his lip and stared at the screen. There wasn't much to see but the empty edge of a driveway and street lined with snow.

Nothing.

Nothing.

Movement.

"Got something." Liam paused the screen and zoomed in. Sure enough, a vehicle was backing out of the driveway.

Reef squinted. "Looks like a black SUV, maybe an Escalade?"

Liam played the video, which featured the vehicle for mere seconds.

"Windows were tinted," Reef muttered.

"We've got more videos to watch," Liam said. "At least we know someone was at the cabin at some point."

"Great."

Liam patted the floor next to him. "Get comfy, man."

"Don't we need to call Kaley's boss, too?"

"All in good time. I want to see if we can find evidence Kaley was actually at the cabin. That will definitely speed up the investigation and give authorities something to go on."

Reef lowered himself back to the floor as Liam made some notes on the first clip and then started a second. And then a third.

Staring at the grainy footage on the small screen made his eyes ache. Surely there was something here, or were they completely off the trail?

"Look." Liam paused the screen. Reef blinked and tried to focus. On the far left of the screen, he spotted two figures.

"This camera is from the cottage next door," Liam said. "I think the far left is picking up the neighboring driveway."

"From the cabin next to the slopes," Reef said. "Can you zoom in?"

"Yes, but it's going to get even more blurry when I do." Liam used the touch screen to zoom closer.

"That's Kaley!" Reef leaned forward, nearly knocking the laptop over.

"How can you tell?"

"That's her white ski jacket. I can't make out her face, but that's her jacket." Reef pointed to the white-jacketed person next to someone wearing black or gray. "And there. You can see her blue headband, though it looks more off-white or gray with this film quality."

Liam nodded. "You're right. That could be her."

His adrenaline blanched. "Could be?"

"I mean, Kaley wasn't the only female skier wearing a white jacket."

"A white jacket and a blue headband," Reef added. "That's a less likely combination."

"We can't say that headband is blue."

Reef gritted his teeth. "We can't say that it's not. And if the video quality is this poor, why are we even wasting our time here?"

"You're right," Liam said. "Sorry, the investigator in me is always questioning. That figure has a bluish colored headband, a clear ponytail, and a white jacket. There's a strong possibility it's Kaley."

The bedroom door flung open, and Brittany barged inside. "You found her? When were you going to tell the rest of us?"

Liam almost jumped out of his skin and glared at Brittany. "We have a lead. That's all. And what in the world are you doing down here?"

Brittany arched her back straighter as if to defend herself. "I'm trying to get everyone together for dinner. It's getting cold."

"I need to make a call." Liam glanced at Reef as if to suggest he needed privacy.

Great. Liam was relegating him to Brittany patrol.

"C'mon, I'll help you gather the others." Reef rose and shooed Brittany back into the hallway.

More than anything, he wanted to help Liam. But he didn't know the numbers to call or who to contact. It was huge that Liam did, because then maybe, wherever Kaley was, they had a fighting chance of catching up to her.

He hated feeling helpless, but at least he could give Liam the space he needed to work. Even if it meant babysitting Brittany.

"Dear God, please watch over her till we get there," he breathed and followed Brittany down the hallway.

Chapter Twenty

What was that smell?

With a groan, Kaley slowly uncrumpled herself. Everything felt dark, with no sense of up or down. With each painful movement, she rubbed against something cold and plastic.

But there, above her head, was a strand of light. It was small and zagged, but there was a corner of light, maybe a way out of this synthetic prison.

Was this a nightmare? Where was she?

But her mind refused to focus or remember. Her only thought was to get to the light.

She poked a finger into the small, lit space. The jagged edge was a zipper. With her finger inserted into the opening, she unzipped it toward her chest to make the gap bigger until fresh, crisp air greeted her.

She was what smelled.

And she was damp.

Bile climbed up her throat. Her clothes reeked of urine, her urine. How long had she been in this … bag?

No, she wouldn't throw up. Not now. But what had happened? Who had done this to her?

Chills swept up and down her body. Maybe she had been drugged. What was the last thing she could remember?

The ski trip. Wasn't she on the ski trip? She and Reef had gone to get pizza together, and there had been an explosion—one of his tires. But they had made it back to the cabin.

Kaley scanned the modest-sized room and elbowed out of the bag. At least the floor was carpeted and soft.

But their cabin didn't have carpet, did it?

Squinting in the dimness, she tried to make out her surroundings. There was a bed in the middle of the room, and some other shadows that resembled furniture.

And there was a door. Two doors.

Which way was out?

She didn't remember this many doors in her room at the cabin. But yuck, this bag!

Tears pricked at her eyes. This couldn't be some prank. She'd never peed herself before, and the smell was awful.

She was finally free of the bag and collapsed onto the soft carpet. At least it didn't smell.

Kaley sucked in fresh air and pressed her eyes shut. From the cabin, they'd gone back to the slopes. She had helped that woman.

Something pricked in her memory. Maybe the fresh air was helping.

That woman. She had tricked her. There had been a man, a tall man with an unyielding face. He had hit her. The woman had questioned her.

Casale.

The name ripped open her memory. The case. The murder. The stalker.

Someone had kidnapped her.

She should run for help, try to escape while no one was watching.

But her limbs failed her. It was as if every ounce of strength had been zapped from her body. What had that man given her?

And how long had she been out? Hours? Days?

Now that the smell no longer overwhelmed her, she detected other pain points. Her throat felt like someone had raked it. Her tongue had swelled inside her mouth like a dry sponge. And her muscles ached as if she had lived in a box for a week.

The tears spilled over. She was helpless to find relief. Her legs refused to work, and her arms burned from the effort of simply climbing out of the bag.

"Help." The word choked in her throat.

But no one heard.

Where were her friends? Where was Reef?

His name made her heart squeeze. Was he looking for her? Did he know she needed him?

Too many questions and no answers. She pressed her face against the carpet and cried until blackness reclaimed her again.

A headache pounded behind her eyes, and Kaley squinted awake. Daylight now filtered into the room, so there was a window somewhere.

The awful smell still clung to her, and the carpet had made a semi-permanent indent on her face. But when she pressed against her arms, her body responded. Hopeful, she tested her legs, which also seemed once more to obey her.

She inched upward to all fours and peeked around the bed. Facing her were two doors.

Her heart pounded. Were they locked? How much of a prisoner was she?

The horror of what had happened to her still burned in her memory, but she shoved it away to focus on her new goal—escaping.

And a close second—getting out of these rancid clothes.

She reached the first door and tried the handle.

Locked.

Frowning, she doggy-crawled to the second, which opened with ease.

Closet.

She pressed down the disappointment and replaced it with hope. Surely if someone had kidnapped her, she was entitled to steal their clothes.

After fully rounding the bed, she spotted yet a third door, encouraging more hope in her chest. Bathroom?

Her legs trembled as she stood and reached for the handle. A tiled bathroom greeted her, and she stepped inside. With the bathroom door open, she turned full circle to survey the whole room. There was one window on the other side of the bed. The shadows of bars crisscrossed on the other side.

This place might as well be a prison. She would look out the window later. She needed water first. Her throat felt swollen, and maybe the headache was from dehydration, not from whatever the man had used to drug her.

Propping her elbows on the vanity for support, she twisted on the faucet and cupped her hands as cold water flowed.

She gulped until she was gasping for breath and swept her gaze up toward the mirror.

Mascara streaked down her cheeks, and her eyeliner had run, giving the impression she was a zombie makeup artist.

Step two. Wash face.

She grabbed the closest towel to wipe away the stains. Now, her pale face and bloodshot eyes stared back at her.

How had Frankl managed to keep life in perspective while in the trenches of concentration camp life? She was only one day into this nightmare, and already, she felt numb.

Well, that matched up with his observations. What had he written? The first stage the prisoner experienced was shock. Maybe she was dealing with a minor case of that herself.

Kaley took a steadying breath. "God, please get me through this." She gulped more mouthfuls of water and eyed the toilet. She needed something else to wear.

Hugging the wall with her hands, she worked her way back to the closet. Her legs still felt wobbly—probably would until she found food.

A few clothes hung on hangers, but otherwise, clothes peeped out of trash bags on the floor. Was this some storage room?

She didn't care. And no matter how musty they were, anything smelled better than what she was wearing.

The sizing was almost perfect, except for a pair of flip-flops a few sizes too big. Was this Val's closet of rejects?

Again, she wasn't picky, nor interested in sorting through it all. She found a pair of faded jeans, black Beatles t-shirt, and even a small Victoria's Secret bag of clearance items someone had forgotten about.

That would work. She'd just have to roll up the pant legs because Val was a few inches taller.

Locking herself in the bathroom, she made quick work of peeling off her clothes. Someone would probably hear the shower water, but if she had to face these people again, she might as well face them clean.

The hot water seemed to revive her wits, and even though her stomach growled angrily, she felt much more alive when she stepped out and slipped into the clean, though stale-smelling clothes.

Hair wrapped in a towel, she unlocked the bathroom and opened the door a crack into her room. Empty. Had no one heard her? How big was this house?

Her toes sunk into the thick carpet as she moved silently toward the window.

She gasped. The backyard stretched past an inground pool toward a river, edged with cypress trees.

A pang of regret stabbed her. It looked much like the Hillsborough River where Reef had once taken her on a jet ski date. That had been their last date before she broke up with him.

Would she still be here if she'd made a different choice?

Pushing the thought aside, she craned her neck for a better view of the house. It was at least two stories, and she was somewhere on the second floor. Based on the river view and immaculate green shrubbery in the yard, Val had money.

And Kaley wasn't in North Carolina anymore.

Was she back in Tampa?

You're coming back to Tampa with me.

Despite her surroundings, Val's words made hope swell in her chest. Was that really the Hillsborough River? Maybe she could escape then. She knew her way around. Reef had shown her.

And maybe Reef could find her.

Even if he never wanted anything else to do with her, he was a good man. He would help her if he could. His care and protectiveness of her during their lunch date and almost car accident had made that clear.

She shoved down more regret. She had been wrong about him. Now, she prayed for a chance to tell him.

Something clicked behind her, and the doorknob twisted.

Kaley squared her shoulders and pressed her legs against the bed for support. *God, help me be brave.*

Chapter Twenty-One

Reef slipped into his jacket and unlocked the door to the snow-covered patio. Several fresh inches lined the railing and bench seats. It all looked too perfect for such a messed-up world.

The cold air slapped his face as dawn warmed the forest with its faint glow. He'd slept fitfully, at best—his dreams haunted by grainy video footage and what it all meant.

Too much time had already passed. Kaley could be anywhere by now.

His boots sunk into the snow, leaving a mark in the otherwise untouched covering.

The mark was so much like sin in the world, marring what God designed to be perfect. And it couldn't be undone, only forgiven.

He was thankful he had recognized his need for forgiveness from a young age, thankful that God had spared him from a lot of bad mistakes. He'd sure watched his mom make enough of her own. But he still had his share of regrets, and his failed dating experiences were at the top of his list. Some of them he had handled better than others. With some of them, he had probably left scars. Surely God didn't mean for him to be single forever? But just when he felt like he might have another chance with the girl who invaded his dreams, she was gone.

He took another step in the snow as his blood rushed hot. Whoever did this needed to pay.

Yet was their sin any worse than his? The thought came from nowhere. He wanted to shout that it was. He had never kidnapped an innocent girl or murdered anyone. He'd only said things he wished he hadn't or seen things he wished he could erase.

But sin was sin in God's eyes.

Reef huffed in frustration, his breath crystalizing before his eyes. He'd come out here to talk to God, not to get a lecture.

Pray for them.

Again, the thought came unbidden. Pray for Kaley? Of course, he was praying for her with every conscious breath, praying that someone would find her and that she'd be safe.

Pray for them.

The scoundrel who kidnaped her?

The thought knocked the air from his chest. He wanted to do a great many things to the person who kidnapped her. Prayer wasn't one of them.

Pray for them.

"Oh, God." The words choked him. It wasn't fair. These people deserved punishment, and he was more than happy to be the instrument to deliver it.

You deserved punishment too.

His chest deflated. Yes, he knew that. He'd come to grips with his sin and confessed it, kept confessing when he stumbled.

But all sin was sin in God's eyes. If God could save him, then God could save the people who had taken Kaley.

God didn't need him to save her. He could do it all on his own.

"Oh, God." Reef tried again. "I want to hate them. But if you can, reach them instead. And keep them from hurting Kaley."

Reef reached the railing but couldn't bring himself to touch it. The surface of the snow was flawless. He wished Kaley could be here to see this with him. She'd once told him she'd never seen snow, and even though she'd never told him, he knew by the light in her eyes when they went sledding that she was as excited as a little kid to experience it.

He longed to wrap his arms around her as he'd done then to keep from falling off the sled.

The sun rose higher as he stood in silence. A family of deer crossed the forest floor beyond him, and the morning song birds twittered as if they didn't have a care in the world.

Maybe Liam was up and ready to go. Reef had already packed the Subaru, and his friend had offered to leave with him instead of waiting for the group. They'd travel faster that way, get to Tampa sooner.

The detective on the case had talked with Liam for a long while last night and invited him to meet up as soon as he returned to town.

As much as Reef wished he could be there, he knew it was better he wasn't. After all, didn't the ex-boyfriend always get blamed for cases like this?

Liam had promised to keep him informed of any leads, which was more than he deserved.

The door creaked behind him, and Liam poked his head out. "Dude, it's freezing out here."

Reef retraced his footprints to the door. "You ready to go?"

"About that." His friend waited for him to get inside and then shut the door.

Reef shook the snow off his boots on the doormat. "You get any news?"

"Yes, we've got a lead." Liam sat down on a bench next to where he'd pulled his luggage. "Thanks to that footage, we identified the license plate on the vehicle."

Whoever was able to read the license plate on that awful footage deserved a gold medal.

"Yeah, they traced it to a rental car agency. Someone named Louis Caputo rented it, and here's where it gets interesting. He's a bodyguard who works for Valentina Russo."

Reef frowned. "Am I supposed to know that name?"

"Dude, remember that mob movie we saw last year that got nominated for all those awards?"

Right now, he was so distracted about Kaley he couldn't remember what movie he saw last month, let alone last year.

Liam sighed as if exasperated. "It was called *Hood*. Does that ring a bell? Anyway, Russo was the director."

"This is all fascinating, Liam, but what does it have to do with Kaley?"

"Caputo wasn't here on vacation. He was on the clock for his employer, Russo. But what interest would a big-time director from California have with Beech Mountain's slopes? I mean, she could ski in Utah."

Reef crossed his arms. "What are you getting at?"

"My point is that Russo has a record. She may be a Hollywood director, but she's a Tampa native."

"Wait, you're telling me that she not only directs mob movies but is part of the mob?"

"It's a theory," Liam said, "considering Caputo and Russo both appear in footage at a private airstrip on Beech Mountain where they left the rental car."

Liam's words finally sunk in. "Wait, was Kaley with them?"

"Hard to say." Liam hesitated. "Right now, it's speculation."

"What do you mean by that? If they clearly appear in footage, then …" Liam's long face made him stop mid-thought. His friend glanced out to the porch and took a deep breath.

"Kaley isn't pictured among them, but Caputo was carrying a duffle bag that looked more like a body bag."

The blood drained from Reef's face. "No."

"We can't prove it's Kaley, and even if she were in that bag, that doesn't mean she's dead," Liam rushed to add. "What would be the point of killing her and bothering to transport a dead body? I think she's alive, but we need to hurry."

Reef couldn't put words to the horror he felt. Imagining Kaley stuffed in a body bag made him want to vomit. She must be so scared. He had to be strong for her.

"The Subaru's packed and ready to go." Reef stepped past Liam. "Let's roll."

Liam didn't rise. "I have a better idea."

As if on cue, Matt emerged from the hallway, carrying a duffle bag. Though he looked worlds better than yesterday, dark circles still hung under his eyes.

"I have an appointment at one o'clock with the detective at the Hillsborough Sheriff's Department, and with Matt's help, we've made all the arrangements to rent a plane. Matt is flying us home, and Macy has offered to drive us to the airstrip."

From out of nowhere, the rest of the group appeared. Brittany and Olivia came from the kitchen, handing them each a breakfast bag. Macy slipped into her boots and jacket, ready to drive them. And Pastor TJ circled them up for a word of prayer.

Emotion squeezed his throat. He had the best of friends, and they were all in this together. Macy had even promised to take care of his tire situation and then drive his Subaru home for him, promising it would be in his driveway tonight.

At Pastor TJ's "Amen," Liam grabbed his bag and started for the door. "All right, we've got a plane to catch."

Chapter Twenty-Two

Val's bulldog of a henchman filled the door frame, his gaze unreadable and stern. Kaley gulped and snatched the towel off her head. There was no reason she should feel embarrassed. The only people who should feel ashamed were the ones who had kidnapped her.

He grunted and stepped aside, as if unwilling to waste words on her.

She crossed her arms and waited. She was not an animal.

He grunted again. "C'mon."

"Where are we going?"

The man glared at her. "Val will see you."

Kaley twisted her wet hair into a top bun, thankful for her habit of always keeping a headband on her wrist. At least she was clean and could hold her head high, despite her circumstances.

Ignoring the trembling in her legs, she edged toward the door, then stopped. There was no way she was going to squeeze past that man. "Lead on."

Still scowling, he shifted his bulk out of the doorframe. "You first."

She swallowed the rising panic. What if he stabbed her with another needle, and she didn't wake up ever?

Fixing her gaze on the hallway, she slipped past him and started for the stairs. Her shadow didn't say anything, but his footsteps thudded closely behind her.

On the first landing, she hesitated.

"Move."

At least she was getting the gist of the house. It was actually three stories, and they were heading to the first. Despite her nerves, she really hoped they would find a kitchen. Her stomach reminded her she hadn't eaten in far too long.

"Stop."

Kaley wanted to be annoyed at his dog-like commands, but the grandeur of the space stole her attention. An enormous room opened before her, and the back wall was a series of sliding doors that overlooked a pool and river view. The space itself held plush seating, a massive entertainment center, and bar.

Bulldog stepped ahead of her and pushed open a set of double doors. "This way."

Sweet relief, it was a kitchen, even bigger than the one in their cabin back at Beech and much more modern. A large island filled the center, and Kaley slipped onto a stool to hide her dizziness and disappointment.

There was no meal laid out for the prisoner, but maybe there would be something?

After rummaging around in a pantry, Bulldog pulled out a box of cereal, which he slid toward her. "Eat."

Kaley bit her tongue. Froot Loops™? She was supposed to survive on sugar-coated cereal? But she didn't dare argue. She helped herself to a paper towel and poured a pile onto it. Apparently, this dog didn't even get a bowl or milk.

While crunching the dry cereal, Kaley eyed a knife set on the far counter. Could she beat Bulldog to it?

Probably not until her sugar rush kicked in.

The doors behind her swished, and Kaley spun on her seat. Val sashayed into the kitchen, wearing a Cheshire cat grin coated with purple lipstick. A red scarf accented her black shirt and dark distressed jeans.

"So glad you're finally up," she all but purred.

Kaley balled her hands into fists on her lap. "No thanks to you."

"Tsk, tsk," Val puckered her lips into a frown. "Not a morning person, are you?" Her gaze dropped to the cereal, and she rolled her eyes at Bulldog. "Come on, Louis, give our guest some real food."

Kaley wasn't sure which upset her more, knowing that she now had to think of Bulldog as Louis, which in no way resembled his personality, or that there was much better food available that he hadn't considered offering her.

Louis shrugged and said nothing.

Val sighed and opened the fridge, pulling out several pre-made party trays that had been partially picked at.

"Do you like fruit and cheese?" She shoved them onto the island in front of Kaley. Before Kaley could even answer, she continued, "We have OJ or cold brew."

"OJ." Kaley popped a cheddar cheese cube into her mouth and tried not to let her growling stomach get the best of her.

Val poured a generous glass and placed it in front of Kaley. "You're welcome."

The cheese almost came back up. This woman expected a thank-you?

"I know you have questions, but right now, you're not in a position to ask them." She poured another glass for herself and sipped slowly. "Right now, I'm offering you an extension on your life in exchange for your cooperation."

Kaley choked. "Excuse me, but what have I ever done to you?"

Val pressed her lips together in a firm line. "Life isn't fair, sweetheart. But I'm a reasonable person. If you cooperate, I'll make sure you get to keep your pretty little head."

Kaley looked away and picked at a cluster of grapes. Not for one moment did she believe Val would keep her word. Whenever she got what she wanted from her, that would be the end.

"Eat up, buttercup." Val downed the rest of her OJ and turned to Louis. "Bring the car around front. We're leaving in ten."

Louis seemed to hesitate and glanced at Kaley.

Val waved him on. "Don't worry about princess. If she tries anything, I'll shoot her."

Tears pricked Kaley's eyes, but she blinked them back. Who was this woman who seemed so hospitable and yet so inhumane?

Now was no time to feel sorry for herself. She needed food to get rid of her headache and be able to think clearly. Ignoring the woman standing across from her, Kaley forced a few more cheese cubes and the rest of the grapes down.

"Follow me." Val motioned toward the double doors. "And by the way, nice shirt."

Kaley said nothing and gulped down the rest of her OJ. Squaring her shoulders, she trailed Val to the front door where a black SUV pulling a modest boat and trailer waited in the circular driveway.

Maybe the odds were stacked against her, but she was still alive. Anything was possible.

Louis came around to open Val's passenger door and then a back door for her. She slipped inside the leather interior, wondering if she'd already been here and didn't remember.

Val twisted in her seat to face her. "Now pay attention. The boat ramp isn't far, and once we get to the houseboat, we have to make quick work."

"Houseboat?" Kaley repeated.

"It's Casale's, and if you know what's good for you, you're going to find me that insurance."

A sinking feeling filled her stomach. How would she even know where to start looking? Her brain felt too foggy to connect any fragmented clues from her meeting with Anthony. Suddenly, an idea gave her hope.

"Wasn't Anthony—Casale—found hung on his houseboat? Wouldn't it be considered part of the crime scene?"

Val shot her a sour glare. "Yes, it's a crime scene. That's why we have to be extra careful."

Kaley's hopes rose. If the houseboat was a crime scene, then maybe there would be a security detail nearby. If she could get away long enough to find a police officer …

"And that's why we also made sure our insider was on duty for the next hour."

"In—insider?" Kaley whispered. Surely, she didn't mean…

Val's lips curled into a sneer. "Darling, the world is not as black and white as it seems. Integrity doesn't drive people. Money does."

Kaley nibbled her lip and shook her head. "Some people want to do the right thing because it's the right thing."

"Oh, buttercup, that's why you're part of a dying breed."

Louis snorted in the seat beside her as if he thought the analogy was funny.

Kaley turned to stare out the tinted window. Maybe a good cop would show up. Maybe she'd have a chance to run. Maybe someone would recognize her. Surely her face was in the news by now or at least in a police database. People had to be looking for her.

Was Reef looking for her?

They pulled into a park she recognized all too well. Reef had launched his jet ski here on their last date together. What she would give to go back in time and relive that moment instead of this one.

The problem with the park was that everything felt too far away. The playground was a good hike down the sidewalk. The bathrooms were at the edge of the parking lot. And the cobwebbed pavilions were either abandoned or occupied by someone smoking pot.

Today didn't appear to be an exception. What was today anyway? Thursday? Friday?

With school in session, the park seemed mostly empty.

"Wait here." Val readjusted her red scarf so that it concealed everything but her eyes. Then, she slipped outside her door and climbed into the boat while Louis prepared to back the trailer into the water.

Kaley continued to peer out the window, hopeful that she'd see a jogger or another sportsman ready to launch his boat.

But would she be able to escape quickly enough, or would she be putting another innocent life in danger?

"Touch that door handle, and I'll cut off all your fingers one at a time."

Kaley jumped and glanced up. Louis was staring at her. Those were the most words she'd heard him say. No doubt he meant them.

She shuddered and shoved her hands under her jeans. *Dear Jesus, help me know what to do.*

Louis shifted his gaze in the rearview mirror from her to the boat and slowly backed the trailer down the ramp.

A moment later, the boat's engine revved, and Val taxied toward a small dock on the side. Louis shifted to drive and pulled forward into a boat trailer parking space.

Without a word, he opened and slammed his driver's side door and lumbered to her side. She wasn't about to touch the door handle after his threat.

Her door swung open. "Out."

She slid to the ground and stepped around him. He grunted and motioned for her to lead the way to the boat.

Kaley padded across the parking lot in Val's too-big flip-flops, careful not to trip in them. Breathing deeply, she inhaled the crisp Florida air. The day was bright and clear, probably thanks to a recent cold front. The humidity would return soon enough.

The Tampa area was her home, and yet she was so much a prisoner right now.

She shook the thought aside to focus on her home court advantage. Maybe she would think of something useful.

Once onboard, Louis untied the rope securing them to the dock, and as soon as they cleared it, Val switched to idle mode and steered them down the river. Kaley slipped past her to a small back seat and watched the peaceful river slip by.

It was impossible to keep from thinking about Reef in this setting. That last jet ski date, they had tackled some deeper questions like where they wanted to be in five years and if they wanted kids. Reef really had no idea about the five-year question. Though he co-owned his water sports business, he was less a planner and more a live-in-the-moment man.

That worried her. She planned out her goals for both short-term and long-term. She was always reading and trying to find ways to advance in her career, which is why she started her master's program. The idea of enjoying the moment, while romantic, seemed impractical.

Of course, he'd said he would always provide for his family, which in his mind included him, a wife, and kids someday.

Still, his not having a five-year-plan worried her. But was he wrong because he was different? Was she too worried about the future that she was missing out on the present?

Kaley studied the water lapping at the sides of the boat. Would she ever have the chance to try enjoying the present again?

She blinked and studied her distorted reflection in the river water. Right now, she would give anything to be on the back of Reef's jet ski where he could take her away from this nightmare.

A single tear slid down her cheek. If she could go back, she'd undo the past.

But she couldn't. And right now, there was no escaping the present.

Chapter Twenty-Three

Val maintained the boat's idle speed as the attractive river houses gave way to older homes. A weathered marina appeared on the left, her clue that they were nearing the cluster of houseboats.

She glanced behind her to check on Kaley. The young woman slouched on the seat, staring at the water as if wishing it could swallow her up. Her face held a tragic beauty, and for a second, Val felt sorry for her.

Whatever. Enough people had stepped on her to get where they wanted to go. It was Val's turn to step on a few.

A short row of houseboats appeared on the right, and Val refocused her attention on the mission at hand. There was no missing Casale's boat. In honor of the Gasparilla boat parade, Tampa's annual "pirate invasion" festival this coming weekend, he had decked it out with Christmas lights and those annoying party streamers.

Now, they partially sagged off the side of the boat, almost covering the name, *Drunken Monkey*.

She snorted. He had been so attached to his stupid monkey. When Big Eddie started to suspect Casale was shortchanging him, he sent some thugs to rough him up. They killed his monkey in the process and let him off with a warning.

If Casale had been smart, he would have cleaned up his act. Instead, something seized up inside him. His deposits from his work on the Cannoli Commission remained suspiciously off, and what's more, he copied their server—complete with emails that would incriminate her in their most profitable fraud scheme yet.

The fool. He had been too sloppy. And now, she had to find that backup before anyone else did.

She could never survive a clean break with her mob connections, but now that she had her feet on the ground, she could be more choosey which projects she accepted. Hollywood had its crooks, but she preferred to keep her reputation intact.

Val steered them close to *Drunken Monkey* and then motioned to Louis to drop anchor. "You ready?" She called over her shoulder to Kaley.

The girl didn't respond, just wiped her wrist over her eyes and stood.

Pathetic. She'd better plug up the tear ducts pronto. Waterworks didn't work on Val.

"Wait here with the boat," Val told Louis as she snapped on a pair of disposable gloves as a precaution. She didn't plan to touch anything, but she could never be too careful. "The guard shouldn't change for at least two hours, but we'd better be on alert in case."

"What about her?" Louis seemed to hesitate.

Val glared at him. "What about her? It wouldn't matter if she were Mother Teresa. I'll shoot her if I have to."

Louis grunted as if satisfied and then dropped down into the captain's seat. She marched past him to the railing, reached for a cleat on *Drunken Monkey's* deck and secured a line to it.

Drunken Monkey was taller than her vessel, so she pushed herself up and swung her legs over the side. Brushing off her jeans, she checked that her handgun remained pressed into her belt holster and then crossed her arms.

Below her, Kaley hesitated. The girl was shorter than she was, but she looked sturdy enough.

Val coughed. "We don't have all day, darling."

Kaley's bottom lip pressed into a determined line, and she half shimmied, half crawled onto the deck.

Either way, she made it, and now the real work could begin.

"What are we looking for?" Kaley asked.

"You tell me."

"I told you …"

Val slapped her across the cheek. "You've had plenty of time to think about your conversation with Casale, and if you still have no ideas, think harder. Maybe you'll see something that will trigger your memory."

She stepped to the side. "Lead the way. And if you try anything, you'll be the next person the police will find dead on this boat."

Kaley's cheeks flushed, but she tipped her chin up and edged down the narrow walkway leading to the main cabin. Trash and litter edged the railway, and Val's boots crunched old candy wrappers and snack bags. Casale was such a slob.

The door hung halfway off its hinges, and Kaley squeezed past it inside. Val followed into the dim interior and suppressed a gag. That smell.

Suddenly, Kaley let out a little shriek and nearly fell back into her.

Val shoved her palm into Kaley's back to push her forward. "What's the matter with you?"

Kaley pointed a shaking finger to a long, dangling shadow. "Is that …?"

"Oh, the rope they hanged him with." Val circled with a sense of dark admiration. "Nice of the cops to leave that in place."

Kaley shuddered, and Val grinned at her discomfort. "Want to try it on for size?"

The girl shot her a repulsed glare, which made Val laugh. Too bad she couldn't afford to keep this kid around for comedy. Most of Val's existence would make her squirm, which would add to the entertainment value.

Val tugged at the rope and then swung it. "I mean, you'd be in good company with Casale and his monkey."

Kaley's eyes widened. "His monkey? He had a pet monkey?"

Twirling the rope's end around her finger, Val nodded toward a dim corner of the room where an old cage lay twisted in a heap. "Actually, it was the monkey they took care of first and then Casale."

The girl looked ready to vomit. "You people are disgusting."

Enough of this. They had work to do. Someone had knocked over a lamp in the corner, and Val strode to it and twisted the light on. The yellow glow made the interior seem smaller somehow, but at least it gave them more visibility.

Oh boy, what a job they had. The inside looked like someone had shaken twelve trash cans and then dumped all their contents on the ground. The police sure had done a thorough job tearing up the place.

Her stomach twisted. What if they'd already found the insurance? She stamped the worry from her mind. It had to be here. Casale had been clever enough to keep it from the men who interrogated and killed him. He must have put it somewhere the police wouldn't look either.

Kaley edged around the rope and seemed to hesitate. Ugh. Hesitation was a character flaw Val couldn't stand.

"Start looking."

Kaley opened her mouth but thankfully must have thought better than to make another lame excuse, another of her pet peeves.

Val stepped back toward the half-hung door and placed her hands on her hips. As much as she wanted to dig into the debris herself, she kept her attention on Kaley. The girl seemed like a push-over, but chances were, she was a flight risk. Her gloves reminded her that her job wasn't to touch anything but to keep a close eye on her captive.

With a sigh, Kaley trudged toward a wobbly desk. The girl must not have any imagination. Not even Casale could be so dull as to leave a drive in a desk drawer. But truthfully, her other options weren't much better. Gasparilla decorations—everything from pirate garlands to mini piñatas to beads and streamers—hung from every square inch of the ceiling, but the room itself was unimpressive. There was the bed which bowed in the middle, a cracked television on the floor, a stained table with microwave, and a mini fridge that was currently leaking into a trash pile.

The smell assaulted her senses once more. The dank air not only stank of trash, rotting food, and mold, but it also stank of death.

Val resisted the urge to wrap her scarf around her face. She'd witnessed more horrible acts than any woman should, and even committed a few herself. Those didn't bother her.

But the smell of death did. There was something so urgent about it. You could mop up blood, but no amount of air freshener could mask the recent scent of death. It had to fade on its own.

How many times could she play this game and keep coming out on the breathing side?

"Just one more time," she muttered. It's what she always told herself.

Kaley twisted to glance at her. "Did you say something?"

"No, keep looking."

"There's not much to see," Kaley said. "I've found three cockroaches, a chewed-on pencil, an invisible ink marker that doesn't work, and a pair of wet socks."

Val felt her blood rising. "It's here. It has to be."

Kaley crossed her arms. "What if it's not?"

Val stomped toward her and jabbed a finger at Kaley's face. "You'd better hope it is, if you want me to keep my end of the bargain, and I have no other hiding place ideas. If you don't find it today, we come back tomorrow morning."

Kaley narrowed her eyes. "And if I don't find anything tomorrow morning?"

So the girl did have some fire. That was fine. She could easily put it out. "If you don't find anything by tomorrow morning, I tie that rope around your pretty little neck and move on with my life."

Kaley spun on her and turned to examine the bed. She shook a pillow and then threw it on the floor.

Val crossed her arms, her own chest heaving. Let the brat have her hissy fit. She had laid out her intentions clearly enough. She lived in exchange for her cooperation. Really, Kaley should thank her. If Big Eddie had found her first, she'd already be dead.

Half an hour passed with Kaley rummaging through and around every inch of furniture. Val's phone pinged. Big Eddie's name flashed on her screen. She had a new text message.

She could ignore him for only so long before he called. Maybe fifteen minutes tops.

A frustrated growl rose in her throat. "Hurry up, we have to leave soon."

Kaley let out an exasperated sigh and stared at the ceiling, frustration etched into her facial features. Even with dust and cobwebs covering her hair, there was a beauty about her face.

Val gritted her teeth. It was her youth, no doubt. Though an adult woman, Kaley still had lots of life left in her.

Others had stolen those years from Val. If she had to steal them back from others, so be it.

She tapped her boot and swore. "Staring at the ceiling seems like a poor use of your time."

But Kaley didn't seem to hear. Instead, her eyes widened, and she spun in a circle, all the while with her gaze fixed on the ceiling.

The girl was daft. Louis must have given her too strong a dosage. Maybe they should leave now and hope she would be able to focus better tomorrow.

Kaley stopped and blinked as if not believing her eyes.

Val tried to follow her gaze, but it was just fixed on the ceiling and all the stupid decorations.

"The party's on Jack," Kaley murmured.

Val stepped closer. Maybe she hadn't heard her right. "What did you say?"

"The party's on Jack," Kaley repeated, this time louder. Then, without warning, she strode toward the desk and shoved it toward a corner of the room. Val winced as it screeched across the floor. Hopefully no one else heard that.

Then, Kaley climbed on it and reached for the decorations. She yanked at several mini piñatas, which sent half a dozen streamers bombing toward the floor.

Val sidestepped them and edged closer. Could the girl be on to something?

Still grasping the piñatas by their strings, Kaley jumped off the desk and yanked open the drawer as if searching for something.

Next thing Val knew, Kaley had stabbed the first mini decoration with a pencil. Pop! Kaley tore the piñata apart and dug her fingers into it.

Seconds later, she tossed it on the floor and grabbed the next one.

Pop. Toss.

Pop. Pop. Toss. Toss.

Kaley's theatrics were impressive, but time was wasting.

Pop! With a cry, Kaley fumbled with something in her hand.

"What is it?" Val bridged the remaining gap between them.

"The party's on Jack," Kaley said, exposing her palm. Amid the paper confetti lay what looked like a flash drive.

Kaley scanned the floor of destroyed piñatas and the monkey one on the desk. "You said Anthony had a monkey. Maybe his name was Jack? The rest of the piñatas are donkeys and llamas, but this one is a monkey."

"Who cares what the monkey's name was?" The girl wasn't daft after all. "Give it to me."

Kaley stepped back. "If I do, what's to keep you from killing me?"

Val drew her gun. "What's to keep me from killing you now and taking what's mine?"

"You promised." Kaley spat the words. "I guess that doesn't mean much to people like you."

Her words stung. She should shoot the girl and be done with it. But she had promised. And she did have to call Big Eddie back.

The perfect plan began to spin in her mind. She lowered her gun and offered a disarming smile. "You're right. I did promise. And even a hood keeps her word."

A glimmer of hope sprang into Kaley's face. "Then you'll let me go?"

"I can't do that." She smirked. "But I can let you live."

Chapter Twenty-Four

Reef stared out the window as the snowy landscape gave way to dull, barren trees. Flying still seemed a stretch for Matt, considering his near concussion, but Matt insisted he felt fine. He and Liam had made all the calls to reserve the plane, and sooner than they could have driven to the closest major airport, they were taking off on a small, private runway in Banner Elk.

It was probably the same runway the kidnappers had used to steal Kaley away. Liam hadn't specified one way or the other, but Banner Elk was a small town. If only he and Liam weren't so far behind in the chase. She could be anywhere by now. She must feel so alone.

He balled his fists and closed his eyes. Taking slow, deep breaths, he tried to calm his raging pulse.

It wasn't working. *God, you know how I'm feeling right now, and it's not very spiritual. Please, please protect Kaley. Let us find her in time.*

Reef glanced to the adjacent seat where Liam was already busy on his laptop. He might not be an investigator like Liam, but he had spent the ride to the airstrip scrolling through the internet on his phone, reading anything he could find about the mob and the possibility it was still operational.

One article explained that after 9-11, America's focus shifted to fighting terrorism. The mafia didn't stop existing. They just stopped drawing the limelight. From what he'd read, they had also branched out to other lucrative, covert operations like fraud and credit card schemes. That thought didn't bring him any comfort. It suggested these people had perfected riding under the radar—and had the resources to make innocents like Kaley disappear without a trace.

A hand slapped his shoulder. "I've got some news." Liam buckled himself into the seat next to him. He'd been so busy pecking at his laptop on the row across from him that Reef hadn't wanted to bother him.

"Talk to me."

"I've been doing some digging on Valentina Russo." Liam thumbed through his phone. It was shocking this little plane had Wi-Fi, let alone that his friend could connect to it. "You'll never guess where her estate is in Tampa."

Reef rolled his eyes. "Then tell me."

"Here." Liam handed him his phone. Reef stared at the image. It was a front-facing picture of a modern three-story home.

He glanced at his friend. "And where is this?"

"Scroll to the next image."

Reef squinted. "Wait, that's a river. Is it the Hillsborough?"

"Bingo."

"I know that area like the back of my hand." Reef returned the phone to his friend. "My colleague Sam and I could easily take a few jet skis down there and have a look."

"Not necessary," Liam said. "There's already an officer in place to monitor Kaley's client's old houseboat, and this estate is up the river from there. He's asked the same crew to also keep an eye on the estate for any suspicious activity."

"Wait, so the houseboat where her client was murdered is on the river not far from this place?"

"Yep, but of course, living in close proximity to someone doesn't guarantee she murdered him, but it sure does give us grounds to stay watchful."

Reef bit back the words forming on his tongue. It seemed more than enough reason to take a closer look. What if Kaley were in that house right now? But then again, he'd never pulled a search warrant and didn't even know what that process involved. Suspicion alone probably wasn't enough.

Another idea struck him. "What about the airport footage you found earlier and the information confirming Valentina rented the cabin where Kaley was held? And didn't that security footage give us enough evidence that Kaley indeed was there? Isn't that enough to search Val's place?"

Liam nibbled his lip. "Maybe. I forwarded all those findings to Reynolds—the Hillsborough detective on the case. As soon as we land, we'll have a meeting and then maybe make that call."

Maybe make that call.

What was there to question? The evidence seemed undeniable that Valentina wasn't traveling for pleasure. But Reef knew better than to push. Liam was doing everything he could—and probably more—to help find Kaley.

His gut twisted. He'd been honest with Liam about his feelings for Kaley, and Liam had indicated his own interest but had never offered more information. Had he and Kaley spoken? Was that why she had been so reserved with him?

He squashed that thought. Liam was his friend and a man of honor who would do his best to find Kaley whether they were personally involved or not.

"What can I do when we get back to Tampa?" Reef asked.

Liam hesitated. "I wanted to introduce you to Reynolds, but then ..."

He didn't need to finish. No one had known they were dating. The thought had already struck Reef that being her most recent ex-boyfriend made him look like a possible suspect.

Liam hurriedly continued. "Not that I would ever think *that*, and besides, you were with Matt when she went missing. But I can't introduce you to Reynolds without it coming to light, and that might not help matters."

He sighed. "Then what *can* I do?"

"I was hoping you could give her family a call. I know it might be hard, but they're probably getting the run-around right now. Some solid hope is what they need most."

No kidding. He could use some solid hope himself.

"I'll do it. What else?"

Liam didn't reply right away, but his jaw muscles seemed to tense. Whatever he was about to say wasn't easy for him.

"Be ready for when we find her."

Reef did a double take. What did he mean? "Wait, I thought you said she was probably still okay?"

"I'm hoping she is, but these people—if this really is the mob—are a tough crowd. She's going to need emotional support—and maybe a lot more."

His words sunk in. To this point, Liam had kept up a positive face. But he was worried.

Reef swallowed the lump forming in his throat. "I'll be there for anything."

"I think Kaley would appreciate that."

He blinked. "Wait, are you saying ...?"

"We're not involved, even if I wish we were." Liam sighed and stared past him out the window. "Kaley was nice to me, and maybe there could be something there with time, but time together is exactly what we didn't get on the trip. But you did. She let you take her out to get pizza, which means you were one of the last people to spend quality time with her. I'm guessing she would want to see you."

His words sent a rush of hope, but Reef quieted the feeling. He also understood Liam's pain, the pain of someone else asking the girl you like out before you ever got the chance. It had happened to him before.

"Thanks for telling me, man," Reef said softly. "I'm here for you—and for Kaley when that time comes."

"Good." The tightness in Liam's voice betrayed his feelings. "Listen, I need to get some more work done, but if you need me, just holler."

With that, Liam slipped out of the seat next to him and returned to his laptop.

Reef gazed out the small window, trying to process everything Liam had told him. If Kaley hadn't let Liam get close to her, then maybe she hadn't given up on Reef. In that case, she needed him more than ever. So yes, he would do everything Liam asked of him and try to stay out of his way. But that didn't mean he couldn't find a way to help Kaley on his own.

Back at her house, Val slipped into the driver's seat of her red Camaro and left Louis in charge of the girl. She had other business to handle.

Big Eddie wasn't a morning person, so he suggested meeting for lunch at Tony's Place. She hoped the reason had less to do with her and more to do with Tony's famous espresso, but the pinch in her gut warned her otherwise.

Although a person couldn't communicate nonverbal cues via text message, Big Eddie almost could. She'd read enough of his short, fragmented texts to know when he was in a good mood and when he wasn't.

Tony's. 12. Sharp.

She wasn't reading between the lines to know he wasn't happy with her. All she could do was hope her good news would soften his anger. She liked to think she was a favorite with Big Eddie, but really, did hoods have favorites? The favorite was the person doing exactly what he was told and returning with the goods.

She wasn't doing either.

The bright red sign of Tony's promised the best coffee and grilled cheese sandwiches in town, but today, it seemed a little lackluster. Maybe it was her mood.

Shifting to park, Val squared her shoulders and pulled out the keys. She wouldn't let him intimidate her. She had her stakes in this affair. She was a big girl now.

Her heels struck the pavement with more force than she intended, but she lifted her chin. *You've got this.*

But as she passed the shop front, she sensed a pair of eyes on her, the gaze so piercing it would have burned her skin if it could have.

A bell chimed as she pressed through the doorway, and she instantly met Big Eddie's glare.

Yes, glare. He sat in a secluded corner but with a clear view of the doorway. Of course, he'd been watching for her.

She pursed her lips into a tight smile and helped herself to the seat across from him. "Hey, Eddie. Thanks …"

"Cut the chit chat." His black eyes seemed like tiny, snake-like dots in his otherwise large, round face. "You've gone too far this time."

She flipped her hair over her shoulder and laughed. She hoped it sounded more casual than she felt. "Oh, Eddie, you've got it all wrong. By the end of our lunch date, you'll be thanking me."

"Thanking you?" It sounded like a growl which he tamed into a cough as the waiter appeared, asking for their orders. Once the young man disappeared, the guttural growling resumed.

"You willfully went around my back. I told you to stay away from the shrink. I told you I would handle her."

Val snorted. "Your version of handling her would have left her in a dumpster with the insurance still exposed. My version has her still useful for our purposes—and any future threats of insurance eliminated."

Big Eddie leaned forward, his thick hands clasped in front of him. "You found it?"

"She found it for me—just like I knew she would." Val trimmed the extra-large smirk she wanted to flaunt into a more modest one. She still had to be careful here.

"And where is it?"

Val didn't hesitate. If she did, he might guess the truth. "Destroyed—no one will ever be able to use that information against us."

Big Eddie pushed back from the table and crossed his arms, as if deciding whether he believed her or not. "And the shrink? I suppose she's already disposed of too?"

She glanced at her ice water. If she weren't careful, she'd slip through the thin ice of their business relationship. "I wanted to talk to you about her. I understand you're not happy with my methods, but I'm loyal to you. I was thinking a peace offering might help. I'll give you the therapist to help pay for any inconvenience I've caused."

He lowered his voice. "You want me to be responsible for disposing of her, is that it? You're not gutsy enough to knock her off yourself?"

Heat rose to her face, but she took a cooling breath. "That's not it at all. I just thought you might profit by her. She's quite the pretty thing, if you know what I mean. Bet you could get a handsome price for her."

A grin snaked its way across Big Eddie's face. "You really are the devil, Val. Most women squirm about that trade, but you won't bat an eye selling a sister to a life of hell."

He paused as if considering his next words. "That's why I like you. But watch yourself. You get too cocky, and I'll take you down. Next time I give orders, I want them followed. I won't be accepting any more peace offerings."

Val sipped her water and nodded as the waiter reappeared with their espresso shots and sandwiches.

She bit into her grilled cheese, cooked to perfection. If a sandwich could be this perfect, so could anything else. Her plans were falling into place, and Big Eddie didn't seem to be holding a grudge, despite his tough talk.

"So I was thinking." She brushed her napkin across her lips. "The Gasparilla boat invasion this weekend would make a perfect cover. There are so many boats and bodies that no one will notice one girl trading hands."

Big Eddie nodded and washed down his sandwich with a sip of water. "Perfect. My men will be in touch."

"Very good." Val chugged her espresso. The meeting was going how she had hoped, but she didn't want to push her luck. The shorter the meeting with Eddie, the better.

"Just swear to me on your mother's grave that you destroyed that insurance."

Val slapped the shot glass onto the table. "I swear." She didn't have good memories of her mother anyway.

"And swear to me you found it all."

A twinge of doubt flickered in her mind. There had been more than one piñata. Had Kaley checked them all?

She forced the thought aside. "I told you I took care of it."

"Good. Fool me once, shame on you. Fool me twice, shame on me."

Someone moved outside the window, and Val didn't need to look to know it was one of Big Eddie's bodyguards.

"I've got the check." She waved her hand. "I'll wait to hear from you about the weekend."

Big Eddie slid his chair back and wiped his chin. "Until then."

Chapter Twenty-Five

Kaley stared at the ceiling from the much-too-soft queen mattress in her room. She'd been staring at it ever since she'd woken up before the dawn.

At least now, warm daylight filtered through the window. A new day had started. But what would it hold? How long would her captors forget about her in this prison of a room?

Yesterday after they had returned to Val's estate from searching the houseboat, Louis had marched her upstairs, and Val—well, she had rushed to the garage the moment they arrived. Kaley had caught a glimpse of her red convertible speeding away from the driveway minutes later. Where had she been off to in such a hurry?

It probably had something to do with that flash drive. Handing it over had felt like giving up her one lifeline.

What was to keep them from killing her now if that was all they had wanted?

And what had Val meant by *I can't let you go, but I can let you live*?

Kaley rolled to her side and off the bed. If all she could do was think, she would go crazy. There had to be a way out... or something she could do to distract herself from a growling stomach. Someone had stuffed a peanut butter and jelly sandwich under the door sometime last evening, but it had hardly been filling.

She strode over to the window again. Just out of reach beyond the barred window was the Hillsborough River. She could see its lazy flow as if it didn't have a care in the world.

An occasional boat passed by, but no one noticed the girl staring out the window. Why would they?

An idea sparked. Kaley spun and hurried to the bathroom. Dropping to her knees, she pulled the bathroom cabinet doors open.

Empty.

She tried the medicine cabinet next.

Also empty.

Don't give up yet.

She crawled to the closet and pulled out the large plastic bags, the ones she had rummaged in earlier to find clothes.

Just maybe she'd get lucky.

She dug her hands into jean pocket after jean pocket. As the bag grew lighter, her spirits sagged.

But then, with a particularly ugly black pair of jeans, she felt a small tube in the front pocket. She yanked it out and almost cried at her good fortune. It was a lipstick container all right, and even better, it was bright red.

She didn't even bother to stuff the clothes back in the bag. Jumping to her feet, she rushed back to the window.

Deep breaths. Stop shaking.

This might be her one chance to let her voice be heard.

She exhaled and drew an H the full size of the pane, followed by an E, L, and P. The P ended up being a little more squished than she would have liked, but she hadn't estimated all the letters evenly because she was writing backwards.

It didn't matter. It shouldn't take a college professor to realize someone needed help.

She studied her artwork for a moment more. *Oh, God, let someone see it.*

Then, she pulled the blinds tightly. Although she missed the sunshine, she couldn't risk Louis seeing the letters the next time he came to retrieve her.

Just the thought of him made her throat go dry. He handled her so roughly, and yesterday, his eyes had raked over the too-tight-for-her-liking Beatles shirt. Now that she wasn't on the verge of passing out, maybe she should dig out something less form-fitting.

It's not like she had anything else to do.

She pocketed the lipstick in case she had another chance to use it and resumed searching the clothes she had strewn across the floor.

They were all name brands, but some of the styles were dated. How old had Val been when she'd worn these? Had she still had a heart then?

"How does someone get to be that cold and cruel?" she whispered. Val wouldn't bat an eye at killing her, but for some reason had decided to keep her. That thought made Kaley's stomach queasy. Whatever it was couldn't be good.

She had to find a way to defend herself or to escape. Maybe there was a pocket knife in here somewhere and she'd missed it on her first go around.

A few nickels and a condom later, she exhausted the search. She tossed the latter aside and slipped the nickels in her pocket. Even though it wasn't even enough to buy a stick of gum, it was a start.

Val apparently didn't own any loose-fitting shirts, but Kaley did find a lightweight flannel she could use to layer. It was better than nothing. She shoved the rest of the clothes back in the bag and then moved on to inspect the rest of the room.

It didn't take long. There was nothing under the bed, and the only other piece of furniture was a small bureau.

She opened the top drawer, and her heart stuttered as she slammed it shut.

That uneasy feeling returned full force. She slowly pulled open the next, but at the sight of more magazine covers, she shoved it closed as well. If only she could unsee those images. Why would any sane woman agree to pose like that? Or had she been given a choice?

Dear God, who are these people?

There were still two drawers left to go, but she didn't want to see any more pictures. Instead, she closed her eyes, opened the drawer and cautiously felt the contents.

The third drawer contained papery-thin fabric items. Lingerie. And a binder buried beneath it.

She pulled it out and peeked at it. The outside was plain and black. Cautiously opening it, she held her breath.

On page one was a young woman's picture. It seemed to have been taken from a distance while she waited for a cab. Below it was a date marked 1999 with "pickup" and "delivery" addresses. That was over two decades ago.

The next page, and the next, and the next several dozen repeated the pattern. No names, just a picture and two addresses.

Who were these women? Something told her that although the binder ended with a date in the 2000's, this "delivery" business hadn't ended. More than likely, the records had simply gone digital.

Biting her lip, she stuffed the binder back into the third drawer and at last pulled open the fourth. It was empty like all her hopes of escaping.

But she had to get out of here. If what she'd found was any indicator, Val's alternative to death would be far worse.

Kaley edged away from the bureau, wishing she could burn it. Could she break off the bureau legs and start a fire with friction? She'd seen survival shows where people made fire from mere sticks.

But with no way to escape, she'd be committing suicide. Still, perhaps she could expose Val for who she was and save the next poor girl.

Or maybe she could use the legs as projectiles and throw them at Louis's head the next time he came for her. That wasn't a bad idea either. She needed ammunition at this point.

Breaking off those legs, thin pegs though they were, would take a considerable amount of effort. She should twist off the drawer knobs and add those to her arsenal in case Louis heard her breaking off the legs.

But first, she stepped toward the window and opened the blinds. She could make those letters even bolder. Pulling out her lipstick, she carefully colored thicker letters.

She didn't choose this nightmare for herself, but she did get to choose how to cope with it. And she wasn't going down without a fight.

Reef slid his cell phone onto his desk, raked a hand over his face, and leaned back in his office chair. A cool breeze fanned Tarpon Springs' salty air through his screened window. On any other day, he'd jump at the chance to be on the water with such perfect conditions.

But today was a long shot from perfect.

And his being gone a few days had clearly been a strain on Sam Winfrey, his right-hand man. The office looked like a warzone. He wondered when they'd have time to file all the guest waivers properly—or if Sam had even been making sure guests filled them out correctly.

Oh well. That was another problem for another day.

Yesterday as soon as they landed, he had called Kaley's parents like he'd promised Liam. But when her dad had picked up the phone, he had asked for permission to swing by. It didn't seem right to tell a man who was desperate for good news about his daughter that the news was only getting worse—and do it impersonally over the phone.

Still, he hadn't been prepared for the meeting. Kaley was the therapist—not him.

Even a therapist couldn't make that conversation go better. *Hello, this is Reef, your daughter's ex-boyfriend. I'm sorry I couldn't protect her from an underground mob but am helping the investigation any way I can.*

Yeah, nowhere in a million years would that have gone well.

Not that they were angry with him. They were just angry and had every right to be that someone had dared steal their daughter away.

If he had to listen to them vent and cry, well, that was the least he could do.

According to Liam, it was the only thing he could do.

He couldn't settle for that. And now that Macy had dropped off his Subaru last evening, he could get busy with his own plan.

The office door chimed open, and Sam's eyes widened the size of scallops they'd caught last summer.

"Dude, what are you doing here? I thought you wouldn't be back until tomorrow." His lanky friend and colleague strode through the door and slung four life vests onto a chair in the waiting room. He must have just finished helping a kayak group.

"It's a long story, and it's not a good one." Reef leaned forward and clasped his hands on the desk. Would Sam be willing to help with his crazy plan?

Sam's tanned brow creased. "Sorry to hear that. Anything I can do?"

"Maybe. How many guests do you have scheduled today?"

"It's a slow morning, so I told Jake not to come till this evening when we have more bookings. I've got one more set of kayakers coming back soon, and then I was thinking of closing for a few hours before Jake gets here."

Reef stood and circled around the desk. "Perfect. I'll help you finish up with our guests this morning and then we can talk. How does brunch at Hellas sound? I can't remember the last time I ate."

Sam grabbed a water from the fridge and nodded. "Sounds great. If you want to put those vests in the storage room and close up here, I'll meet you there in fifteen."

"I'm going to load up some skis on the double trailer first— if you're game for some unofficial surveillance on the Hillsborough River."

His friend's eyebrows shot up, but the grin spreading across his lips gave him away. "You know I can't say no to river time. I look forward to learning what this is all about."

Reef offered a half smile. "Be careful what you wish for."

After loading the jet skis, Reef still arrived at Hellas before Sam. A waiter greeted him at the hostess station. "How many."

"Two," Reef said. "And could we sit by the window if you have a free table?"

"Of course." The man ushered him past a group of interior tables to a window seat in the next room.

Reef's stomach squeezed. This was almost the same spot where he and Kaley had eaten a late dinner after their island date on Anclote Key.

"Something to drink?" The waiter's voice interrupted the memory.

"Water's fine, thanks." Reef smiled and then let his gaze wander to the waterway across the street.

It had been such a perfect date. Kaley had looked so cute in her raggedy beach shorts and tank top. She'd also looked a little shy and unsure. She'd never been out on a jet ski before, and all she knew was that they were having a picnic lunch on Anclote Key.

He couldn't have asked for better conditions. It had been a warm October day with nothing but a gentle breeze. The sea was almost flat, paving the way for a smooth ride toward the island.

She had admitted to never driving a jet ski before, and he had been quick to remedy that problem—even though it landed him in the ocean. He had talked her through the basic functions of the ski when without warning, she gripped the handles/gas and accelerated, throwing him off.

The look of horror on her face was priceless, but he was laughing too hard for her to take herself seriously. Before accelerating again, she had asked if he were ready, and he had properly secured himself.

They'd even seen a pod of dolphins. Her eyes had lit up like a little kid's at Christmas. One had swum right next to them on its side, staring up at them as if curious about them too. He'd been able to snap a picture before the dolphin disappeared with the rest of its friends.

On the island, they'd swung on the hammock he brought, talking and enjoying the scenery in silence. That was something he appreciated about Kaley. She didn't have to fill every second with conversation. She could simply enjoy stillness and beauty.

Everything had gone so right on that date. How had it all fallen apart only weeks later?

"Oh, I know that look."

Reef jumped and swung his attention back around as Sam slipped into the seat across from him.

"Hey, man." Reef pulled himself up in his chair. "Thanks for coming."

Sam folded his arms and leaned forward. "It's a girl, isn't it?"

"What?"

"The reason you want my help with river 'surveillance.'"

Color crept up his neck. Or was it just hot in here?

"Yeah, it's a girl."

"Please tell me it's not that loser who sent you into a tailspin a few months back."

Reef sighed and rolled his eyes. "She's not a loser, and I wasn't in a tailspin."

Sam held up his hands. "My bad. If you prefer to call it a depression or coma, that'll work fine as well."

"Sam."

"I've never seen you like that, man, and it wasn't cool."

"Sam."

"What?" Sam frowned at him, and then after a long minute, groaned. "Of course, it's that one."

"Her name is Kaley, and she's been kidnapped by the Tampa mafia."

Sam's eyes widened. "Get out. The only place left for the mafia is the movies."

"That's what I thought too, but Kaley's client said they were after him—and he ended up dead. And now, they've got Kaley."

Sam let out a low whistle. "I didn't like her after the way she treated you, but that's tough stuff."

"Yeah, it's a rotten situation." Reef glanced back out the window. How could the day look so perfect, as if the world hadn't gone mad?

"So how does this involve you, me, and our jet skis?"

Reef turned back to Sam. There was no judgment in his friend's voice, and he respected that. Even if Sam had a bone to pick with Kaley, he was a loyal friend.

"We suspect she's being held in a house on the Hillsborough River."

Sam's sun-bleached eyebrows crinkled. "Then why haven't the police called in a warrant?"

"That's the thing. They have probable cause to suspect the owner and the property, but they're hesitating. I want to take a stroll down the river and see if there's anything to see from the water." Reef ran a hand through his hair. "I know it's a long shot, but I can't just sit around and wait for someone to find her body. I totally get it if you change your mind and don't want to come, but I …"

"I'm coming," Sam said. "You want to launch in the regular place?"

Reef's chest swelled. He could always count on Sam.

The waiter returned for their orders, and Reef asked for the check as soon as the food came out. Time was wasting.

He didn't know what they'd do if they found something, but somehow, being on the water felt like the right next step. His dad liked to say the water and sky could clear a man's mind, and Reef had found it to be true. If only it had cured his mother's addiction.

"I say, Reef, what's the plan when we get there?" Sam's question pulled him back to the present.

"We'll make it up as we go," Reef said. "My hope is we'll find some reason to call in for help."

"That's a relief."

"What's a relief?"

Sam grinned. "I was starting to worry I was your backup."

Reef laughed, and it felt good to break the tension in his chest. "You're the Robin to my Batman, Sam. But yes, I hope to call my investigator friend with the break he needs to issue a warrant."

"Be careful what you wish for," Sam said slowly. "Consider what we might find."

Reef swallowed hard. "I'm praying God shows us the way and that Kaley is still safe. I can't even imagine—"

"If she's there, we'll find her."

He met his friend's gaze. "It means a lot that you're with me on this."

Sam nodded. "I may not like her, but she deserves a chance. If she's there to be found, we'll find her."

Chapter Twenty-Six

Reef tied off the second ski to the dock while Sam pulled the trailer away from the loading ramp and parked. Lowry Park seemed quiet for a Friday, but perhaps people were saving their gas money for tomorrow's Gasparilla boat parade. Either way, it worked fine for him. The less crowded the river, the more room they had to explore.

Waiting for Sam to join him gave him a little too much time to think. He needed action. Sitting still reminded him of his last trip with Kaley down this river. Thinking about her, locked away somewhere nearby but barely out of reach, was enough to make him lose his cool.

Sam jogged over, and his spirits lifted. They'd be on their way soon. At least he'd be doing something—despite Liam's warning to stay out of the investigation.

It was a free river. If he happened to be on it, that was his business.

"Where to?" Sam slipped onto the other ski and stuck two short poles into the storage compartment, along with a small cooler.

"I thought we would try to find Russo's house first," Reef said. "It should be a short way down river from here. After that, I want to cruise around and see what there is to see. I think the dead man's houseboat was somewhere on the river, too, but I'm guessing that's been removed."

Reef paused. "What are the poles for?"

"They're fishing poles." Sam snapped the compartment shut and untied the rope holding his ski to the dock. "I figured if you wanted to do surveillance on a house, it would look a little less suspicious if you were actually doing something other than staring."

"Good thinking," Reef said, "although most people don't fish off jet skis."

"What can I say?" Sam whipped on a camo baseball cap. "We're just two rednecks killing time on a Friday."

Reef laughed. "There's a reason I keep you around."

Sam grinned and started the ski. "Someone's got to think of the details. You're brilliant but more of a big picture guy."

He started idling down river as well. "You're not wrong."

Sam's words rubbed a memory. Kaley had seemed uneasy with his lack of goal-planning. He had goals, of course, but they weren't mapped out on paper.

Was that what she wanted—a details guy? He shook off the thought. Right now, she probably wanted her freedom and wouldn't care if an entrepreneur like him or the most goal-centered accountant helped her get out of there.

Ugh, he shuddered at the thought of being an accountant. It had to be one of the most boring jobs on the planet. She said one of her ex-boyfriends had been one, but what's-his-face wasn't here now. Technically, Reef wasn't supposed to be here either, but he wasn't a quitter.

He pulled out his phone and glanced at his map app. He had pre-entered the address for Val's house. It should be coming up on the right.

"Anything in particular I'm supposed to be looking for?" Sam called from beside him.

"If Google maps is up-to-date, the house should be beige with a terra-cotta-colored tile roof. Other than that, I dunno—anything that looks out of the ordinary. I mean, someone waving a white flag or an S.O.S. sign would be perfect, but I doubt it's going to be that obvious."

"So red lettering that spells *help* would be a good place to start?" Sam's jet ski jerked closer to shore.

"Uh—yeah?" Reef tried to figure out what had caught Sam's attention or if perhaps something was wrong with his ski.

Then he saw it. There was a window, and in the window, red bold letters spelled the word *help*.

"Kaley." His mouth went dry as his gaze moved from the window to the rest of the house, which was beige with a clay-colored roof.

This was the place, Russo's house. And if Kaley was in there, he was breaking her out—warrant or no warrant. He idled closer to shore. A small motor boat was lazily secured to a dock, but there was also a concrete boat ramp with a canopied space in the yard to store a larger yacht. Only, the space was empty. Maybe Russo dry-docked a yacht somewhere else.

How long would it take for someone to notice a pair of jet skis near the dock?

"Man, what are you doing?" Sam hissed at him. "What happened to look casual?"

Reef pulled away from the dock and closer to his friend. "You saw that lettering. If that isn't the writing on the wall, I don't know what is. And that's definitely Russo's house."

"Okay, but we need to think here. We won't be helping Kaley if we draw attention to ourselves."

Reef snapped a picture and then let his ski coast past the estate. Then, he circled up next to Sam. "Yes, we think, but we act too. I'm texting this picture to Liam."

"Who's Liam?"

"My cop friend who is working with the case detective. Maybe this will be the evidence he needs to get boots on the ground."

"I hope so." Sam pressed his lips into a thin line. "There's definitely something off about that place."

Reef pressed send on the text and tried to steady his pulse. "Right? What's the worst I could get for trespassing? Because it almost feels worth the risk."

Sam hesitated. "Whoa, you've got a business reputation to consider. Give Liam a chance to reply first."

A sharp reply formed on his lips, but Reef swallowed it. There was no point arguing with Sam. Logically, yes, he should be careful. But his heart didn't want to talk reason right now.

His phone pinged, and he glanced at the screen. It was Liam. *Where are you?*

Reef pecked a reply while watching the river. *On the river.*

Seconds later, another ping. *I told you to stay away.*

He forced a long exhale before replying. *It's a free country. Are you sending someone out? This is clearly not a hoax. Kaley is there.*

"Dude, watch where you're going." Sam's voice cut into his thoughts. "You almost rammed me."

"Sorry," Reef muttered. "Wish there were somewhere we could park. It's hard to text and drive."

"Rick's on the River is about a mile from here."

"I don't want to go that far."

His phone pinged again. *We don't know Kaley is there, but yes, I'm sending this to Reynolds.*

Enough side stepping. Reef dialed Liam's number and pressed the phone to his ear.

"Reef." There was no hiding the sigh in Liam's voice.

"Yo, man, what are we doing here? That's the clearest sign for help we could have asked for. Are you seriously going to let someone else's red tape keep you from busting Kaley out of there?"

"Reef." Now, Liam's tone held an edge. "I have to follow due process. I'm working this up the proper channels. It takes time."

"What if Kaley doesn't have time?" Reef bit his lip. He didn't want to sound like the whining boyfriend.

"I'm working as fast as I can. Listen, I need you to get out of there before someone reports you for violating due process."

"The river is open to the public, Liam. And I have all the proper registration and tags for my ski."

"Whatever, just stay out of sight. I'll call you when I have anything." Liam hung up without giving him a chance to respond.

Sam whistled. "Sounds like that went well."

Reef slammed his hand onto the wheel. "Yeah, so well. If red tape gets Kaley killed …" No, he couldn't think like that.

"Breathe, man. She had to be alive to write on the window. Focus on that for now."

"You're right. And she's a fighter. Now, she needs someone fighting on her side."

"She's got us," Sam said. "So until your red-tape man gets back to you, how about we go fish?"

Reef's spirits lifted. Even if he couldn't legally break her out, he could at least keep watch until Liam's help arrived—assuming they would come. They had to come.

"Yeah, let's go fish," he agreed.

Reach under the pillow. Grab a bureau knob. Throw.

Kaley lay on the bed, practicing her steps. She'd planted her weapons throughout the room—on the bed, under the bed, on the covered windowsill. Basically, any place she imagined herself being pushed into a corner, she'd hidden weapons.

She sighed. She could barely call them weapons. Bureau knobs would only go so far stalling an attacker—or serve to make him angrier.

But the shepherd boy David had killed a giant with a river rock and a sling shot. Maybe she could do the same with a dresser handle.

She had just replaced it under the pillow when her door burst open. Kaley jumped upright, both relieved her weapons were hidden and worried she wasn't holding one.

It was Louis. She stood to her feet and edged toward the window sill, in case she needed her version of a river rock.

He stood in the doorway and crossed his arms. "Move. Val wants you."

Relief spread through her. At least he didn't have any intentions of tying her to a bed post at the moment.

She slipped past him and hurried down the now-familiar steps. What did Val want with her now? Hadn't she found the drive?

Val perched on the corner of a couch, texting. Behind her were the double set of sliding doors leading to the patio and pool. The sheer beauty of the spot filled her with regret. Under any other conditions, being in this place would feel like a luxury vacation.

Val glanced at Kaley and then snatched a piece of fabric off the couch next to her, tossing it at Kaley.

Without hesitating, she grabbed it and looked at Val for an explanation. "What's this?"

"It's a scarf, stupid," Val snapped. "Wrap it around your head. I don't want to draw attention to ourselves." She picked up another scarf and began wrapping it around her hair and face.

Kaley fumbled with hers. She'd worn scarves before but never like some kind of Arabic head covering.

"You look ridiculous, but it will have to do." Val yanked a sliding door open. "We've got to act while my guard is on duty this morning."

"On duty where?" Kaley asked.

Val's only response was to glare at her as if Kaley were supposed to read her mind.

Louis gripped her arm from behind and shoved her after Val. Kaley yanked free and quickened her pace. Apparently, there would be no breakfast this morning.

They were heading back to the motor boat.

Oh no. What if they saw her letters in the window?

Val climbed into the motor boat first, and Kaley tumbled in behind her, landing on the floor. Her captor swung her head toward the commotion.

"Clumsy!" She snorted and without reaching to help Kaley up, moved to the captain's seat.

Kaley's heart pounded hard. That trick had worked, and it was worth the bruises if she could keep Val from glancing at the house.

Louis was another story. Though he seemed engrossed with undoing the moorings, he was always looking around, checking their perimeter. It would only be a matter of time …

His head swung back toward the lawn.

"Louis!" she gasped.

He jerked her way and scowled. "What?"

Kaley searched for an excuse. Her gaze landed on two fishermen. "Is—is the Hillsborough good for fishing?"

He cocked an eyebrow. "Fishing? Since when do you care about fishing?"

"I—I was only wondering." She squinted at the jet skis, and her pulse quickened. Wait, she knew that jet ski. But it couldn't be…

The next second, Louis was next to her and shoved her into a seat facing away from the fishermen. "Sit down and shut up."

Her new direction planted her firmly in line with Val's glare. "Stop gawking at people. No one can read your mind, and if you draw unnecessary attention to us, I will personally drown you."

Kaley hugged herself and glanced at the river. The two fishermen on jet skis were behind her.

Maybe this was her chance. She could jump overboard and swim toward them. But they were several hundred feet away. She'd never reach them before Val caught up with her.

And what if it wasn't Reef but someone who had his model of jet ski? What if the fishermen were so absorbed in their sport that they didn't even notice her escape attempt? Val would drown her for sure.

But her time was running out regardless, and there were worse fates than drowning.

The motorboat jerked away from the dock, and Kaley's hopes faded. She had hesitated too long. Chancing a look behind her, the jet skis seemed even farther away now. She didn't have a prayer.

The quiet river offered some solace, and at this time, Val didn't try talking to her. For a few moments, she could enjoy simply being on the water and being alive.

She didn't feel thankful for much right now, but she could be thankful for that. *Thank you, Jesus, for this moment.* Her next one wasn't promised.

The river ride ended too quickly, and Val maneuvered the boat right next to Anthony's old houseboat. Her heart sank. Why were they coming back here? She'd already found the drive.

But asking questions would only annoy Val. Kaley watched and waited to be bossed around.

Val slipped on a pair of gloves as Louis secured the motorboat. There was no pair for Kaley. Apparently, they didn't care about her fingerprints.

The thought made her squirm again. Were they going to try to frame her? But there was no way she could have murdered Anthony. She'd been on her way to North Carolina when—She shivered thinking about the poor man's fate.

Was she next in line?

Val's phone chirped, and the smile spreading across her face suggested she was happy about something.

"Perfect, our guy is on duty for another hour," she told Louis. "That should be plenty of time."

He nodded. "You want me to stay here again?"

"Yes, and phone me if you see anything suspicious." Val climbed onto the houseboat and paused at the top. "Uh, princess? This isn't a pleasure cruise. Get your bum up here. Oh, and grab the bags from under your seat."

Kaley leaned forward to peer under her seat. Yuck! Cobwebs and dirt covered two fabric grocery bags. She pressed a shoe onto them and pulled them out, reluctantly picked them up, and hurried to the railing.

After flinging the bags onto the splintering deck of Anthony's old houseboat, Kaley shimmied up the side and searched for Val who had already disappeared inside. The woman waited for no one.

Louis grunted from the motorboat and muttered something she wished she hadn't heard. Face flaming, she scurried after Val inside the boat.

Back in Anthony's quarters, the woman spun in the center of the room, surveying the remaining decorations.

What did she want with those? Kaley had already found her the flash drive.

A fear pricked her chest. What if it wasn't the right one? What if …

"Take all the piñatas and garlands down so we can check them." Val waved her hand with a flourish. "Make it fast but be careful. We need them in one piece."

So that's what the bags were for. But why? She knew better than to ask. "Won't someone notice they're missing?"

Val whirled to glare at her. "The police are done here. They removed the crime scene tape. I'm sure vandals are the least of their worries."

"Then why do they still have a guard posted?" As soon as the words left her mouth, Kaley regretted them.

The woman's nostrils flared. "Shut up and do as I say."

Kaley found a lopsided chair and balanced herself on it while reaching for the garland Anthony had tacked up. The tacks pulled out easily enough. What had her client been thinking as he pinned up all these decorations? Had he been savoring Jack's revenge? But how did hiding a flash drive in a monkey piñata accomplish his revenge?

She grasped a llama piñata and paused. Surely all these extra decorations were total overkill unless—

Her gaze snapped toward the lights strung in and out with the garland. There were an excessive number of lights too. At night with those on, anyone could see through the windows.

No one would care about the garlands and streamers and piñatas. Anthony had just used those to help conceal the flash drive. But with the lights, he must have been wanting to send a message.

The question was—how?

Kaley left the lights in place as she stuffed the llama into the bag and moved her chair to the next garland. Her mind raced back to her own desperate attempts to draw attention to her window. What if Anthony had concealed a message in the glass?

Her thoughts tripped over themselves as the dots connected. Anthony had an invisible ink marker in his desk, which she had overlooked in her initial search for Val. He must have used it somewhere.

"Hurry up, we haven't got all day!" Val snapped from across the room where she'd smashed another mini piñata which appeared to be empty.

"Sorry." Kaley mumbled. "The garland is all woven in and out of the lights."

The lights. They looked like ordinary LED lights, but up closer, they were different. They had a purplish hue—and if she were a betting person, they were probably UV light, which would reveal any invisible ink markings on the windows.

Her heart raced. There was more "insurance" hidden in plain sight, but what was she to do with that information?

And more pressing, why was Val having her take down the decorations?

It still didn't make sense. And it *really* didn't make sense why Val had her here helping when anyone who wasn't a hostage could easily remove tacks from a wall.

There were too many questions. Right now, she needed to focus on surviving long enough to find answers.

Kaley cleared her throat. "All done." She stepped down from the chair and scooted it against the wall. "What next?"

In response, Val struck a match on the desk and held it out to Kaley. "You're going to burn this boat."

Chapter Twenty-Seven

"Wha-at?" Kaley stared at the match in Val's hand. If Anthony's houseboat burned, no one would ever know what final clues he'd written on the windows. Val would win, and any remaining secrets would go up in smoke.

"You heard me. Torch the place."

"But that's arson."

Val rolled her eyes and whipped out a handgun. "Shooting you is murder, and it doesn't bother me at all."

Hands trembling, Kaley stepped forward and took the match. Thank goodness it had a long stem, but it was burning fast. Setting fire to someone's property was wrong. But what choice did she have?

God, forgive me. She sucked a deep breath and then tossed it on Anthony's mattress. Within moments, flames were licking at the sheets.

"Let's get going, princess. We don't want to be anywhere near here when someone calls the fire department." Val turned and slipped out the doorway.

Kaley snatched the bags and rushed toward the closest outlet. Grabbing a light string, she slammed the male end of the plug into it and jerked her chin up.

Though the afternoon sun was brighter than ideal, she scanned the scrawled message that made her heart hammer even harder.

"Any day, princess!" Val's tone was sharp.

Kaley yanked out the plug and stumbled through the doorway where smoke was already starting to seep out.

Arms crossed, Val glared at her from the motorboat. "Get in. What in blazes took you so long?"

"My bag caught." Kaley coughed and covered her face—partly to cover the cough and partly so she wouldn't lie to the woman's face.

Louis harrumphed next to her and snatched the bags from her hands. "Thought I saw lights in there."

"There is a fire," Kaley mumbled and lowered herself into the boat. When she landed, the backside of Louis's hand crashed against her face.

"Mouthy," he spat.

She fell against the side of the boat and covered her face with her arms to protect herself from another blow.

Val swore and glanced nervously over her shoulder. "We don't have time for fighting. Get us out of here."

Louis grumbled but strode toward the captain's chair. Yanking the wheel, he spun the boat around. "Where to?"

"Down river." Val fell into the chair across from him. "I need a drink. Let's go to Rick's and kill some time. It's going to get stuffy on the river real soon with fire officials and all their jazz."

"What about her?" Louis's jaw tightened.

Kaley pushed herself as far into the side of the boat as she could, wishing there were a hole that would swallow her up. The left side of her face ached and already felt puffy.

Val sighed. "Thanks to you, she's going to have a shiner. Good going, genius."

Louis snorted but didn't respond. "I say we chuck her in the bay and then get a drink. She's outlived her usefulness."

"I make the calls with princess." Val snapped at him. "You're too short-sighted. And if you bruise her again, you're going to have to answer to Big Eddie. For your sake, you'd better hope we can cover that up with makeup."

Louis stiffened, but something about his movements looked jittery. Was he nervous? Who was this Big Eddie he should be afraid of, and what did any of it have to do with her?

Val's face brightened, and she plunged a hand into one of the bags of decorations. "Hold that thought. Today might be your lucky day."

Kaley squinted with her one good eye and tried to follow her movements. Unless it was some extra-strength pain killers, she wasn't interested.

"Ah-ha!" Val held up a small, black piece of fabric. "I grabbed Anthony's pirate garb while princess was Grinching his decorations." She tossed it to Kaley. "Put that on."

The eye-patch fell short of where she huddled, but Kaley crawled forward to retrieve it. She shrank from the idea of wearing a dead man's costume. She was much too close to meeting his same fate than she'd like.

But doing what she was told seemed like the better way to avoid more abuse from Louis. She gently tugged the fabric cover over her eye and secured the strap around her mangled braid.

"Perfect!" Val clapped her hands as if this were a costume party. "We have our own pirate princess now."

This woman's mood swings were off the charts.

Val started chatting with Louis about something else and turned her back on Kaley.

In a way, being ignored was a relief. Kaley hugged her knees to her chest and placed her chin between them. She only wished she had another eye patch, so that if the tears she'd been damming up broke loose, Val wouldn't see.

A patch might cover her black eye, but it couldn't cover the growing ache in her chest. She was desperately afraid and lonely. All her cries for help seemed to go unheard.

Just like Anthony's final cries for justice would soon be lost at the bottom of the Hillsborough. Once again, he had shared his final secrets with only her.

"I'm sure that was Kaley." Reef idled in the water, his irritation rising with each wasted minute.

"She was wearing a scarf—you couldn't even see her face." Sam frowned. "Would you please stop circling me? I'm getting dizzy."

"Sam, it was her body language. She looked—broken almost." Reef swallowed hard and fell into pace next to his friend. If anyone had hurt her—

"I agree that something seemed off, but we can't assume it was Kaley."

Reef waved in exasperation toward the estate. "And what about the giant red help scrawled in the window?"

"All right, we'll follow them, but I think we should phone your cop friend first. He should at least know where we are and what we're doing in case we get ourselves in over our heads."

Reef sighed and fished out his watertight case from the compartment in the jet ski. Calling Liam would take even more time—and his friend was already annoyed they were snooping around in the first place.

But his emotions were playing him hard right now, and he needed Sam's level headedness. So he dialed Liam's familiar number.

To his relief, the call went to voicemail.

"Hey man, it's me again. Listen, we're still on the Hillsborough River—fishing—and a motorboat just left Russo's dock. There were two women, but they were both disguised with head scarves, so we couldn't see their faces. They were with one guy.

"My gut tells me one of the women was Kaley, but I promise, we're not taking chances here. I want you to know we're heading down river after them. They have a good five-minute start, which feels almost too long, but Sam said to keep a safe distance. I'll call you if we see anything strange."

He hung up and stuffed his cell phone back into the watertight box, then glanced at Sam. "Ready?"

"Lead the way."

Idling downriver at least felt like progress. There was no sign of the motorboat, but at this point, it could be halfway to Tampa Bay.

They rode in silence for a few minutes. With each passing moment, his senses seemed to heighten as if a red alert were just around the corner.

What was it? Something …

He cocked his head at Sam. "Do you smell that?"

"Yeah—smoke," Sam said. "Maybe someone has a bonfire."

"Look!" Reef pointed to smoke snaking toward the sky. "That's pretty close to the river."

Sam didn't respond but started moving faster. They'd be pushing idling speed at this rate, but Reef didn't care.

Something was wrong. That wasn't a bonfire.

They rounded the next corner, and his chest tightened. There was a line of dilapidated houseboats, one of which might belong to Kaley's deceased client.

"*Drunken Monkey*," Sam read the name of the houseboat on fire.

"That could be the dead man's boat. We need to call Liam stat." Reef snatched the watertight box again and popped the lid. "Here, he's on speed dial. Call him."

Sam straddled close enough to grab the phone. "What are you doing?"

"What if Kaley's in there?"

"Man, the boat is on fire! You can't go in there."

"Here, I'm going to tie up to you. Keep the skis far away from the debris." Reef looped rope around his steering wheel and tossed it to Sam.

"Dude, you're crazy."

"I have to know if she's in there." He snatched his extra sun-protection buff from the compartment to cover his face. "Call Liam, and if he doesn't answer, call 9-1-1."

Sam pressed the phone to his ear as Reef slid into the murky river. Gators were his last concern right now. He swam to the edge of the boat where he'd spotted a rope dangling. He hoisted himself up, and thankfully, that part of the boat wasn't consumed in flames.

The main fire seemed to be inside the boat, but based on the condition of this houseboat, the whole thing would be engulfed in no time.

"Kaley!" He shouted her name, then sucked in a deep breath before plunging forward. Smoke engulfed the doorway. Would he even be able to see inside?

Eyes burning, he pushed through what was left of the doorway. Ash fell onto his sleeve, singeing skin through his rash guard. The fabric was designed to protect his upper body from the sun, not scorching embers. He winced and took another step. "Kaley!" He shouted through the buff covering his mouth.

If she had been here, she wasn't here now. Flames licked the floorboards just feet away, and he retreated out the same way he'd come.

Below him, the boat seemed to groan in on itself. The flames must be eating out the hull. He didn't have much time.

He took off running toward the edge of the boat as a splintering sound crackled beneath his feet. His left foot came up empty, but his right foot pressed against solid wood. With a cry, he pressed all his weight onto his right foot and propelled himself over the edge—hoping it would be enough to escape the flaming chasm opening beneath him.

Reef sat on the bumper of a first response vehicle, wincing as a paramedic checked him over. Smoke continued to plume above the houseboat that now lay half submerged in the Hillsborough. Fire trucks hadn't been able to save it—but they did keep it from catching neighboring vessels on fire.

Sam still waited on the other side of the river with the jet skis. He owed his friend big time for putting up with him today.

But for all they'd been through, he still wasn't any closer to holding Kaley in his arms. He had been so close—he was sure of it. Yet all he had to show for his efforts were singed skin and a bigger ache in his heart.

"You are lucky to be alive." Liam's voice came from behind him.

Reef swung his head around but winced again as burnt skin rubbed against his rash guard.

"You should take that off, and let me have a look," the EMT said. "You've probably got a few third-degree burns."

Reef sighed. "I'll be fine."

Liam shook his head. "Do what he says. Better him looking at those burns now than you ending up with an infection in a few days."

With another sigh, Reef slowly peeled off his rash guard. There were definitely some tender spots that made him grit his teeth.

"All things considered, you don't look too bad off," the EMT said. "There are a few spots, though, that I'd like to treat."

"Do what you gotta do." Reef sucked a pained breath between his teeth and focused on Liam. "Talk to me. Any news?"

"Yes and no." Liam propped up a knee on the bumper next to Reef. "We sent a scout right to Russo's house to check out that help message you texted me. Turns out, it's gone."

"But you have my text. I didn't make it up."

"I know you didn't." Liam ran a hand through his hair. "It makes me think you were right, and someone is meticulously covering tracks."

"If someone found that message, then Kaley—" Reef couldn't finish. What would her captor do to her when she found out about the message?

Liam pressed on. "I also think your theory about Kaley being on the motorboat is possible. If Russo kidnapped her, she thinks Kaley knows something and must have thought there was information on this houseboat. They either found it—or decided to torch it so no one else could."

"Then maybe we can go after that boat." But even as he spoke the words, hope faded in his heart. That motorboat could be anywhere by now. "Or can you at least get a warrant to search Russo's place?"

"Reynolds is working on it," Liam said. "I forwarded your picture, and between that and the evidence already mounting up against Russo, we should have the paperwork soon."

Soon. But would soon be too late for Kaley?

Shooting pain spiked in his left shoulder where the EMT was disinfecting the burns. He grunted and squinted at Liam. "If they went downriver, she might not come back."

"We're looking to see if Russo has any colleagues in Tampa Bay," Liam said. "But yeah, I agree with you. If she felt like her estate was under scrutiny, she'd move Kaley."

Reef didn't say anything. He almost welcomed the pain shooting down his back. It was the closest thing to a distraction he had going for him.

"Listen, man, I'm sorry I doubted you," Liam said. "We should have set more surveillance around Russo's place. As it is, the guard set to watch the houseboat didn't report seeing anything. You're better surveillance than trained personnel."

He nodded and forced down the angry words forming in his throat. Reynolds' team had been sloppy. Any surveillance guard who didn't notice a burning houseboat needed his vision checked.

"All set," the EMT said. "I would wear really loose cotton shirts until those heal. You're lucky they're not more serious. If they don't act like they're healing, call a dermatologist asap."

"Thanks." Reef picked up the singed rash guard but didn't bother putting it on.

The EMT eyed his bare chest as he packed up his supplies. "That your jet ski on the water?" He nodded toward where Sam still waited with the two skis.

"Yeah," Reef said. "Why?"

"You'll want to stay out of the sun. I know the big Gasparilla invasion is this weekend, but I'd watch it from your television. The last thing you need on top of those burns is a sunburn."

Reef's head swirled. Maybe Russo had moved downriver for another reason. He collected his wits long enough to respond. "Sure thing."

As soon as the man had walked away, Reef spun to face Liam. "The Gasparilla invasion. That's it."

"What's that got to do with anything?" Liam asked.

"It's the perfect cover for Russo to escape with Kaley," Reef said. "If we don't find Kaley before then, we're not going to find her."

"The invasion is a nightmare with all those boats and bodies. How do you propose we go about finding her?"

Reef stared hard at his friend. "Reynolds is the one with the resources. Get Kaley's picture on every law enforcement officer's desk. Use drones. Have FWC out there checking every registration."

Liam slowly nodded. "If we can find Kaley's DNA at Russo's estate once we get that warrant, then we'll definitely have more fuel for our case and the need to search the surrounding area. I'll contact Reynolds about our suspicions. And I'll let you know once we have that warrant."

"Sounds good." It wasn't good by any means, but it was a start.

"And Reef? Try to stay away from any more burning boats, okay?"

Reef smirked and stood. "No promises, but I'll do my best."

Chapter Twenty-Eight

Kaley rubbed her burning cheek and blinked back the tears. If Louis kept hitting her, she was going to need a full-face mask, not just an eye patch.

"Enough!" Val smacked Louis on the shoulder. With her other hand, she ended the call from the maid who had tattled about Kaley's message in the window.

Thanks to that maid, she might have another black and blue.

"We're almost to Rick's, and we don't need to attract any attention," Val said.

"No one probably saw your stupid message anyway," Louis mumbled and turned back to the steering wheel.

Val glared at her. "Someone did, thanks to princess here. We can't go back to the house tonight. Lucky for us, I had my team move my yacht to the marina. We'll dump this boat there and take the yacht the rest of the way down the river to the bay. No snoopy investigator will find us then."

She edged next to Louis and started whispering. Kaley turned her head away but strained to hear.

"But what about the house?" Louis asked. "Won't they find something?"

"I'm having every last inch of her room detailed. There won't be any DNA for them to find."

Kaley bit her lip and dared to hope Val could be wrong. All the team needed was one strand of her hair or one fingerprint, right? Surely Val's cleaning team couldn't be that thorough.

But this was the woman who had burned a dead man's houseboat to cover her steps. She was capable of anything.

Minutes later, their boat came to a stop in front of a riverside restaurant. This must be the Rick's on the River that Val had mentioned.

Her stomach grumbled. That PB&J sandwich was a long time ago. Was it too much to hope they'd get her something?

"Get up." Val kicked her leg, and Kaley jumped to her feet. Val grabbed her forearm and squeezed tightly enough to leave a mark. "And if you try anything while we're here, you'll regret it. Just shut up, sit at the table, and let us do the ordering."

Kaley swallowed and hoped that meant she'd get something to eat.

When Val released her death grip, Kaley climbed onto the dock outside the restaurant and followed Louis to an open-air table far away from the other customers. Val pulled out a menu stuffed into the center of the table and handed one to Louis. She didn't bother offering her one.

A moment later, a young waitress sauntered over. "What can I get you?"

"Water with lemon," Val said, not bothering to look at the woman.

"Beer for me." Louis winked at her and rattled off a brand.

"Nice patch, but where's your pirate hat?"

Kaley jerked her head up. Was the waitress really talking to her? "Uh…"

"Her costume is in progress," Val cut in and then raised her voice, loud enough for anyone in the surrounding tables to hear. "She's on the spectrum."

"Oooh." The waitress smiled extra wide at Kaley, who felt her face burn.

Of course, Val was lying, but even if she weren't, there was no reason anyone should talk down to someone on the autism spectrum.

"And what can I get you, dear?"

"Just water for her too," Val answered for her. "And we're ready to order."

The waitress returned her focus to Val, who ordered two sides of wings, and then Louis added something else.

Just please let one of those wing baskets be for me. It was either all the slapping, or she was getting lightheaded.

Kaley didn't bother paying attention to Val and Louis as they made small talk. There was no need to pretend being nice when Val made anyone within earshot believe she was "special." No one would believe she needed help even if she made a scene.

She stared at the river beyond them, wondering how a place she once found so peaceful and beautiful could turn into such a cage for her.

The food came soon, and Val slid a basket with wings and fries her way. "Don't say I never did anything for you."

If she expected a thank-you, she wasn't going to get it. Kaley ignored her and focused on the food. It was simple, but she couldn't remember anything tasting so delicious. Was this what people called a last meal?

Better not to think that way. She needed her strength and the calories, so she ate every last French fry and drained her glass.

"I see our little pirate was hungry." The waitress's words made her jump.

"Always is." Val forced a smile and stared at her, as if daring her to say a word.

"Uh, bathroom?" Kaley said.

"Oh, it's inside and to the right."

Val hopped out of her seat. "I'll go with you. Don't want you getting *turned around.*"

Kaley didn't protest. This was her one chance to use the bathroom and maybe leave a clue.

Val was close enough to breathe down her neck the whole walk inside. Right outside the bathroom, Val paused. "I'll wait here. Make it quick, though."

Kaley nodded and pushed open the door. There were two private stalls, and she quickly locked the one farthest from the door.

Now was her chance. She pulled the small lipstick from her pant pocket and scrawled on the back of the door. Yanking out a strand of hair, she also slipped it into the woman's receptacle. Then, after quickly using the facilities, she washed her hands and hurried out before Val could come looking for her.

Kaley held her breath. As long as Val didn't use her stall too, her ploy might work.

But Val only grunted and strode toward the exit, as if Kaley had taken too long.

Louis was already at the boat, and Kaley followed Val onto it without a struggle. Resisting was pointless anyway.

Her one hope now lay with a scribbled lipstick message. Maybe a guest would report it. She could only hope the after-hours cleaning crew didn't wash it away without a thought.

It took the last of Reef's energy to drag himself over the threshold of his little lakefront house. He had dropped off the skis at the shop and waved goodbye to Sam. Even little movements were painful, but he tried not to think about it.

These days, everything was painful, mostly his heart.

He had failed. They hadn't found Kaley. He felt like they'd been so close, but he had no evidence. Maybe the house search would turn up something, but if Russo were as conniving as she had proven so far, he doubted it.

Shower? Food? Sleep? He needed all three if he were going to be worth anything tomorrow. With a sigh, he trudged to the freezer and pulled out a frozen pizza. After setting an alarm on his phone, he collapsed onto his worn leather couch and closed his eyes.

Twenty minutes, that was all he needed for now. Twenty minutes, then pizza, then a shower …

His phone vibrated.

"What do you make of this?" Liam's text read. An attachment below it showed "loading."

Reef groaned. Of course, his phone was almost dead.

He rolled off the couch in search of his charger. He found it on his nightstand and stuffed the charging cord into the end of his phone.

The image finally loaded, and he blinked. What was that?

Another text pinged. *A waitress found it on the door of a stall at Rick's on the River and called the police.*

Reef's heart stuttered at the image. Someone had scrawled Pirate 9-1-1 in red lettering on the stall door.

His hand trembled as he texted back. "Red lipstick?"

"Yes."

Heart racing, he scrolled through his past images for the one he'd taken of the window message and then compared them side by side.

They looked identical.

He sent the screen capture to Liam. "They're the same."

"That's what I thought." The dots next to Liam's text told him his friend was still texting. "And there's more. We found a hair sample in the trash."

Reef dialed his friend. "Tell me Rick's has surveillance cameras."

"They do," Liam said. "And we've already requested them. We interviewed the waitresses, and one says she thinks she knows who did it. She said there were three customers and one was a woman with a pirate patch over one eye. She didn't say much— and her companions joked that she was 'special.'"

"Kaley," Reef whispered.

"We can't jump to conclusions, but I think there's a strong possibility this trail is hot. And if Russo knows it, Kaley is in even more danger."

Reef's head pounded. What was he supposed to say to that?

"And the invasion is tomorrow."

"What can I do to help?"

Liam chuckled on the other side. "Officially, nothing. Unofficially ..." There were muffled voices in the background.

"Hey, man, I have to go. I'll swing by your place when I get off my shift."

"I'll be here." Reef hung up and stared at the picture until his timer went off.

Why was Kaley dressed up like a pirate? But her message had worked, and if the surveillance videos were reliable, Liam and his team would be able to recognize Kaley, eye patch or not.

Still, they had lost her again. Her captors could be anywhere in Tampa Bay by now. But something was keeping them here. What was it?

"Leave us another clue," he whispered. "Don't give up. We're coming."

"Why is she even here?" Louis's voice was low, and his tone, menacing as ever. "If we'd knocked her off after you got the drive, we wouldn't be on the run."

"I pay you to do what you're told, not to question my decisions." Val's words sliced through the air.

Kaley almost wished she couldn't hear. She dangled her legs off the edge of Val's yacht, anchored in the bay a long way from shore. The guy who had swapped vessels with them at the marina had long since taken off. From what she had gathered, they would keep a healthy distance from any other vessels before lining up for the invasion in the early morning hours.

The sun dipped low on the horizon. Watching the sunset from the back of a yacht was something she'd only dreamed about doing. Now, she wished more than anything to be home and far away from here.

But wishing didn't make things happen. And with the way Louis was talking, she should probably try to enjoy this sunset because it might be her last.

Only, he didn't know that she still had some bargaining power. She hadn't told Val she'd seen Anthony's final message, and she wasn't going to until she needed the leverage.

Poor Anthony. That man had been obsessed with avenging Jack the monkey. If only his painstaking plans had made a difference for him. Even so, maybe his insurance could buy her another sunset.

Footsteps sounded behind her, and something hit the deck. Kaley jumped and twisted to find Val glaring at her. "This isn't a pleasure sunset cruise, sweetheart. You get to earn your keep." She nodded at the bag of tangled decorations they had pulled off Anthony's houseboat.

"I want this place looking like a party before morning. We're going to blend right in with the other boats for the Gasparilla invasion." With that, she spun on her heels.

Kaley fingered a strand of garland that looked more knotted than Christmas lights forgotten in the attic. This was not going to be an easy job, and with daylight fading, she'd better hurry and get this mess at least sorted before dark.

After unscrambling the garland, she found some half-broken piñatas. With a sad smile, she fingered a particularly beat looking llama. Had Anthony planned to make some big reveal during the invasion? Was that when he had planned to leak his flash drive or tip investigators off to his second location of incriminating documents?

"Jack's revenge," Kaley murmured. If she got out of this alive, she might be able to see Anthony's plan through and help serve justice to the people who had wronged not only him, but also countless others in the fraud scheme.

His last clue—the writing on the windows—had revealed what kind of dark trenches this mob had been digging. Granted, Anthony's hands weren't exactly clean either since he had been working for this group, but he had tried, in his own crazy way, to make things right.

Or at least to get revenge.

Fraud and secrets never die. Dig them up with my pirate bones in Oaklawn. – Jack

She'd lived in the Tampa area long enough to know that Oaklawn was the oldest cemetery in Tampa, but where exactly had he buried Jack's remains? Was it possible there was an actual pirate grave? If so, hopefully it was obvious. No one had time to examine hundreds of graves for a clue.

But that was a problem for another day. Right now, she had to finish stringing up these decorations before her arms gave out. Val and Louis had already gone inside the cabin. There would be no place for her to sleep there—and even if there were, she wouldn't camp anywhere near Louis.

She'd spotted a pile of towels in a compartment near the controls. As long as it didn't rain, she'd curl up with those on one of the deck seats.

When the cabin light went off, Kaley let the last strand of garland fall to the deck. She could barely see her hands in the blackness. Apparently, Val wasn't taking any chances being found or of her escaping. She had made sure to go far enough out in the water that Kaley couldn't even dream of swimming for shore—let alone know which way led to the shore.

Still, the choice to turn off the standard yacht lights seemed foolish. The last thing they wanted was for a fishing yacht or something bigger to run into them.

But whatever. She was too bone-tired to care. Kaley pawed her way across the deck to the controls, yanked several towels out of the compartment nearby, and collapsed onto the closest deck lounge seating.

It was cool to the touch, and she shivered. She'd probably be covered in dew by morning, but at least for now, she could stay dry-ish.

She slid her weary body across the leather cushions and stretched out. The one perk to sleeping on deck were the stars. Above her, shining more brightly than she'd seen in a long time, were millions of stars.

"He counts the number of the stars; He calls them all by name," Kaley whispered the verse from Psalm 147.

If God knew every star by name, He certainly knew how lonely and lost she felt right now. She snuggled under one of the towels as her thoughts drifted back to Frankl's story. If she ever had the chance to finish her master's, she knew what her thesis would be.

Frankl had theorized that knowing one's meaning in life was the key to surviving suffering. He had been so close to the truth, but just a rock's throw shy of it. The key to finding one's way through suffering was understanding that a person's meaning or life purpose came through a relationship with Jesus Christ. The Source of meaning made the difference.

And right now, God knew and saw her, His child. Her identity as His daughter was secure, and He would always be her faithful Father. She clung to that thought and stared at the stars until her eyelids drooped as the boat's gentle rocking lulled her to sleep.

Chapter Twenty-Nine

A pickup door slammed, and Reef squinted in the pre-dawn light. There was no reason Sam should be at the shop this early. After his visit from Liam, he'd texted Sam to let him know he was taking out their yacht so Sam wouldn't worry, but why—

Footsteps pounded on the planked walkway and stopped just in front of him on the dock. "No way, man. You can't take the yacht out by yourself."

The edge to Sam's voice surprised him. "Sam, you know I'm the best—"

"Doesn't matter. You can't captain the yacht, avoid the other boats, and try to find your girl without committing suicide." Even in the dim light, Reef could see Sam's arms crossed. "Remember the first—and only time—we agreed to take customers on our yacht in the flotilla?"

How could Reef forget? The Gasparilla flotilla involved hundreds, if not thousands, of private boats, along with the fully rigged pirate ship, the *Jose Gasparilla*, to reenact Tampa's legendary pirate invasion. "Yeah, it was pure madness, the only time we ever got a scratch on *Serenity Now*."

"Right. I tried calling you, but you weren't answering, so as soon as I got your text, I came over—first to try to talk you out of it and then to join you since I figured that was impossible."

Reef grinned. His friend knew him so well.

"Please tell me your investigator buddy we met yesterday somehow got in all the paperwork for you at the last minute and secured dock space?"

"Yes, I have all of that, thanks to Liam," Reef said.

Sam helped himself into the yacht. "Well, at least we're doing this legally."

Reef started the engine, and *Serenity Now* purred to life. "There will probably be forty or so law enforcement boats, but most of them are going to be too busy checking for DUIs and the proper number of life vests to be able to help us. That's why Liam pulled some strings. He agreed the team needed eyes on the ground, so to speak."

"Which is exactly why you need a captain." Sam gripped the wheel. "The only person better than you is me. And you can't exactly stare through binoculars looking for Kaley while making sure you don't crash into the craft next to you."

"Hey now …" Reef started to argue but clamped his mouth shut. He could debate their captaining skills later. "You're right. Thanks."

"Glad that's settled." Sam huffed. "Speaking of binoculars, did you grab the ones from the office?"

"Ah, nope." Maybe it was a good thing Sam was coming after all.

Sam let out an exasperated sigh. "Did you get any sleep last night?"

"I'll sleep when I'm dead." Reef hopped onto the dock. "I've already staged my Subaru at Craig's Park, so we'll load *Serenity Now* on the trailer there."

"How'd you get back here?"

"Bike."

"In the dark? You're crazy." Even though he couldn't see his friend's face in the early dawn light, he could hear the teasing in his voice.

"Be right back." Reef jogged toward the office, unlocked the door, and hurried to his desk, yanking the lower drawer open. After grabbing a pair of binoculars, he also strode to the mini fridge and helped himself to two iced cappuccinos. Thank goodness he had restocked the other day. They were Sam's favorite and perhaps a much-needed peace offering.

He wasn't a big fan, but he needed the caffeine to drive away the fatigue pinching at his eyes. Once he locked the office behind him—making sure the sign read *Closed*—he ran for the dock.

Sam had left the last tie-offs for him to undo and was reclining in the captain's chair while scrolling through something on his phone. "You know," he said, without looking up, "the guidelines say the invasion doesn't start until 11:30 am. We need to get there early, but dude, it's barely dawn."

Reef pressed a cold cappuccino into his hand. "It's almost a fifty-minute drive to the Gandy ramp, and we want to be in the water by 8 o'clock before the rush hits. Plus, I have a tracker for our boat that Liam will be following, and we also need to set up my laptop and make sure it can receive the drone footage."

Sam choked on his first gulp and pounded his chest. "Drone footage?"

"Yes, Liam is setting up a team of surveillance drones, giving us an aerial of the invasion. We're hoping they'll give us a bird's eye view for a better chance of finding Kaley."

His friend continued to stare at him as if he were crazy. "You were going to captain a ship, search for Kaley, and monitor drone footage in the flotilla?"

Reef offered an apologetic smile and took a gulp of his own beverage. When Sam put it like that, he may have been a tad optimistic about his abilities.

"You need your head examined." Sam sipped his cappuccino more carefully.

"Some people call it love." He winked at his friend and then capped his bottle. He could take only so much of that medicine at once.

"Then you, my friend, are a lost cause."

"Good thing I've got you for a friend."

Sam snorted and shoved him away. "Yeah, good thing. Now go undo those tie-offs and we'll get this party started."

"Aye, captain." Reef retreated to the sides of the yacht and un-looped the rope from the cleats. As much as he didn't want to endanger Sam today, relief washed over him, knowing that his friend could focus on maneuvering the boat, and he could focus on finding Kaley—using the drone footage and his own eyes on the "ground."

Even with the video surveillance from Rick's on the River, and confirmed identities of her kidnappers, finding her in the flotilla would still be like looking for a needle in a haystack. Still, it was their one shot. If Val were using the invasion for a trade-off of some sort, this might be their last chance to find Kaley before she disappeared in the underworld.

Minutes later, Sam idled *Serenity Now* out of the docking area and steered her past the Sponge Docks. It shouldn't take too long for them to reach Craig's Park, and at this hour, the boat ramp shouldn't be busy. From there, the next stop would be Tampa Bay.

"Can't thank you enough for this." Reef stored the tie-off rope under a seat. "Our odds today are small, but I feel like they just got better with you being here."

Sam grunted. "Your odds of survival are better. Can't believe you were really going out alone."

"In my defense, Liam gave me permission." Reef slumped into the seat next to Sam.

"Doesn't make it any safer."

Reef forced a laugh. "Nothing about rescuing my ex-girlfriend from mobsters is safe."

Sam's jaw tensed. "So we're really dealing with the mob here?"

"Liam filled me in. Russo's been sending large sums of money to an LLC in Tampa—pretty consistently for years now. There's a shallow front that it's a charity for rescued animals, but after some digging, investigators confirmed there's no such operation. It's a cover for something else.

"And this Louis Caputo character who was in the surveillance video with Russo and Kaley has a prison record for embezzling funds. He started the bodyguard stint after his last release, but there's a paper trail connecting him with Russo that goes way back. Something stinks in Denmark."

"What?"

Reef pulled a baseball cap off the dashboard and tugged it on. "Oh, it's the one thing I actually remember from my senior literature class. We had to read some Shakespeare play—and every time half of us forgot to turn in our essays, the teacher would say, 'Something stinks in Denmark,' because a character in the play said that. Basically, she was mad at us for being bad students."

"Look at you, quoting Shakespeare."

"Full of surprises, right?" Reef chuckled.

"So how do you and the investigators figure you'll find Kaley? Do you have a tracking device?"

"Wouldn't that be nice? No, we're simply looking for any sign of Kaley, Russo, or Caputo. Kaley's *pirate* message indicated they would be in the flotilla."

"That's the best lead you have?"

The skepticism in Sam's voice wasn't lost on Reef. He'd been fighting the futility of this search all night, but they had to have hope. Kaley had given them two messages—the one in the window and the one on the bathroom stall. If she could just give them one more.

He and Sam rode in silence, the water splashing against the sides of the boat. The breeze they generated sent goosebumps up his arms, and other than the rash guard he was wearing, he hadn't brought a jacket. But the forecast all week had been unseasonably warm, and anytime he thought about Russo and Caputo, his blood ran a little hotter. They had dared to steal Kaley, and today, he planned to steal her back.

"God, guide our way," he whispered into the wind.

So cold. Kaley shivered awake in the pre-dawn light. Dew had coated her towels, and they were little protection from January's morning breath.

There had been more towels by the captain's seat, right? With a groan, she flung the damp towels off her and shuffled down the deck. There were no lights on in the cabin, so Val and Louis were probably still sleeping cozily.

She bit back bitter tears. There was no use crying about how unfair her situation was. Right now, she had to focus on getting dry and warm.

The covered captain's seat wasn't damp from the dew, and Kaley sank into it. The towels should be nearby.

Bingo. The panel squeaked slightly as she tugged out the last two towels. She wrapped them tightly around her and curled up in the chair. At least here, she was slightly protected from the breeze too.

But though her eyelids felt heavy, she couldn't sleep. Any moment, Louis could wake up, find her in his seat, and hit her. What if she dozed off, and Val wasn't happy with her decorations?

"You have to rest," she mumbled to herself. She'd be useless if she didn't snag one more hour. Rotating slightly, she managed to straighten out by propping her legs on a little ledge. Maybe this would be more comfortable.

Tucking her head inside her towel cocoon, she closed her eyes again. So sleepy. Almost warm.

What felt like moments later, a slamming door jarred her awake. She shoved herself upright in the chair and whirled to face the early riser.

Val didn't even glance her way but strode past her to the deck. She stuffed a cigarette in her mouth and flicked her lighter.

Were those bags under her eyes? Maybe Kaley wasn't the only one who hadn't slept well.

Quietly so as not to attract Val's attention, Kaley slipped from the captain's seat to the back side of the boat, careful not to drop her towel-blankets. The seating there was damp from dew, and she didn't want to sacrifice a towel to wipe it dry. Instead, she stared over the railing toward the sunrise.

Hues of pink, purple, and yellow streaked across the sky, followed by the sun's golden orb. Kaley closed her eyes and soaked in the warmth on her face. It was the reminder she needed that nothing could separate her from God's love. Whatever this day might hold, He would see her through.

"Your garlands fell in the front." An acrid voice behind her spoiled the moment.

Kaley took a steadying breath and turned to face Val. "I'll fix them."

"You better." Val sucked her cigarette and exhaled the smoke. "Can't have our boat looking less than a party."

Kaley slid past her and found herself breathing more easily on the other side of the boat. Val's presence and her nasty smoke made her uneasy.

Sure enough, her longest garland had slipped through the railing along the boat's edge and now hung precariously close to the water.

Kaley eyed the swim ladder, and an idea flashed in her mind. She could use it to scrawl a message on the side of the boat—a message that would seem fitting for a pirate boat but be in her red lipstick that hopefully police would recognize as her writing. If Val questioned what she was doing there, she could say she was fixing the garland. And the odds of her or Louis seeing her message were slim to none.

It was her one chance to leave a last message.

Val was still puffing on her cigarette, and there was no sign of Louis. Silently, she swung herself over the side while gripping the swim ladder and cautiously stepped down, one rung after the other.

Still gripping the railing with one hand, she stuffed her hand into her pocket and retrieved the precious lipstick. It only had to last long enough for her to write two words.

Her lipstick ran dry on the last letter.

"Are you down there?" Val's voice shrieked from somewhere above her, causing the lipstick to slip from her fingers. Not that it mattered.

Kaley cleared her throat and snatched the drooping garland. "Just getting the garland, like you said." She climbed the steps as quickly as her shaking limbs allowed. Val couldn't find the message. She just couldn't.

Forcing a smile, she held the garland high for her to see. "It was caught on the ladder." Kaley dropped her gaze to the railing and resumed wrapping it, all the while holding her breath.

"Well, hurry up. I'm hungry."

She paused. "We have breakfast?"

"We do once you make it," Val snapped at her. "Louis said there's pancake mix inside and ingredients in the mini fridge."

Louis. The last place she wanted to be was in a confined space near him.

"Oh-kay," Kaley said and sent up a silent prayer. "I'll get started right away."

"Good, because once you finish, we need to start heading toward Hillsborough Bay to get in position."

That would be her chance for someone to spot her message—as long as neither Val or Louis found it first.

Scanning the window for any sight of Louis, she pressed the cabin door open. Water was running behind another door—must be the bathroom. Maybe he was taking a shower. Maybe he would take his time.

She kept the door cracked open and headed toward the kitchenette. Making pancakes wasn't exactly rocket science. Val must be a spoiled brat not to know how.

At least the little space had all the utensils and ingredients she needed. Someone who'd been here before knew how to stock a basic kitchen. Soon, she was flipping her first pancake on the tiny one-serving-sized skillet.

The smell made her stomach growl. If she ate the first one, she'd at least guarantee getting something.

She was still chewing when the door slapped the frame behind her. "What do you think you're doing?"

Kaley swallowed. "Making pancakes like you said."

"I didn't say you could eat them."

Kaley forced restraint into her voice. "The first one is never the right consistency. I didn't figure you'd want anything less than perfectly fluffy."

Val grunted and stepped closer as if to verify Kaley was telling the truth. "There's a coffee maker in the corner. Start a pot, will you?"

This must be how Cinderella felt. At the moment, though, Kaley felt much less kind than the fairy-tale princess.

With another pancake rising on the skillet, Kaley investigated the coffee pot. She'd be lucky not to burn breakfast while trying to hunt for the coffee filter and grinds.

Thankfully, the kitchen was tiny, so she found those items quickly as well. When Louis came out of the bathroom, Val was hogging all the space around her. The woman was like an impatient child, smelling the coffee and eyeing the growing mound of pancakes.

"Here." Kaley handed Val the plate where she'd stacked four pancakes. "You can get started with these. There's butter in the fridge, but I haven't seen syrup."

Val smiled as she received the warm plate, but the reason probably had less to do with Kaley and more to do with breakfast. Louis helped himself to an extra plate and pushed it in front of Val, who grudgingly handed over two pancakes.

Sheesh, it's not like those two didn't have dinner.

But Kaley was glad for her one pancake. If nothing else, it would settle her stomach and hopefully keep the lightheadedness at bay. She continued to scoop batter onto the little skillet while her captors ate in silence behind her. Only after she delivered four more pancakes did they start to slow down enough to talk between bites.

"You get a hold of Big Eddie's guy last night?" Louis asked.

"Yep." Val chewed loudly.

"Where's the rendezvous?"

There was a pause, and Val dropped her voice an octave. "Outside the Tampa Convention center. He pulled some strings to get us docking spaces next to each other to make the swap easier."

Swap. Kaley gripped the counter ledge to steady herself. Was she the swap? Swap for what, and for whom?

The one pancake she'd had threatened to come back up. None of the answers she could think of were good ones.

But the bay would be full of boats and other people. Surely there would be someone to help her, some way she could escape. Or maybe the teeming crowds were exactly what Val wanted so that no one would notice if one woman disappeared.

Stop it. Kaley forced the thought from her mind and quickly rescued a pancake that was turning a little too brown. She had to stay present and focused if she were going to have a chance.

Chairs scraped on the floor behind her, and Kaley glanced back. "I have two more almost done."

Louis made a bloated motion above his belly and then scowled. "Just more coffee. I drink my own pot."

"Well excuse me." Val chugged the rest of her mug. "You already drank over half the first one."

"Make another pot," he growled at Kaley, and she shrank closer to the counter as he stomped past her out the door.

"Just be quick about it." Val dumped her plate in the sink. "We'll be taking off soon, and anything loose is liable to make a mess or break." With that, she slipped outside and kicked the door closed with her foot.

Kaley sighed as she stared at the dirty dishes—the ones Val had left in the sink. Louis's were still on the table. They'd left the two pancakes, and without asking, she stuffed one in her mouth while turning off the burner and wiping the remaining batter into the trash. She secured the other pancake in a zip-lock bag and slid it in her pants pocket. It might be her only shot at food later in the day.

After starting a second pot, she washed, dried, and put the dishes away. Suddenly, the boat jumped forward, and she collided into the stove, thankful she'd finished her chores in time.

The coffee was done brewing and sloshed inside the pot. If Louis wanted it, he could come get it himself. Her trying to deliver the pot only guaranteed she'd spill it all over him. She smiled at the thought but decided his reaction would be too dangerous to risk.

She peeked out the window. Val and Louis were seated opposite each other with Louis at the wheel. They were shouting above the breeze created by the boat rushing forward. At least now that they'd picked up speed, the ride didn't feel quite so choppy.

Leaving the coffee for them, she helped herself to a glass of water and sat at the table, staring out the window.

Under any other circumstances, she would love to have her quiet time here with the beautiful ocean view. Closing her eyes, she imagined her worn Bible and a cup of her own coffee in front of her.

"Maybe one day, Lord?" She sighed. Right now, all she could do was pray. Pray that she could find an escape during the Gasparilla festivities. Pray that she'd written her message high enough so that the water wouldn't wash it away. Pray that someone would be paying attention and see her today.

Yes, God saw her. But she needed someone to be His eyes and ears.

Chapter Thirty

The sun had risen over an hour ago, and time seemed to be going both torturously slow and far too quickly. Inside the cabin at a desk made for people much shorter than him, Reef tugged his baseball cap on and off while staring at his spinning laptop screen. He'd spent the last half hour fighting his way through various two-factor authentication processes, reinventing more difficult passwords, and hopefully gaining access to the drone footage webpage.

"C'mon," he groaned. The screen icon kept spinning. With his luck, the whole program was frozen, and he'd have to start over.

Sam poked his head inside the cabin. "You get that thing working yet? The bay is filling up fast, and you've got plenty of boats to scan for Kaley if you want."

"If this thing would ever start working." Reef sighed. "Seriously, I can't babysit this. I've already called Liam twice, and I can't bring myself to tell him I still can't access the website."

Sam glanced at the screen. "Looks like it's thinking."

"It's been doing that for over a minute."

"Hmm, well, I'm heading back to the wheel. Call me if you need me." Sam snagged a bottle of water from the mini fridge before disappearing through the doorway.

"I need a hacker, apparently," Reef muttered and glanced back at the screen. It had opened to a webpage with five different video screens.

"Finally!" He moved the mouse to inspect each one. It looked like all five drones were operational, but only two were in the air. That made sense since the boat invasion didn't actually start until 11:30, at which time he would focus on monitoring the active drones.

Until then, he would use his binoculars to scan as many boats as he could see from the cabin's roof while sporting a fake spyglass and pirate hat.

This pirate party did make for the perfect cover.

With one last glance at the screen, he replaced his baseball cap with the black, feather-plumed hat and stuffed the other gear under his arm.

He squinted into the bright January sun, reflecting brilliantly off the water. Sam was right. There were already hundreds of boats staging early for the invasion.

His heart sank. He could barely see with the blinding glare, and there were so many yachts. Was this plan a complete fool's errand?

"Quite a sight, right?" Sam nodded to him.

"Yeah, um, I'll be right back." He retreated inside for his polarized sunglasses and sucked a deep breath.

Did Liam and Detective Reynolds even think he had a chance? Or were they trying to keep him preoccupied and out of the real investigative business?

Reef shook the thought aside. No, the more eyes they had on the water, the better. They were going to have one other patrol boat disguised as a Florida Fish and Wildlife Commission vessel, but that was it. Two against these odds weren't very positive.

In fact, they were virtually impossible.

Nothing is impossible with God. The verse from his Sunday school days came back to him. He wanted to believe it, but the twisting feeling in his gut made him doubt he actually did.

He glanced at the laptop screen on his way out. One drone was giving a wide aerial of the bay, dotted with hundreds of tiny specs. And one of those might have Kaley on it.

"I need to find that one, Lord," he whispered.

His cell phone vibrated in his pocket. Liam.

Our boat is in position. All drones are operational and will be in the air before the invasion starts. I'm at HQ. What's your position?

Reef dropped a pin of his location and texted it to Liam with a thumb's up. Then, he slid on his sunglasses and with a determined step, started toward the ladder he'd installed. Sam had added some nice touches with party flags. At least *Serenity Now* didn't look out of place next to so many other boats decked out from bow to stern.

Sam met him right before he started climbing and swung several pairs of bead necklaces over his hat.

"Where'd you get those?" Reef removed one that got snagged on his sunglasses.

Sam grinned. "Stole 'em."

"What?"

"Dude, you are way too uptight. Of course, I didn't steal them. Some guys on the boat next to me offered to throw me some, and I thought they'd help complete your costume."

"Keep a few for yourself." Reef tossed some at his friend and smiled. "And thanks. That was good thinking."

The playful sparkle in Sam's eyes faded. "Listen, I get that today is important—and serious. But patrolling this yacht like the Terminator isn't going to make us look casual, so try to act like you're having fun up there?" His gaze darted up the ladder.

"Yeah, I'll do my best." Reef started the climb. "I already tossed a folding chair up there, so it will look like I'm just a pirate waiting for the show."

"Have fun in the crow's nest." Sam laughed at his own joke. The roof of the cabin was no more a crow's nest than he was a pirate. "I'll make sure we don't ram any boats so you don't go flying overboard." Sam slapped him on the shoulder and slipped back into his captain's seat.

The cloudless day was already warming quickly and would be in the mid-seventies by afternoon. In other words, the weather was perfect—for a sunburn. Thanks to his rash guard and pirate hat, hopefully that wouldn't happen. His skin was still sore from yesterday's burns.

Reef set up the folding chair and pulled out his binoculars to scan the boats. Whenever he caught someone staring at him, he'd lower them, wave and swig water from his bottle. He hoped that most partygoers would soon be too drunk to notice him.

He chided himself for the thought. No, not even for his own benefit should he wish anyone to deaden their senses with alcohol the way his mom used to. It had destroyed her, and he'd seen it destroy too many of his peers as well.

Setting down his water, he resumed his binocular search. There were plenty of young women dancing, drinking, or sunbathing on the boats, but none of them were Kaley.

Already his exposed hands were smarting in the sunlight. He took a quick break, climbed down, applied some sunscreen, and checked the drone footage. There was nothing out of the ordinary.

His heart sinking, he started his second shift on the cabin roof. Minutes faded into an hour or more, and water space became more crowded by the second. His phone pinged, and he set aside his binoculars. He already felt like he was seeing double from his constant searching.

Blinking to refocus, he read the text from Sam. "Invasion starts in five. You'll want to be on deck in case the ride gets bumpy."

Reef sighed. He already felt like a failure, as though he were giving up. But Sam was right. Sitting on a lawn chair on a flat roof during the most packed boat parade—perhaps anywhere—was a recipe for disaster. Besides, he could monitor the drones from his laptop inside the cabin.

After folding and securing his chair to a tie-down on the roof, he descended the ladder. To his surprise, Sam wasn't at the captain's seat.

"Sam?" he called and peered inside the cabin. His friend was bent over the laptop, staring at something.

He slipped through the doorway and stood behind him. "What is it?"

"The laptop—it started making this beeping noise. I thought your battery might be low, so I came in to check if it was plugged in. That's when I noticed the red square flashing around one of the drone footage screens."

Sam moved back so Reef could take a closer look. "Dude, I gotta get back out front. This invasion starts any minute now, and we don't want to get run over for standing still."

"Yeah, go do your thing." Reef waved his friend away and focused on the screen.

There. It was a yacht—barely the minimum length for the flotilla. Like many others, someone had decorated it with garland and party streamers.

But it wasn't those decorations that held his attention. On the side of the boat, right under the railing on the side, someone had scribbled two words next to the swim ladder.

Love, Pirate.

The wording itself didn't mean much, but how it was written made his breath catch in his chest.

It was in red handwriting, the same color, slant, and style as the one he had seen in the window and the one Kaley had written in the bathroom.

That's her. He texted Liam. *Send me a pin.*

No sooner had he texted the words than the yacht lurched forward, and shouts erupted from all around him.

The invasion had begun.

Kaley clung to the kitchen table, which someone had wisely bolted to the wall, as the yacht sped through the bay. She thought Louis's driving was crazy before. That was nothing compared to his riding neck-and-neck with other yachts to greet the pirate ship.

She'd never actually been to watch a Gasparilla invasion before—she didn't like crowds. Now, she was at the epicenter of over a thousand boats all full of partygoers ready to celebrate the annual event.

Another yacht missed the side of theirs by what seemed like inches, and Kaley winced, bracing for impact. None came, except that their yacht lurched and paused, yanked right and then left, to forge a way through the mayhem.

Maybe you had to be crazy to captain a yacht in this invasion. In that case, Louis was the perfect choice. He had returned only briefly to claim his pot of coffee and snarled something at her she hoped she'd heard wrong. He was always in a fouler mood when he crossed Val, and they had been arguing about something.

√She hoped it wasn't about her.

In the distance, she spotted a vessel that towered above the others. Its pirate flag waved proudly in the breeze.

That must be the main boat. What was it called? The *Jose Gasparilla* maybe? In any event, if she remembered right, the private yachts would escort it to downtown Tampa where the mayor would hand over the key of the city to the pirates.

Beads would be flung. Beers would be doused. Revelers would revel.

And would she, a prisoner in her own hometown, go unseen?

A commotion to her left drew her attention once more to the window beside her. Another yacht rushed to fill the gap left by their previous neighbor and actually brushed their railing. The scraping noise made her cringe.

Shouting erupted on the deck, and she craned to look. A partygoer from the other boat was yelling at Louis who met the man with a string of curses.

The man seemed stunned at Louis's violent reaction. Sure, there were probably scratches, but this was all a party to him, right?

The man was so close to her that if a window and wall hadn't separated them, she could reach over and touch him. As if reading her thoughts, he glanced her way, a confused and riled look on his face.

"Help me," she mouthed and then repeated the words out loud. Could he hear her? She repeated them again more boldly, urgency in her voice. "I've been kidnapped."

He stared at her for only a second more, eyes wide, and then staggered farther back into his boat as Louis's bulky form blocked the view from her window. Val must have taken over the wheel.

She closed her eyes. *Dear Jesus, please get me out of here.*

Moments later, the cabin door flung open, slamming against the wall. "What are you doing by the window?" Louis seethed and strode toward her.

She shrank against the chair. "I—I didn't think you'd want me on deck."

"I don't want you staring out the window either!" Louis yanked her by the arm and dragged her to the steps leading down to the sleeping quarters.

"Please—" she gasped. The last place she wanted to be was in a confined space with Louis.

He flung her into the room and gripped the doorknob. "Stay here." With that, he yanked the door shut.

So this is where he and Val had spent the night. There were two twin beds hugging separate walls, and a small bathroom off to one side. She darted inside and relieved herself before she peed her pants. Louis could scare anyone half out of her wits.

She eyed the tiny shower with longing. Her hair felt so greasy, and a shower would feel amazing. But she couldn't risk it. And with the unpredictable movements of the yacht through the parade of other boats, the room was constantly tilting. Instead, she helped herself to a wash cloth, washed her face and tightened her hair into a bun. At least that way, she didn't have to think about her hair being gross.

With caution, she peaked outside the bathroom door. The cabin was still empty. There were no windows like in the little kitchen and living area. Her heart sagged as she curled her legs into her chest on the less messy bed. She had no way of escape now and no way to signal for help.

She could only hope her prayers had wings.

Chapter Thirty-One

There was no time for patience. With every second, Kaley got farther away. With one hand gripping the edge of the table to keep from sliding all over the room, Reef dialed Liam with the other.

"Hey, man, I was just going to call you," Liam said.

"Send me her pin."

"On its way, but listen, someone else has spotted her."

Reef's heart pounded. "Who?"

"Another boater." Liam spoke to someone in the background, and every wasted second made Reef want to jump out of his skin. "Hey, sorry, a boater called 9-1-1 and reported a woman in distress. He said she called to him for help, said she'd been kidnapped. His pin location was close to the yacht we suspect might be Russo's."

His phone pinged as the pin location arrived. Even though it was already old information, it was better than nothing. "I'll call if we spot the yacht. Thanks." Reef hung up and staggered to the doorway to find Sam.

The pin location was about half a mile ahead of them, which in this flotilla, might as well have been twenty.

"You got something?" Sam called over his shoulder, never taking his eyes off the water or his hand off the wheel.

"Last known pin location." Reef lifted his phone to Sam's line of vision. "Can you try to steer in that direction?"

"We're all going the same direction as that pirate ship." Sam seemed to force a smile for his sake. "But don't worry, we'll catch them."

Sam's optimism was exactly what he needed. Because as far as he could see, in this crowd, there was no way they could make up the distance between them.

Combining a bucking bull with a high-speed boat race might accurately describe Sam's driving style the next few minutes. Even with his feet staggered, Reef still had to grip the railing to keep from face planting on deck.

He held his breath as they inched closer to the pin dot on his phone. Of course, Kaley wasn't there now, but maybe if her driver weren't as reckless as Sam, he might not be too far ahead.

His phone pinged again with an updated pin location. There was no time to ask how Liam got new information. Maybe the boater who reported Kaley was keeping tabs on her. Could he hope for such concern among partygoers?

"New location." He updated his maps and held his breath. Squinting at the screen, he gasped. "We're on top of her!"

"Where?" Sam cried, barely avoiding a collision with another boat.

"Hold on." Reef glanced up. There, on the side of the yacht next to them were the words in red, *Love, Pirate.*

It was now or never. He squeezed Sam's shoulder. "Don't go far."

"What …?" But Sam never got the chance to finish his statement. The two yachts both turned to steer closer to the pirate ship and tilted precariously close. "No, Reef!"

But Reef had taken off running on the deck. Without hesitating, he jumped from the deck of *Serenity Now* onto the other yacht's stern.

He hit the deck hard as it tilted almost twenty-five degrees, sending him sliding toward the edge. A loose garland from the other side flapped toward him, and he snatched at it to slow his slide.

"What the …?" Voices argued from the stern. Any moment, someone would discover him. He hadn't thought this through. He was completely unarmed. And if they suspected he had intentionally jumped on their yacht, he was in trouble.

He had to act stupid. No, he had to act drunk.

The thought repulsed him. He'd seen his mom drunk so many times. Maybe those experiences, painful as they were, wouldn't be wasted.

As heavy footsteps closed in, he rolled onto his stomach and started laughing.

"You there!" A sharp, deep voice yelled from somewhere above him. "What are you doing?"

Between laughs, Reef started to sing off key, "Yo-ho-ho, and a bottle of—" He smirked and squinted at the man above him. "You got any of that rum? I appear to have lost my bottle."

The man scoffed and kicked his leg. "Get up—and get off my yacht."

"Yer yacht?" Reef patted the wooden deck with his hand. "Well, where's mine?"

The vessel lurched forward, and someone screamed up front. A woman's voice, "Get back here, Louis!"

"Fall into the bay for all I care," the man muttered and strode back the way he'd come.

The woman shrieked again. "These boaters can't drive! Two have almost shoved me into another craft. Don't leave me at the wheel again."

"A drunk fell onto the stern," came Louis's retort. "I don't know what to do with him."

"Fell from where?"

"Another boat, I guess. Someone is bound to miss him soon enough, and we can return him once this rat race ends."

"Get rid of him now!" The woman hissed back. "We can't have anyone finding her."

"She's in the cabin. No one will see her."

Her. They had to mean Kaley. He was so close—perhaps mere feet away—from where she was being kept somewhere below deck. He would not, could not, lose her now.

"Get rid of him!"

"Do you want me to drive this boat or not?"

"Fine, I'll take care of him."

245

The boat hurled this way and that as the flotilla neared the bay. Would he have a better chance finding Kaley now? Should he wait until they reached a dock or act now while there were only two for him to fight? Or were there more people below deck? And what if this woman was armed? He couldn't take any chances.

He started chortling and chanting "Ninety-Nine Bottles of Beer on the Wall" as she approached.

"Get up, you drunk." She kicked him in the side. Hard.

"Wal, hey to you too!" He cackled and held up a hand, squinting to get a better look. If his online research were correct, the woman was Valentina Russo herself. "Help a guy to his feet?"

"Where's your boat?" she demanded.

"If you help me up, we can look to-geth-er!" He slurred his words and continued to hold up a hand.

"Whatever." She grabbed his hand to yank him up, and in that moment, he used her as leverage to jump to his feet. Her eyes went wide, but she had no time to scream as he completed a fast action knock-out strike. He caught her limp body before she hit the deck and quickly dragged her toward the bow.

The captain's chair was still out of sight when he started his act again. "Help! She hit her head." He looped an arm around her shoulder to hold her up as the wheel came in sight. It was a good six feet from the entrance to the cabin. Louis couldn't leave the wheel and stop him from entering.

Louis swore. "What happened?"

"We both fell when the boat went all tipsy." He hiccupped and patted the woman's head. "I'll set 'er down inside, and then she can rest."

"Set her down right here." Louis's eyes darted between them and the boats crashing in around them.

"Naw, it's too bright." He pretended to squint into the sun. "Just set 'er down inside and be back."

Ignoring Louis's protests, he swaggered with the woman toward the cabin. The curses grew louder, but Louis's voice didn't get closer. He didn't dare leave the wheel without getting them all killed.

Once Reef kicked the cabin door shut, he dragged Russo down a few steps toward a closed door. To his relief, it didn't seem to be locked.

"Kaley!" He called and shouldered it open.

"Reef?" She squeaked as she jumped off a mattress.

Her voice was pure music to his ears. Dropping Val in the doorway, he lunged forward and enveloped her in a hug.

Kaley burst in to tears. "How did you get here?"

He brushed her hair from her face, taking in her every feature. "There's no time for that now. Louis is still driving the boat out of sheer necessity, but we've got a small window to get out of here before she wakes up."

"Val," Kaley gasped. "Did you …"

"Just knocked her out. She won't be unconscious long."

Kaley skirted her body but never let go of his hand. Her hand in his felt so good, so right.

"We've got to move fast. I'll block Louis and you run to the stern. I'll meet you there, and if we have any luck, Sam will still be right next to us."

"Sam?"

"My friend. He's driving our boat—*Serenity Now*."

"What if he isn't there?"

√Reef forced a grin. "We improvise." He tugged Kaley to a crouched position inside the main cabin door. "Ready? As soon as I open this door, you run. I'll be right behind you."

Kaley nodded, but the color had drained from her face. He didn't tell her that he felt exactly the way she looked.

He squeezed her hand and then let go. "Now!" he whispered and swung open the door.

No surprise, Louis yanked his head toward them. "Hey!"

"Run!" Reef didn't need to tell Kaley twice. She took off around the side deck toward the stern just as he told her. Louis lunged at him but missed, and Reef didn't engage. Louis would have to choose between them all getting killed or them getting away.

Reef darted after Kaley and banked on Louis choosing self-preservation.

She had paused on the stern, scanning every which way. "Is that her?" She pointed toward a boat behind them.

Reef waved his arms in response to signal Sam. "Hey!" he shouted, continuing to wave furiously. Sam shoved his way into position beside them, definitely scraping paint off both yachts.

Kaley fell against Reef at the impact, and he held her firm. "We've got one chance at this, okay?" He pulled her toward the far side of the stern, and she latched onto the railing. "On the count of three, we run as fast as we can and jump. Got it?"

Her eyes were wild and wide. She was scared. So was he.

"Take my hand." Reef held his out to her. "We'll do this together."

Without hesitating, she grabbed it. "Okay."

Sam was in position, but how long he could hold it, Reef couldn't say. "One-two-three!" Reef yanked Kaley from the railing, and they sprinted across the narrow deck, making a desperate leap for *Serenity Now*.

Her legs crumpled upon impact, and Kaley leaned her shoulder forward to roll onto her side. It was far better than trying to stop herself with her hands. There were some childhood rough housing experiences with her brother that paid dividends in adulthood.

She hadn't even caught her breath when she blinked and found Reef kneeling over her. "You all right?"

Kaley elbowed her way to a sitting position. "Yeah." She blinked at him again, and this time, felt the moisture behind her lashes.

Why fight it? She choked on a laugh and let the tears trickle down.

Reef reached forward and touched her arm. "Hey, you sure you're all right?"

She sniffed and smiled. "I'm so glad to see you." Without caring how she looked or what he would think, she threw her arms around him. She hadn't made friendly contact in days, and his touch overwhelmed her.

Reef hugged her back with such gentleness and firmness that she started crying again.

He was real. She was free. And he cared.

Kaley pulled back and wiped her face with her palms. "Sorry, it's just …"

"You don't need to explain." His hand squeezed her shoulder. "I'm so glad to have you back."

The yacht suddenly twisted to the side, sending Kaley into Reef's chest again. He gripped her and tried to steady them both.

"Whoa!" He gasped.

"Uh, Reef?" A man called from the front. "Can you guys get up here?"

Reef helped her to her feet, and they raced toward the front to the captain's seat. A man with a Bucs baseball cap kept his eyes on the crowded water in front of them.

"Sam, Kaley. Kaley, Sam." Reef made quick business of introductions.

"Glad we found you," Sam said. "But Reef, we're not out of this yet."

"Did you lose the other boat?" Reef motioned to the chair next to Sam, and Kaley gratefully sank into it. Her adrenaline rush was fast fading.

"Yeah, he pulled off to the side, and I lost visual. But do you see that boat right off the stern? He came out of nowhere, and I can't lose him."

Reef nodded, his jaw tense. "Thanks, Sam. Keep an eye on him. I'm taking Kaley to the cabin and calling Liam. Holler if you need me, and I'll come running."

To her relief, Reef offered her an arm, and she latched onto it as they slipped into the cabin. It was much smaller than the other one, but it felt safe. How long had it been since she'd felt safe?

But were they safe now?

"I don't like that Russo sicked a watchdog on us." Reef said as if reading her thoughts.

He pulled out a chair at a small table, and Kaley once more fell into it. When would she get her energy back? Was she in some kind of shock?

She gritted her teeth and forced herself to focus. "If it was Russo."

Reef looked up from where he had been tapping on the laptop screen. "What do you mean?"

"Val talked about someone called Big Eddie. I got the impression that she was transferring me to him."

Reef's eyebrows creased. "Why?"

Kaley swallowed. Her throat felt tight. "I was trying not to think about it."

Reef clenched and unclenched his fists, then dug into his pocket. Frowning, he slapped his pant pockets and groaned.

"What?" Kaley sat up straighter.

"My phone. It's gone."

She felt the blood drain from her face. "Did you lose it on Val's yacht?"

"Either there or when we made the jump." Reef ran a hand through his hair, then bent forward and started typing on the keypad.

Kaley's mind raced. "Is it password protected?"

"Yeah, that will only stop pros for so long, though. But ..." Reef's voice trailed off.

"But what?"

"This could work to our benefit. Let me get off an email to Liam first, though, so he knows not to call my phone."

"Liam's helping?" She felt a surge of warmth. Who else from their group had helped make her rescue possible?

"Yes." Reef's answer was tight. Was that because he was busy or because he wasn't sure how she felt about Liam?

That conversation could wait. Right now, if Val and Big Eddie were tracking them, they needed help.

The boat suddenly lurched forward, and something scraped the side. "Reef!" Sam called from up front.

"Stay here." He twisted the laptop to face her. "You can use my email and send Liam anything you can think of that he might need." With that, he sprinted out of the cabin.

Kaley stared at the blank message screen. Where should she start? Wait, she'd overheard Val and Louis talking.

Tampa Convention Center. Docking spaces. Make the swap.

She started typing. *Hey, Liam. It's Kaley. I'm okay, with Reef and Sam. I think Val and Louis are going to the Tampa Convention Center. They said something about having docking spaces to make a swap. Not sure if that was supposed to be me.*

She took a steadying breath. *But Sam thinks someone is following us. Can you send help?*

The boat swayed, and hurriedly, Kaley pressed send. But as the floor returned to level, she took another breath and studied the screen. She had more to say.

Think, Kaley, think.

Pursing her lips, she opened another new message and typed Liam's name in the address field.

Hey again. Someone is definitely pursuing us. Boat keeps rocking. Listen, if I don't make it, Val only got half the 'insurance' that Anthony had on her. She doesn't know it, but the rest of it is—

A violent crash shoved Kaley into the table, knocking the breath out of her. She snatched at the laptop and snapped it shut, hugging it to her chest, as her chair tipped and hit the floor.

Her elbow scraped the deck, and she cried out, but refused to let the laptop go. Curling into a fetal position, she tried to protect the laptop and her head.

Glass shattered behind her. She jerked her gaze to where the window should have been.

And screamed.

Chapter Thirty-Two

The *Jose Gasparilla* had arrived in the bay to claim the key to Tampa, and the pirates had landed. On them.

"What the?" Sam gaped as a man with a skull bandana wrapped around his head swung onto their deck and landed in a graceless heap.

"I've got him. Get us out of here!" Reef snatched a life vest and charged the man. His high school running back days were way in the past, but with the right momentum, he could take the guy down.

The man was starting to stand when Reef slammed into him and shoved him overboard. The man yelled and grabbed at him but only grasped the life vest. He hit the water hard.

And then Reef heard the crash and Kaley's scream.

"There's more of 'em!" Sam shouted. "I can't get out of this traffic jam fast enough."

"Kaley!" Reef cried and took off running again. The cabin door was jammed, but the window gave him an eyewitness view to the chaos inside.

A giant of a man, glass slivers coating his long black-sleeved shirt, snatched at Kaley, but she shoved the overturned table between them.

He snarled at her, half his face concealed with an eyepatch and pirate hat, and sprang again.

Enough of this. Reef backed up, got a running start, and put his weight into his shoulder. It collided with the frame, and the door blew open.

To his satisfaction, it fell directly on the wanna-be-pirate. "Run, Kaley!" He called from on top of the door. There was no telling how long he could keep the man pinned.

"One second!" Kaley called back.

Reef grunted as the man beneath the door cursed. Why was she wasting time? The table blocked her from view, but he thought he heard a tapping noise. Was she trapped by something?

"Kaley, get out of—"

But the door beneath him suddenly twisted to the side, sending him off balance and into the wall.

This guy might be twice his size, but he could use leverage against him. Reef crouched and then pounced on his back, locking his arms around his neck. If he could get the right choke-hold, the man would be out in seconds.

The man tried to claw him off, but Reef wrapped his legs around his waist and squeezed tighter. Moments later, the giant fell to his knees, gasping for air. Within seconds, he went limp.

Reef grunted and rolled off him, panting. The man wouldn't be out forever, and they needed to secure him.

"Kaley, you there?"

"Yes!" She popped off the floor from behind the table.

"There should be rope in the cabinet behind you. We need to tie this guy up, and then go help Sam."

Reef made quick work of tugging the man's arms behind him so Kaley could secure them with the rope. He started to tie a knot, when something slammed into the yacht, and the three of them rolled toward the wall.

As the unconscious man plowed into him, Reef barely avoided snowballing into Kaley. She shrieked and ended up falling between the overturned table legs.

"You okay?" He grunted, pushing the man off him and finishing the knot.

"I think so."

But she was shaking hard.

He pulled himself slowly to a standing position and stepped toward her. Window shards crackled under his shoes. "Watch out for the glass. It's everywhere."

She untangled herself and rose. "We—we've stopped?"

Shouts rang out from beyond the destroyed cabin door, and Reef strode forward. "Stay behind me. I've got a bad feeling."

Kaley bit her lip and nodded. Her breath made his neck tingle. More than anything, he wanted to get her safe and out of this mess.

But his heart sank the minute he saw the captain's chair was empty. He crouched down inside the frame and scanned the deck. "Sam?" He whispered urgently.

If anything happened to his friend, he would never forgive himself.

"Hands where I can see them!" A voice growled so close that Reef fell backward into Kaley.

Reef raised his hands and nudged Kaley to do the same. A pair of leather-clad men also dressed in pirate gear hemmed them in from both sides of the shattered doorframe. Masks covered the top half of their faces, and both aimed handguns at his head.

Reef felt for Kaley's hand and gripped it. He couldn't lose her again. Not when he just got her back. But there wasn't much he could do with two guns aimed at his head.

Worse yet, a third guy appeared, shoving a bleeding Sam into the room in front of him. It looked like someone had pistol-whipped him in the forehead. But at least he was conscious—and alive.

"What's the order?" Pirate number one pressed on an earpiece.

Another nodded and stepped forward. "Get the girl. No survivors."

"No!" Kaley released his hand and slipped around him, standing to her full petite frame. "You leave these two men here alive, or I'll never tell Val where Anthony hid the second part of his insurance."

The man glared at her. "You're bluffing."

"No, I'm not."

"There are other ways we can make you talk."

"I'll die first."

The second pirate interrupted. "We're wasting time. And there are too many witnesses here with this window blown out."

"Fine." Pirate number one reached forward and yanked Kaley's arm.

"No!" Reef grabbed her other hand.

Kaley offered him a small smile. "It's okay." She squeezed his hand and then let go.

The next instant, a second man clamped onto her other arm, and they hauled her overboard. A small engine revved, hinting that perhaps they were using a speedboat to escape, even though a boat that size was illegal in the flotilla.

The third man retrieved the unconscious giant and hurled one last insult. "Hope you took a good look, because you're never gonna see her again." He snickered and jumped overboard after his friends.

His heart stuttered. Not seeing Kaley again was not an option.

Reef shook himself and focused on the present. "Sam, are you all right?"

His friend nodded with one hand pressed against his head. With the other, he held out his cell phone.

"I think it still works. Call your friends. We can't let them win."

Reef took the phone and hurried to the lopsided edge of *Serenity Now* in time to snap a picture of the fleeing speed boat.

"We won't," he muttered and dialed 9-1-1.

Her brave front melted the moment Kaley spotted Val's yacht docked next to the Tampa Convention Center. As the speedboat pulled alongside it, doubts rolled over her in waves.

A hundred things could go wrong before Liam found them. And what if Liam never received the email she'd frantically sent?

Following the doubts came the regret. The last several days, she'd prayed for a chance to tell Reef how she felt, how wrong she'd been. She'd had her chance—and she'd missed it. Granted, they'd been running for their lives the whole time they'd been together, but surely, she could've spared the breath to tell him she loved him.

Yes, loved him. The man had risked everything for her. And he hadn't given up on her. He'd been looking for her all this time.

She choked down the emotion that was making her throat constrict. She couldn't cry in front of Val, Louis, or any of these men. She had to keep her head squarely on her shoulders if she had a chance.

"Get up." A man yanked her arm and pushed her toward the ladder. At least during the chase, her red-lipstick had been washed away. One less thing to explain, the better.

Val sat at the captain's chair, her face consumed with a scowl. "Can't get enough of us, can you, princess?"

Kaley bit her tongue to keep down a sarcastic retort. She couldn't win this cat fight, not on these terms.

Val glanced from her to the four men with her. One remained unconscious. "Well, what happened? Tell me the man who caused all this trouble is dead."

For a moment, no one spoke.

"C'mon, we don't have all day. Big Eddie's yacht will be here soon. I need a report."

The leather-clad man gripping her arm released her but shoved her forward. Kaley staggered to regain balance only inches away from Val.

"She said there's more insurance," he said.

"What?" Val launched to her feet. Her gaze jumped between Kaley and the men so quickly it was a wonder she didn't get whiplash.

Val stepped forward and shoved Kaley into the other seat. "I'll deal with you in a minute."

Kaley blew out the breath she'd been holding. At least Val's wrath wasn't directed at her for the moment—and so far, she'd seen no sign of Louis.

"But I asked you a question," Val continued. "Is that wretched man dead?"

The three men exchanged glances, and the leader finally cleared his throat. "She said if we killed him, she would never tell where the insurance was."

"Then he's alive?" Val shrieked. "You idiots!"

"There were too many witnesses," another man blurted. "We were drawing too much attention."

Val cursed under her breath and paced the small space separating her from the men. "At least you're wearing masks, but the speed boat is traceable. Lose it until we can get it overhauled. And what happened to him?" She tapped the unconscious man with her foot.

"The dude must have got him in a choke-hold. He's fine but will have a killer headache when he wakes up."

"Tell me about it." Val rubbed her neck and flicked her other hand at the speaker. "Take him and the speed boat." She turned to the other two. "Now what's this about insurance?"

Both men pointed at Kaley as if ratting out a classmate to a teacher. "Ask her. She said you only got half."

Kaley sat up straighter and beat Val to her interrogation. "That's right. Anthony left another clue that you didn't see."

"Didn't see when?" Val narrowed her eyes.

"When you burned Anthony's houseboat."

"Correction. *You* burned Anthony's houseboat."

Kaley wanted to punch the woman but kept her voice level. "It worked out. You didn't see his message in the window."

"You're bluffing."

"That's easy for you to say—unless the police beat you there."

"What?" Val hissed.

"That's right, if you don't hurry, they'll find it before you do."

"Well then you'd better start singing, because you have another ship to catch." She nodded toward the leather pirates. "They're going to deliver you to a whoring *whole new world*."

Val laughed at her vile Disney-song pun, but Kaley wasn't smiling. She crossed her arms and glared back. If Val wanted to crack cruel jokes, fine. It bought Liam and his team more time to assemble.

After a few seconds of silence, Val stopped chuckling and frowned. "So where is it?"

Part of Kaley didn't even want to tell her, but she also needed Val to take her there—if she had a prayer of getting rescued again. "It's in Tampa's Oaklawn cemetery, but you'll never find the site without me. There are hundreds of burial sites."

One of the pirates shook his head. "No way, we're supposed to deliver her to Big Eddie's boat as soon as it gets here. That was part of the deal."

Kaley arched an eyebrow at Val and crossed her arms. Val was going to have to choose between slighting Big Eddie or letting someone beat her to insurance that would cost her whatever was left of her reputation.

"And how do we know she ain't bluffing?" Another pirate asked.

"Because splitting up the insurance is smart, and even though Casale was a rat, he was devious." Val retrieved her head scarf from a compartment and tossed a second at Kaley.

"And what about Big Eddie?"

"Big Eddie's gonna want this insurance as much as I do," Val said. "So stop squawking and do your jobs."

"But our job was the girl—"

"Figure it out."

A small tan sedan with darkly tinted windows honked just beyond the dock, and Kaley's heart sank. That would explain where Louis had been all this time.

Val jerked Kaley to her feet and marched her to the gangway. "All right, sweetheart, you get to lead us to this insurance site, but know this—whether your cop friends beat us there or not, you've already dug your own grave."

Chapter Thirty-Three

Nothing was worse than a rat except a rat's shrink who started calling the shots. Val flipped an AC vent toward her and spun the radio volume to blaring. Beside her in the driver's seat, Louis cast her an annoyed glance and squeezed and released his death-grip on the steering wheel several times.

Good. If she were getting under his skin, she must be driving the chick in the back seat crazy.

Val tugged down her visor and pushed open the make-up mirror. The last week had not been kind to her. When today was over, her legal team would do damage control on any reports about her involvement in the affair. Meanwhile, she'd be on a yacht to Cozumel where her alibi placed her before Kaley even disappeared off Beech Mountain.

And then she'd schedule another round of Botox to help erase the stress of this week.

Her gaze latched onto Kaley in the back seat, and her heart writhed just a little. As disheveled as Kaley looked with her messy bun and make-up-less face, she still radiated youthfulness and beauty.

Such a waste. The young woman had messed with her plans too many times. She was her biggest liability, too, and only first-hand witness to her involvement.

Val wasn't a villain, though. She'd make it quick, painless—and poetic. The Glock 23 handgun in the glove compartment would see to that. A point-blank shot to the head would end the girl's misery.

She couldn't hide a smirk. Whatever gravesite Kaley led them to would become her own.

As Louis pulled into the small cemetery parking lot, Kaley fought a growing sense of anxiety. Other than one van and a homeless person camped out under the shade of a palmetto tree, the place was dead. What if Liam hadn't gotten her message?

Another problem gnawed at her. Although this cemetery wasn't huge, it was big enough. How was she supposed to find the grave? Didn't cemeteries usually have a map or marker or some way to locate specific graves?

But the grave she was looking for wasn't specific. All Anthony had written was that they could dig up the insurance with "his pirate bones at Oaklawn."

A pirate's grave had to be a prominent landmark, considering this was Tampa, home of the world's biggest celebration of pirates. But what if she were wrong? What if the grave was obscure, and she couldn't find it?

With a wry smile, she thought back to the day she had attempted to help Liam navigate the church van and failed miserably. Now, he could very well be waiting for her right where she told him to be—and all the while she might be unable to find the site herself.

Louis yanked open her passenger door and grunted for her to move. Hesitation held her to the seat like Velcro.

"Get out," he mumbled. She didn't dare risk angering him, so she forced herself into the afternoon air. How could such a pretty day hold so much trouble?

Focus, girl.

Val appeared from the other side of the vehicle as she retightened her scarf around her face. Something bulged underneath a leather jacket she'd slipped into. "Now, where's this gravesite?"

Kaley craned her neck in search of some form of signage. "Um, I just need to find a gravesite directory or something."

Val spun on her heels and raised an eyebrow. "I don't see one."

Kaley took a step away from the car. "Maybe we'll find one once we start walking."

"Hold on there, missy."

Louis placed a restraining hand on her shoulder and looked to Val for more instruction.

Val sashayed closer to her, her scarf edges flapping in the wind. "We're not going to spend all afternoon ambling around in a cemetery like sitting ducks for your cop friends. We get in and we get out. Period."

Kaley tried to wiggle her shoulder free, but Louis didn't budge. "But I've only driven past this place. I don't have a map of it or anything."

"Then what did Anthony's message say?"

"He told me the name of the grave site."

"Hmm." Val pulled out her phone and tapped on her screen. Moments later, she held out the screen toward Kaley while still holding firmly onto the body of the phone. "This should help then."

Kaley squinted past the glare on the screen. Val had pulled up a website called findagrave.com and selected Tampa's Oaklawn Cemetery. Now, the screen showed search fields for first name and last name.

"Type in the name Anthony wrote, and this should show us where the gravesite is," Val said. "And hurry up. We don't have all day."

Would pirate work? Kaley pecked the letters on the screen into the last name field and pressed search.

0 memorials found.

"Well?" Val twisted the screen to see for herself. "What? Nothing?"

Kaley twisted her hands together. "I need an actual name."

"You told me you had an actual name," Val hissed.

"It's more like a title."

Val narrowed her eyes at the search results again. "Pirate? That's what you typed in?"

Kaley bit her lip and nodded. "Anthony said he'd hidden the insurance at the pirate's grave. But I don't know the pirate's actual name."

Val cursed and shoved Kaley back toward the car. "This is a wild goose chase."

"Hold on. She might be on to something," Louis muttered behind her.

Kaley twisted to see that he'd pulled out his phone as well.

"There is a pirate's grave in Oaklawn."

"And how do you know that?" Val glared at him.

"Google."

She snorted. "So what's this pirate's name?"

"There are actually two."

Kaley took a baby step away from the car. If these two tried to exclude her from the search, she'd have to run for it.

Val made a waving motion at Louis. "And?"

"Their names are Hubbard and Perfino," Louis said. "Huh, Cuban pirates."

"Cut the fluff. Let's find these markers and get out of here."

"Uh, the article doesn't say where they're located, except for something about palm trees."

"I'm surrounded by idiots," Val muttered and pecked at her phone again. "So ..." Her voice trailed off. "If this find-a-grave website is right, both sites are close to each other." She glanced up from her phone and pointed. "That way."

Louis turned to the lead the way, and Kaley fell into step behind him. A concrete wall bordered the parking lot, and he scaled the wall.

There must be a main entrance somewhere else, but she didn't bother proposing they find it. Instead, she climbed the wall after him.

Val grunted as she landed on the other side. "No fancy moves, princess. I've got my little friend on you—and his friends all run faster than you can."

Kaley stiffened and cast a glance behind her at Val.

She was gripping something under her jacket. It had to be a handgun. How good of a shot was she?

And what kind of head start could Kaley get before having to find out?

If the parking lot was any indicator, the cemetery would be mostly empty. Most of Tampa had probably lined downtown to participate in the Gasparilla festivities.

Still, there was one hunched-over man with a cane slowly creeping along a brick pathway. Off to the left, she spotted a small group of maybe five people who seemed to be part of a guided tour. No one seemed to notice them.

Where were Liam and his team?

In the distance, she heard the zooming of cars on I-275. She was so close to being free and so close to hundreds of people who could help her—if they only knew she were here.

"I like this place." Louis stopped to examine a woman's statue. She was in a kneeling position, but something was wrong.

Kaley blinked. Her head was missing.

Louis caught her gaze and jeered. "How about we play reenact the statue? You're the statue."

"Quit stalling, you two." Val's tone was sharp as a knife.

Louis snorted and strode farther ahead. Kaley pretended to busy herself looking for the gravesites and tried to forget about the gun Val had trained on her every move.

But she found herself wanting to read the various tombstones. These had once been living and breathing people like her. Now, a tombstone with two dates and a dash marked their lives.

She wanted her dash to be much longer than it was. She wanted to do so much more with her life. Surely God wasn't done with her yet?

But if He was about to call her home, what epitaph would someone write on her grave? Or as Frankl might have asked, what had been her life's meaning? She hadn't done anything extraordinary to be remembered by, and even if she had, those things wouldn't define her.

Tears pricked her eyes. The best way to define her life was not by *what* she'd done but by *Who* she belonged to.

"Loved by Jesus," she whispered. That would be her epitaph. Could she dare presume to add Reef's name too?

"What are you mumbling about?"

Kaley jumped at the nearness of Val's voice. The woman was dogging her every footstep.

"Just reading the graves." She quickened her pace. Maybe if she found the sites first, she could find some clue that Liam and his team were here waiting to rescue her.

"Over here!" Louis called to them, and her heart sank. He must have found the markers already.

Kaley used his command as an excuse to jog away from Val, though the woman panted closely behind her.

"I found 'em," Louis said as if he deserved some kind of medal.

Kaley peeked around him at the markers. There wasn't much to them. They were flat with simple inscriptions, and both shared the phrase "a Cuban pirate." Had they known each other or worked together? Perhaps she would never know.

Val pointed. "There's dirt next to Perfino's marker where someone dug recently. Maybe that's where Anthony buried something."

Louis and Val stared at her. Apparently, they expected her to do all the dirty work. It wasn't like anyone brought a shovel.

With a sigh, she bent down and started scooping the earth with her fingers. There was no way she could outrun anyone from this position. If Liam didn't show, this was where her story would end.

Her fingers brushed something small and square, and she caught her breath. Had Anthony dug such a shallow grave?

Val kicked her leg with the side of her shoe. "Well? We don't have all day."

"I might have something." Kaley winced and yanked the box free. It was a small card box a little bigger than her hand. Slowly, she tugged the lid up.

In scraggly handwriting, someone had scrawled the note, "RIP Jack." It was placed on— were those ashes?

Kaley wrinkled her nose. Had Anthony cremated his monkey?

"Give it to me." Val snatched the box out of her open hand. Fine, if she wanted to dig around in a monkey's ashes, she could go right ahead.

Kaley took the moment to climb to her feet.

"It's empty!" Val shook the box upside down, and Jack's remains wafted to the ground.

"Maybe there's something else buried." Louis gestured to the dirt. This time, he took the trouble to start digging around himself.

"You!" Val pointed an ash-covered finger at Kaley. "Where is it?"

"All Anthony's message said was to find the pirate's grave." Kaley cast one last hopeful glance over Val's shoulder. If the box were empty, maybe that meant someone had gotten there before them. But other than the small tour group, no one else was in sight.

Louis grunted. "I got nothing."

Val shoved her hand into her jacket pocket, and something pressed through the fabric in Kaley's direction. "Get back in the car."

Kaley staggered backward, holding up her hands. "Please, let me go."

Val snorted and started toward her. "Really, after all this, you think you get to go home? And here I thought you were a smart girl."

Her eyes darted past Val. The tour group had made a dramatic turn toward them.

"And right over here, we have two alleged pirate graves." The woman's voice seemed louder than necessary. "However, as much as Tampa residents might like to think their city is the resting place for two notorious pirates, there isn't much evidence to prove these two men were actually pirates."

The next moment was a blur. Tour group members jumped between her and Val, and suddenly, she was hemmed in on all sides.

"Jack!" The tour guide shouted, and a man beside her tackled her to the ground, covering and all but smothering her.

Val's shriek pierced the grounds. Someone fired and was met with a return blast.

Kaley gasped for breath. She couldn't see anything with the man on top of her.

"Secure." The woman's voice called.

The man rolled to the side and extended a hand. "You all right, miss?"

Kaley scanned the ground. Val was face down in the dirt, her hands cuffed behind her. Another "tour guide" member had shoved Louis into a tree and was cuffing him as well. His right arm was streaked with blood.

"I'm—I'm fine." Kaley accepted his hand and shakily rose to her feet. The woman strode over to her.

"Kaley Colbert?" The alto voice was firm, but kind.

"Yes, ma'am."

The woman's stern face broke into a smile. She couldn't be much older than Kaley.

"Detective Avery Reynolds." She extended one hand to Kaley and pressed a finger to an almost invisible earpiece with the other. "All clear. Target is secure."

Kaley's jaw hung open. "You're—you're with Liam?"

"That's one way to put it." Avery's face broke into a grin. She nodded toward the parking lot, just out of sight. "Bracken is running comm in the van, and your man Mitchell is with him."

"Huh?" Kaley couldn't clear the fog from her head. She cast a glance the direction Avery had indicated.

A man was sprinting across the cemetery. His baseball cap flew off, and he didn't look back to retrieve it.

Reef. Reef Mitchell.

He reached her faster than she could blink away the tears welling in her eyes and engulfed her in a hug.

"You're safe. You're safe!" He breathed into her hair. "I'm so sorry. So sorry."

"For what?" She pulled away to look into his eyes.

"For letting them take you again—for not being able to stop them—for not doing more—"

She held a finger to his lips. "Shh. None of that matters. I need to tell you something."

"I love you," he blurted breathlessly.

Her cheeks flushed. "I—I was going to tell you that I love you."

The widest smile spread across his face. "You mean it?"

"Yes, and then you had to go and beat me to it." She playfully punched his shoulder.

He winked and kissed her hair. "Not that it's a race."

Kaley rolled her eyes and laughed. "But if it were, you won."

His voice dropped an octave, and he tugged her chin upward, closing the distance between their lips. "Holding you in my arms is the win of a lifetime."

Chapter Thirty-Four

She hadn't planned to have her first kiss with Reef in a cemetery surrounded by an investigative team disguised as a tour group. That's just how it happened.

Behind them, Reynolds cleared her throat, and Kaley pulled away. If the heat flooding her face was any indicator, she was beet red.

And Reef couldn't look more pleased about it.

Reynolds coughed again. "When you have a moment?"

"Yes, sorry," Reef laughed. "I just—I didn't know if I'd ever get to tell her."

The smirk on Avery Reynold's face was part amused and part skeptic. "That's sweet. Can't say I've seen your kind of determination."

Reef wrapped his arms around Kaley's shoulders and sent her a look that made her insides want to melt.

Reynolds motioned for them to follow her to the parking lot. "We need to get Ms. Colbert checked out and get her testimony. I want to gather so much evidence on Russo and Caputo that they won't be going anywhere for a long time." She motioned for them to follow her to the parking lot.

The mention of Val and Louis brought Kaley's head back into the game. "What about the others?"

"You mean the men on the boat who hijacked you?" Avery asked.

"Right, and there was another boat they were waiting for—Big Eddie's boat."

"Big Eddie?"

"Yes, from what I pieced together, he's the underground's current version of a mob boss. Val got nervous when she talked about him. Her original plan was to deliver me to him for—" Kaley shivered.

Avery stopped walking so she could face her. There was a sudden kindness in her expression that encouraged her to continue. "For what, Kaley?"

Kaley glanced at Reef, whose face had gone tense. "I—I think he runs a trafficking ring."

Reef reached for her hand and squeezed it as if he might never let go.

"Unfortunately, there's a lot of trafficking in the Tampa area," Avery said. "It would be great to get a bead on this Big Eddie. Breaking up his ring would be a step in the right direction."

"They had dock space right outside the Tampa Convention Center," Kaley said. "That's where Val left her yacht."

"It's not much to go on, but it's a start," Avery said. "I'll send a team to investigate."

They reached the parking lot, which had transformed from a sleepy place with a homeless person and van to a crime scene. There was no sign of either Val or Louis who must already be in one of the cars with flashing lights. Fine by her.

Kaley shivered and felt Reef's intense gaze. "You okay?"

She swallowed and nodded. "Yeah, I hope I never have to see Val again."

"There's a chance you'll have to testify, but we have plenty to hold her for now," Avery said. "Attempted homicide, kidnapping—"

"Fraud, money laundering," a voice behind them added.

Kaley spun to find Liam outside his undercover minivan serving as a communications center.

"Liam!" She released Reef's hand and embraced him in a hug. "Thank you for not giving up on me."

"We would never." Liam returned her squeeze but then released her quickly. "Reef wouldn't quit his crazy schemes, so someone had to keep him in line."

Kaley pulled back and exchanged glances between Reef and Liam. "Crazy?"

Liam pressed his lips into a thin line and seemed to be forcing a smile. "I'm sure he'll fill you in on everything later." He directed his focus toward Avery. "But here's what I came to tell you. I've barely scratched the surface, but that flash drive we recovered has enough evidence incriminating Russo on involvement in everything from credit card theft to fraud and more. It's all connected to a scheme dubbed the Cannoli Commission. Cracking this could be huge."

"Flash drive?" Kaley asked. "You mean—"

Avery nodded. "We got here before you did and retrieved it from the box. I then replaced the empty box for Russo to uncover and hopefully buy us a distraction."

"There's a second flash drive we found on Anthony's houseboat, but I don't know what she did with it." Kaley sighed. "Probably destroyed it."

"Doesn't matter," Liam said. "This one has more than enough." He motioned to Avery. "You're going to want to take a look."

"For sure." She glanced at Kaley. "Colbert here says there's a chance we might find Russo's accomplices docked at the Tampa Convention Center. Are the drones still in the air?"

"Yes, want me to put surveillance in place?"

"Give me an update when you have one, Bracken."

"Will do." Liam turned to Kaley and Reef. "Glad to have you back, Kaley, and I'll see you around, man."

Reef reached forward and shook his hand. "Definitely. Thanks for everything."

With a tight nod, Liam retreated to his communications post.

"Is he okay?" Kaley whispered to Reef. "He seemed—"

"He's on the job, Kaley." Reef took her hand again.

She felt another pair of eyes on her. "And three's a crowd, right?" Avery said.

Kaley's face warmed. Who was this detective who seemed to have such a pulse on people? She'd like to get to know her, under different conditions.

Avery hesitated. "You're the—friend—from his church Bracken mentioned. Is that right?"

"Maybe?" Kaley could only wonder what Liam had told her. "We all go to Crossroads Christian Church."

"I see." Reynold's expression was unreadable. "Bracken has been trying to get me to check out his group for years."

An ambulance pulled into the parking lot, followed by another emergency response vehicle. Avery waved over the ambulance, which pulled to a stop in front of them. "We'll get you checked out, and then I'm taking you back to HQ." She glanced at Reef. "I'll be in the comm van. Come get me when the medics are done with her."

"Will do," Reef said.

A medic stepped out of the ambulance and strode toward me. "Are you the patient?"

Kaley glanced down at her dirty borrowed clothes. "I'm fine, but I think she wanted me to get checked out."

"Does anything hurt?"

"I—I don't think so. I'm just tired and thirsty. And I'd really like to go home and call my family."

"I'd call them for you, but I lost my phone somewhere, remember?" Reef's smile melted her insides. "But phones are replaceable."

An idea squeezed inside her brain as the medic checked her blood pressure. "Wait, did you download that tracking app we used during the drive up to Beech?"

"I did, why?"

"Could we find your phone that way?"

Reef tapped his chin. "You're right. Assuming it's not at the bottom of the bay, we might be able to track it—"

"Straight to Val's yacht," Kaley said.

Reef grinned at her. "You're a genius. Will you be okay here if I go check with Liam on tracing my phone?"

"Of course." Kaley went through the motions of answering the medic's questions and was glad a preliminary round of poking and prodding satisfied him of her overall wellbeing.

What she needed now was a hot shower and her bed. Her adrenaline was all dried up. If she could form sentences for another hour, she'd be proud of herself.

The medic draped a blanket around her shoulders and pushed a cold water bottle into her hands. "You're all right, ma'am, but you should get some rest. I don't know what you've been through, but you're about to pass out from exhaustion."

"You're not wrong about that." Kaley offered a wry smile. "But tell that to the gal in charge."

"I'll see what I can do."

Kaley crept over to a shady, unoccupied part of the parking lot and leaned against a tree with her blanket. She'd rest her eyes for a minute.

What seemed like only moments later, a gentle hand was shaking her awake. "Kaley, I'm taking you home."

"Reef?" She rubbed her eyes. "Sorry, I'm just so tired."

"I told Reynolds that headquarters can wait. She agreed and said to get a few hours of sleep and then check in later tonight or in the morning. She's got enough on her hands to keep her busy for a while anyway."

Kaley didn't argue. No place sounded better than home right now.

Reef glanced toward his Subaru, parked near the Gandy boat ramp. Daylight was fading, but he could still see Kaley's silhouette inside.

The afternoon had not been as simple as he'd wanted it to be. By the time he and Kaley had caught an Uber to the boat ramp parking lot, Sam was still there. Because he didn't have Reef's keys, he'd had to call in Jake to bring his truck to pull out *Serenity Now*. Jake had arrived right before they had.

While he helped Jake and Sam with the yacht, Sam had kindly offered to let Kaley use his cell phone to call her parents and boss. She'd been more than happy to wait in the Subaru.

Reef was grateful. Although getting Kaley home where she could rest and feel safe was his priority, he hadn't felt right about leaving Sam and Jake to deal with their yacht without him.

Poor Sam. He'd also had to wait for an FWC agent to arrive so he could file a report about their yacht. Apparently, he'd had to get in line. This year's Gasparilla had more than one boating accident. *Serenity Now* was definitely scratched up from the hard hits, but Reef hoped everything was cosmetic. They'd find out once they could get her back to their own docks.

Reef helped direct Jake through the traffic jam in the parking lot until Sam had cleared the ramp with the boat.

Moments later, Sam climbed down the yacht to the pavement and strode toward him. "Jake and I will drop her off at the shop, and then I'll call Jim to see when he's free to come take a look at her." Sam ran a hand over his face, which was already starting to bruise. "Looks like we'll need to cancel our dolphin cruises for a few days."

"I'll handle all those calls tomorrow," Reef said. "I owe you, man. Get some rest, and we'll get all this sorted out soon."

Sam smiled as wide as his swollen face would let him. "I'm just glad the good guys won today, and your girl is okay. A boat is fixable."

His girl. Yes, she was. Even Liam knew it, though he could tell his friend was smarting about it.

Understandable. Kaley wasn't an everyday catch. She was a once-in-a-lifetime woman. And she was his.

"Let me get your phone back, and you can be on your way." Reef jogged over to his Subaru and tapped on the window. He'd made sure to tell Kaley to keep it locked until he returned.

She rolled down the window. The fatigue written on her face was painfully obvious, but her eyes sparkled. "Everything okay?"

"Yeah, Sam needs his phone back, and then I'm taking you home."

She passed him the phone through the window. "Please thank him again for me."

He squeezed her hand. "Will do. Be right back."

When he finally settled into the driver's seat moments later, the day's tension began to fall off him in waves. Driving his own vehicle with his own girl was the closest thing to normal that this day had offered.

"Everything okay with the boat?" Kaley broke the silence.

"It will be." Reef reached over and covered her hand in his. "What matters most is that everything is okay with you."

Kaley didn't reply right away, but a few seconds later, was sniffling in the seat beside him. She wiped her face with the back of her hand.

"You can cry." He squeezed her hand. "You don't have to be brave with me. Be yourself."

She laughed a little. "I know. And I'm thankful for that. I'm just tired."

"Home is our next stop. Want me to drop you off at your parents' place?"

She nodded. "Yes, please. I don't want to be alone tonight. After my short call to my mom, I have a feeling she's going to have a Thanksgiving feast waiting, but all I really want is a shower and bed. After I moved out, they made my room into the guest room, and I won't have any problem falling asleep in my old bed."

"Good." Reef smiled to himself, imagining Kaley as a little girl or even a carefree teenager, living at home. He wished he'd known her then. But he was grateful to know her now.

"I also called Blake." Her voice grew even quieter.

"What's wrong?" He tried and failed to keep worry from seeping into his voice.

Kaley sighed and leaned into the passenger headrest. "It's the office. I guess the damage from the arsonist was pretty extensive. He said it'll be several more weeks before any of us can return to work. He's had Meg reschedule all our regulars for next month and is dealing with any sensitive cases himself."

"You could use a break after all this." Reef turned into Kaley's family's neighborhood. He knew how to get there without directions, thanks to the recent visit he'd paid them. At least this time, he was returning their daughter.

"Yes, but I also need to work," Kaley said. "Master's programs aren't cheap, and I don't have a roommate anymore at the condo. I mean—I'm fine, but it would be nice not to dip into savings."

A thought struck Reef. He and Sam were heading into their busy season with spring break right around the corner. Having help in the office would be nice. They were already behind on filing paperwork, and their social media sites could use a facelift. Plus, it would mean he'd get to see Kaley every day of the work week.

He tried to keep from getting carried away. Maybe she wouldn't be interested. Or maybe …

"Would you want a temp job at the shop?" He held his breath. Moment of truth.

"What? Your shop?" Kaley gasped.

Was that excitement or are-you-kidding-me?

"For real?" She squeaked. This time, he glanced to his right and caught her wide, smiling eyes. "You'd hire me? The girl who threw you off a jet ski?"

"Well, I know a guy, and we can definitely use office and marketing help." He winked at her. "No jet ski driving skills required, but we can promise on-the-job training. The pay wouldn't be as good as at your office, but there are a lot more perks."

"Such as?"

"Oh, there's one-on-one jet ski lessons, free admission to sunset dolphin cruises, kayak excursions—"

"What about dating my boss?" Kaley wrinkled her nose. "Isn't that weird?"

His heart stuttered. "Wh-what?"

Her face flushed, then fell. "I—I thought that maybe you'd want—but if I'm wrong—"

Reef yanked the wheel into her parent's driveway and shifted to park. The next instant, he took both her hands in his. "I want that more than anything."

"But dating my boss is weird."

"Sam can be your boss. Weird problem eliminated."

She laughed, and the sound was music to his ears. "Thank you."

"You can sleep on it—I mean the job part, not the dating part." Why did the cab suddenly feel so warm? "The dating part is decided, right?"

"It's absolutely decided." She leaned in and kissed him. "But we'd better go inside before my parents surround the vehicle. Knowing my mom, she saw us coming before we even hit the driveway."

"Right." More than anything, he wanted to kiss her back and give her parents something to talk about.

But there would be time for that later. Right now, he needed to see his girl safe and sound to her parents' door—and shake her daddy's hand.

Chapter Thirty-Five

Three weeks later.

She didn't have much time. Kaley slipped out of her sandals and raced to the bathroom. Reaching into the shower, she yanked the water on and then tugged open her closet door.

"No idea what to wear," she muttered. Talking with Reef hadn't helped. He had told her he had a big surprise for her this evening, and it involved one of the promised "perks" of her job. Did that mean she should wear a swimsuit and shorts or dress up and look nice?

"Wear whatever makes you feel pretty, because you're always pretty to me," he'd said.

Her cheeks blushed again just remembering the conversation. He had it *bad* for her.

A smile softened her lips. She was perfectly okay with that.

But her head-over-heels-in-love boyfriend refused to give her any other advice on what she should wear.

She let out a contented sigh. It was good to have normal girl problems again instead of trying to escape a Hollywood kidnapper. After her interview with Avery Reynolds, the detective had promised to keep her informed of anything that related to her. For the most part, she'd heard very little from her—other than that they had plenty to keep Val and Louis behind bars and she probably wouldn't have to testify in court. That was a relief.

As for Liam, he'd been avoiding her like the plague at church.

Poor guy. Liam had a heart of gold. He hadn't been the man for her, but his girl would come along soon. She was already prepared to like her and plan double dates.

Her gaze fell on a black knee-length number with subtle flecks of gold edging the bottom and neckline. It could pass as a casual little black dress or a beach coverup. Perfect. She could wear a bikini under it—just in case Reef planned on her getting wet.

After all, their job was the water.

Their job. In the almost-month she had been working at Reef's Water Adventures, she'd come to take pride in her role. She'd reinvented the office space and updated the scheduling systems. She'd even installed an automatic reminder text system to those who had booked excursions and digitized the release forms. Sam said they'd never run more smoothly.

Besides the task side of her job, she loved the environment. Seeing the water everyday was magical, and Reef had moved her desk so that she had a water view.

Reef. He was the real reason she had come to love her temporary job. While some couples might worry that working together could strain their relationship, the opposite had been the case for them. Although they were both exceptionally busy during the day, they shared lunch together every day, which often involved a short walk to Hellas or another local shop. Other times, he'd leave something special for her at her desk—flowers or bakery items. Ugh, she needed to lay off Hellas bakery treats for a while.

Kaley rummaged through her dresser for her swimsuit as her mind continued to run over the last few weeks. They reminded her of her summers in school. Sure, she'd had summer jobs like most college kids, but her jobs had been such a nice break from the regular schedule.

But summer always came to an end, and her time at the shop would soon. Blake called earlier to tell her that she could come back to work in a week. She hadn't told Reef yet and almost didn't want to.

After a quick shower, she towel-dried and added some light-hold gel to her hair. It brought out her natural waves, and there was no point trying to straighten those when salt water would be involved.

Her phone pinged. *Be there in five*, Reef's text said. She'd need to hurry. After dabbing on tinted moisturizer, a dash of mascara, and her favorite lipstick, she slipped into the coverup and a strappy pair of flats, then grabbed a small clutch for her phone and wallet.

When the doorbell rang, she was ready for it.

Reef's face lit up when he saw her. "Wow, don't you look like a million dollars!"

"So this is good for wherever we're going?" She brushed the skirt of her dress to hide her nerves.

"It's perfect. You're perfect." He leaned in for a kiss. "You ready?"

She took his hand. "Absolutely."

He proved tight-lipped during the drive to the docks, refusing to offer any clue. But his fingers tapped the steering wheel every time they hit a red light. Whatever he had planned, he was either excited about it or a little bit nervous.

No way. They'd only been dating a month, but it was Valentine's Day weekend. It was too soon for *that*, right?

Now she was even more nervous. They'd talked about so much in the last month, and taking their time getting to know each other better was something they had both agreed on. So no, he couldn't be proposing … yet.

In that case, what was he all nervous about?

He pulled into his regular parking space, jumped out, and got her door. She took one step onto the pavement and froze in her steps.

"Is that—*Serenity Now* behind the shop?"

Reef sighed and reclaimed her hand. "You're too observant for your own good."

"She's okay? She's all fixed up?"

"Just wait and see. It's supposed to be a surprise, remember?" He tugged her toward the sidewalk that would lead around the office to the docks out back.

"Oh, sorry." But she wasn't really. She could barely contain her excitement. A few weeks ago, she thought they'd received some bad news about the damage sustained to their sunset cruise yacht, but Reef hadn't wanted to talk about it. She figured he didn't want her to worry or think it was her fault, but she had been worried. That yacht was one of their prime sources of income, because dolphin sunset cruises were wildly popular.

Having that yacht back in working order would be such a relief ...

"Surprise!"

Kaley staggered into Reef and couldn't keep her mouth from gaping open. They had just rounded the corner onto the gangway, revealing the full view of *Serenity Now*. There, collected on her deck, were about a dozen people.

Olivia, Pastor TJ and his wife, Macy, Matt, Liam, Brittany ... the whole crew from Beech Mountain was assembled, plus Sam, his girlfriend, and Avery Reynolds herself.

She looked from Reef to them and back to Reef. "This is the best surprise!"

"The best is yet to come," he grinned. "C'mon, we've got a sunset to catch."

"Welcome aboard." Sam offered his hand as she stepped into the yacht.

"It looks amazing, like it's brand new."

"You'd never know she had a scratch." He beamed at her, and she could tell how much having the yacht back meant to him.

As soon as she was aboard, Olivia was at her side, linking her arm in hers. "Well don't you and Reef look like an item tonight. Didn't I tell you—"

Kaley laughed. "Yes, you were right after all, and I'm not afraid to admit it."

Her friend smirked at her. "You're welcome."

"And what about Matt?" Kaley cut her gaze toward the other side of the yacht where Matt leaned over the railing. "He looks rather handsome himself."

Olivia released her arm and jabbed her in the ribs. "Now just because you up and got a boyfriend doesn't mean you get to play matchmaker."

"He's a good guy, and I'm pretty sure he likes you."

Olivia rolled her eyes. "But he's Matt."

"I'm simply saying that if you can be right about me, I can be right about you."

"Kaley!" Brittany's squeal interrupted them. Seconds later, she was at Kaley's side. "I'm so honored you and Reef invited me. This is absolutely gorgeous."

"I'm glad you could come," Kaley said, "although Reef gets all the credit for planning this."

Brittany's smile faded, but there was a new seriousness to her countenance that greatly improved it. "I'm sorry about what happened at the ski resort. Honest. I was—well, jealous, I guess—and I went off on my own. If I had only …"

"It's not your fault," Kaley said. "I'm glad we can all be here tonight."

Relief flooded her features. "Really? That means a lot. And is there any chance Reef has a younger brother?"

Kaley couldn't help but laugh. "He's an only child, but he does have a wide friend circle. I hope we can all hang out sometime."

And she meant it sincerely. Brittany wasn't anything like her, but as Kaley was discovering with Reef, people with different personalities and perspectives could help her see the world in ways she never imagined.

"Ready to set sail?" Reef called from the steering wheel, and a cheer went up from the yacht.

"Make yourself at home," Sam added and started playing Jack Johnson tunes through the sound system. "There's water in one cooler and watermelon slices in the other."

After exchanging hugs with Pastor TJ and his wife and giving Macy a high-five—the girl was not a hugger—Kaley made her way to the railing where Avery was talking with Liam. The detective looked much different wearing shorts and a nice linen shirt as opposed to undercover civilian clothes. She'd even let her hair down, which angled around her defined chin and facial features. In the fading daylight, it proved to be an attractive auburn color.

Maybe Liam was seeing what she did, or maybe he was catching up on investigative talk?

Regardless, the moment he noticed her, he seemed to stiffen.

"So glad you could both be here," she said.

Avery offered a relaxed smile. It was good to see the woman knew how to put her hair down—literally and figuratively. "I don't turn down free sunset cruises."

"Yeah, this is great," Liam said quickly. "I've got some questions for Reef about this yacht—my uncle is into boating. See you around." With that, he hurried away.

Kaley couldn't hold back a sigh.

"He's fine," Avery said. "Just give him space."

Did this woman have a sixth sense? Kaley would have to assume so. She didn't want to try explaining—especially if somehow, they were talking about different things. "Yeah, I hope so," was all she said.

"Do you want to talk about the case or just enjoy the view?" Avery changed the subject.

Kaley laughed. This woman was so refreshing. "Can we do both at the same time?"

"I think so," Avery grinned. "I'll start with the good news. You'll never have to see Russo or Caputo again. They're both facing charges that could give them life in prison."

"That is a relief, but I'm sure a life sentence isn't how Val imagined her star-lit career ending," Kaley said.

"You reap what you sow, to quote the old saying."

"It's a biblical principle," Kaley said.

282

"I wouldn't know." Avery gazed out over the waters. The sun was dipping lower, and someone on the other side—who sounded like Brittany—started calling out dolphin sightings.

But Kaley didn't budge. This successful, intelligent woman had a story that seemed to be missing the most important piece.

"The bad news," Avery continued, "is that even though we secured Val's yacht, thanks to Reef's phone, there's no sign of the so-called Big Eddie everyone was talking about. The trail has gone cold for now, but that doesn't mean we're giving up because Anthony—Casale—deserves justice." Her tone held a strange fierceness, as if this case were somehow personal. Perhaps it was simply the trait of a dedicated detective.

"I really appreciate everything you've done and everything you do that I don't have a clue about. Thank you for that."

"My pleasure." Avery turned to face her again. "I'm glad your story has a happy ending. So many don't." She excused herself to get a beverage. There was something heavy to her words, something that demanded respect and space. One day, Kaley would like the chance to know this woman better.

Finding herself alone for the first time all evening, she slipped next to Reef at the wheel.

"Hey, Miss Popular," he teased. "Having fun?"

"This is perfect." She kissed him on the cheek. "Thank you. I've come to love the water so much. I'm going to miss it."

The words slipped out before she could stop them.

"What?" Reef raised an eyebrow. "What's wrong?"

"Nothing—I don't want to spoil the evening."

"Talk to me, sweetheart."

She sighed. "Blake called today and said I can come back to work in a week."

"That's great news," Reef said. "Why does that have you all sad?"

"Because, well, because I'm going to miss all this," she made a waving motion, "and working with you every day."

"I'll miss you too, Kaley, but we'll still see each other all the time. You're amazing at being a therapist, and your patients need you." His gaze was so affirming it made her heart flutter. "And maybe you can work with me on weekends when I have shifts. You'll still be a part of this—as long as you want to be."

The sun dipped below the horizon, falling farther out of sight with each second. She didn't know what tomorrow's sunset or the sunset after that would hold, and she didn't need to.

A sense of peace flooded her, and she reached for Reef's hand on the wheel. "Count me in."

Author's Note

Mark Twain said, "Write what you know." With this book, I certainly took his advice. The setting of Beech Mountain, North Carolina is part of my own story in a special way. While my husband James and I were dating, our church group planned a ski trip to Beech Mountain, much like the one Reef and Kaley embark on in this story. Born and raised in Florida, I had never seen fresh snow fall, let alone attempt to ski in it. Writing Kaley's frustration with the learning curve is something I came by honestly.

James taught the other new skiers and me the basics, and I felt so special to be his girlfriend and have such a thoughtful date. Later, when my writing imagination kicked in, I began to wonder, "What if James and I hadn't been dating but had broken up? How awkward would that experience have been?" Awkward on steroids. Then the suspense lover in me began to spin the story of Kaley and Reef as well as a celebrity villain that no one would suspect. And so, this story was born.

But my experience with Beech Mountain didn't stop with a ski trip. After James and I had been dating for just over a year, he planned a surprise engagement trip to—you guessed it—Beech Mountain. Since my Sunshine State doesn't offer fall foliage, James invited some friends and me on a fall hiking trip. Though I wondered if he might pop the big question, I wasn't sure, and my best friend wasn't budging with any clues. One of our late afternoon hikes took us to Wiseman's View, a stunning overlook of the mountains and canyon below. I was cold, craving hot chocolate, and ready to head back to our cabin, but James wanted to show me one more vista and "get a picture." With my best friend recording the moment, James dropped down on one knee, spoke the sweetest words, and asked me to marry him—to which I happily said yes!

Now, Beech Mountain is one of our favorite road trip destinations as a married couple. As we eagerly await the arrival of our baby in August, we're dreaming about future trips with our little boy. James already plans to teach him to snowboard as soon as he can stand up.

The good news is that I have writing material for days from this setting and am so excited to bring you more stories in this series that revolve around Beech Mountain. Will Reef and Kaley tie the knot? Will Liam's disappointed heart heal and find the woman who's right for him? And Avery—will she discover the most important Piece that's missing from her life?

Until next time, I'll be working on the nursery, cramming in a few writing projects before my due date, and praying over this story as it prepares to enter the world. Thinking about you reading these words makes me smile, because I know that when you do, my story will be in your hands and hopefully blessing you in some way. I look forward to sharing more adventures in fiction with you soon!

~ Kristen

You can connect with her at KristenHogrefeParnell.com. Sign up for her monthly newsletter and receive a free story.

Young Adult Fiction by Kristen, published under her maiden name Kristen Hogrefe, includes:

The Rogues Trilogy

The Revisionary
The Revolutionary
The Reactionary

Discussion Questions

1. During her ordeal, Kaley realizes that she can't control what happens to her, but she can choose her response to it. What circumstances are you facing right now that are outside your control? What freedom can you find in choosing your response to them?

2. Although our pasts shape us, they don't have to define us. Kaley wrongfully judged Reef based on his childhood experiences, and the assumptions she made were largely responsible for their breakup. How does Kaley move forward and discover she was wrong about Reef? Have you ever misjudged someone? What next step did you take—or should you take?

3. Our expectations often cause us to miss opportunities. What expectations do you have for a current or future relationship? Take some time to evaluate if they are realistic and biblical or if they might need to be adjusted.

4. Brittany rubs Kaley the wrong way, and Kaley struggles to find common ground with her. In the end, she realizes that Brittany's differences are an opportunity to see the world from a completely different perspective. Do you know someone who is your polar opposite? How might befriending this person be an unexpected blessing?

5. Val takes the trauma from her past and uses it as a weapon—and a reason to believe she has the right to take whatever she wants from other people. When we allow our past hurts to rule our lives, we create our own path of destruction. Is there a hurt or trauma from your past that you need to seek healing from? How might you start that process?

6. Kaley is a Florida girl who has never seen snow, and skiing turns out to be more difficult and uncomfortable than she expected. When was the last time you took a trip or tried something outside of your comfort zone? What did you learn from the experience?

7. At one point during her ordeal, Kaley stares up at the stars and remembers this verse from Psalm 147:4. "He counts the number of the stars; He calls them all by name." Do you believe God sees you and knows you? How can that truth comfort you with a situation you're facing today?

8. As Kaley prepares her notes from meeting Anthony Casale, she feels inadequate to access his situation—even with her skillset. What does James 1:5 say we should do when we lack wisdom?

9. Kaley prides herself on her ability to "read people," but throughout the story, she misjudges Reef and later makes the poor decision to help a skier (Russo) on her own instead of getting ski patrol's assistance. Her tendency to solve problems herself lands her in big trouble! What problems are you trying to solve on your own today? Who might you ask to come alongside you and help?

10. People say that "opposites attract," and in many ways, Reef and Kaley are different. However, Reef thinks back to their dates and how she was willing to go outside of her comfort zone to try new activities that he enjoyed. If you're in a relationship today (dating or married), how can you step into your partner's world and show that you care about his or her interests?

Made in United States
Orlando, FL
29 November 2022